Skin of Tattoos

Praise for *Skin of Tattoos*

Hoag is a talented writer, summoning Mags' world on the page with remarkable empathy and detail ... None of the characters seem hastily constructed or come off as clichés. Their pressures and motivations are clearly stated and genuinely felt, and readers will quickly become invested in Mags and his confrontation with an uncertain future. The overall experience is surprisingly nuanced and wholly enjoyable. A well-crafted and engaging book. —Kirkus Reviews

Skin of Tattoos is full of the inevitability of lost lives; of those who can't escape the deeply worn tracks of their predecessors. I started to become totally engrossed in Mags' world; the characters Mags engages with are flawed and have agendas, which make them untrustworthy and far from predictable, and Mags himself is a complex character...A great debut novel. —Kiwi Crime Reads

The plot twists and turns through a labyrinth of unexpected betrayals, difficult alliances, and the politics of gang life. This is a great book for anyone willing to get out of their comfort zone and to vicariously step into another person's shoes and bleak existence. —UnderratedReads.com

A compelling, and at times chilling, tale of the inner workings of what it is to be entrenched in a gang lifestyle. The "codes", the rules, the crimes and even the betrayals. Ms. Hoag has written a truly extensive and intensive story that will have you turning the pages.—CMashLovestoRead.com

The research is extensive and her understanding of Salvadoran gangs quite vivid. An ending that lets readers know that some endings are new beginnings.—Just Reviews

The book is fast-paced, and Mags is a sympathetic and credible narrator. Hoag does a masterful job of putting the reader though gut-wrenching cycles of fearing for him and hoping for him, hoping for him and fearing the worst. It's book that demands to be read in one sitting.—Alison McMahan, author, screenwriter, filmmaker

As a criminal-defense attorney who has done too many RICO cases, I am grateful to see a portrayal of this world that gives society a better idea of the odds at stake, the motivations at work, and the lack of easy answers available in the world of gang offenses. The work makes an accessible beach read while also refusing to let the reader off easy.—Clare Lyon, lawyer & author

Romance, intrigue and of course, suspense. Definitely a different look at Los Angeles. I cannot wait to read more from this author.—DealSharingAunt.com

This well-crafted, realistic novel with its twists and turns will leave you breathless. Read the first chapter, and you'll be hooked. Hoag provides such a perfect glimpse into the lives of the Los Angeles Salvadoran gang members that you will care what happens to these well-developed characters. The superb writing and the escalating tension will hold you until the very last page.—L.C. Hayden, author

Lyrically written, with several twists and turns that left me breathless til the very end, this novel is a must read for anyone interested in the perils of gang life.—Matthew Peters, author

Skin of Tattoos

Christina Hoag

Three Jandals
Press

Skin of Tattoos
Copyright © 2016 by Christina Hoag

Third edition published by Three Jandals Press, 2022
All rights reserved.

Three Jandals Press
Santa Monica, California, United States of America

Also by this author

Fiction
Girl on the Brink
Law of the Jungle

Nonfiction
I Am the Famous Carlos:
The Story of the Jackal, the World's First Celebrity Terrorist
Peace in the Hood:
Working with Gang Members to End the Violence

ONE

Night in L.A. can be heavy as a medieval cloak or it can sparkle and crackle. It can burn you with its current, protect you or betray you. It can be like a jaina with a wet pout and curves that clap into your cupped hands. Tonight L.A. was just heavy, swimming in sweet syrup heavy.

I stood on the sidewalk and breathed in a lungful of darkness. For the first time in twenty-six months and thirteen days, I was free to go to the corner store and buy a Snickers. At least that was my excuse for slipping out my first night home, in case anyone asked. But they didn't. Moms and my sisters went to bed, my brother Frank wouldn't be home til the next day and Pops was working his night job. I bounced.

The quietness rang in my ears like I'd been punched upside the head. I had to listen to find noise. It was there. A siren whooped, a car door slammed, but they were faded, comfortable noises like a pair of old jeans. Noise wasn't up close like in lockup with all its yelling, buzzing, clanging—the constant rumble of hundreds of angry fools. And it was dark. No lights blaring into every little crack of privacy all the time.

I walked past the store flashing the Tecate neon sign behind a barred window, feeling the moon watching me. I was going to see Blueboy. A parole violation for sure. He was on the D.A.'s gang affiliate list and so was I. I was home and free, but not home free. Not by a long shot. But I had to see Blue. We went way back, to before we were both jumped in to the Cyco Lokos. That was a lifetime and a half ago. Just seven years. But they were gang years, which kind of count like dog years. We were thirteen.

Blueboy lived in the armpit of the 110 and 10 freeways. If he was home, he'd be slouched on the couch watching TV with the lights off, like we always did when his mom was working nights at the hospital.

He was going to be surprised when he saw me. I didn't get word to my homeboys about my release date. I missed the hell out of them, but I wasn't getting back in the crazy life again. I couldn't do more time. That's what getting all involved was going to get me. Or killed. Same difference.

It felt rich just to push one foot ahead of the other and to go wherever I wanted, whenever I wanted. I stuck my arms straight out and walked like that for a while, looking into windows. People watching TV, eating. Women carrying babies, wearing curlers. Tetas.

I pushed open Blueboy's gate. The pitbulls next door barked as I ambled down the driveway to the illegal garage conversion where he lived with his mom and sister. Blue flickers from the TV flashed through the missing slats of the window blinds. He was home. For the first time since eight o'clock that morning, when the State of California spit me out to a bus stop, my bones didn't creak.

I drum-rolled my knuckles on the door. The blinds rustled and then the door burst open.

"Mags! What the fuck, fool?" He hugged me. I hugged him back. Hard. "Why you didn't tell me you were coming home? I thought I was seeing things."

"Just got home today." Big smiles splashed on our faces.

He stood back to let me in. "Damn, you got buff, homes. You been working out?"

"That's all I did inside, work out and go to school. You know how it is."

Blueboy looked the same. Tall and bony with vanilla ice cream skin and the bluest eyes I've ever seen. Eyes like the desert sky. Everybody thought he was white, which pissed him off. He was as Salvadoran as I was.

"I can't believe you're back. Lotta shit going down with the clica lately, dog. You seen anybody yet?"

Before I could answer, someone called my name. I knew who it was. I turned. Paloma stood in the doorway. All the organs in my body stopped working, except my eyes. Lean dulce de leche legs, a slender neck that swung into all kinds of curves, face framed by a dark thick mane. Her lips parted, revealing a hint of bright white teeth. A lit fuse zoomed from me to her and her to me and back again. My ribcage ached. It was still there, what we had before I got locked up. I thought my feelings for her were long gone down a bottomless black hole but now here they were, bouncing back up at me. Fuck.

"Sup Paloma," I croaked. Seeing her had suddenly rusted my voice.

"When did you get out?" she said.

"Girl, go back to your room," Blueboy ordered. "You got breakfast shift in the morning, or you forgot?"

She threw her brother a resentful look, then disappeared. The palms of my hands had sprouted seeds of sweat. I wiped them on my jeans, hoping to hell Blueboy didn't pick up on our eyes eloping.

I cleared my throat. "I gotta get me a candy bar, homes. You coming?"

He rolled his eyes. "You and fuckin candy bars. I can't understand how you never got a face like a pizza from them fuckin things."

Outside, the cool air dried my sweat and the freeway's seashell roar blocked the echo of Paloma's voice calling my name in my head. We turned down an alley to get out of the sightline of any passing five-o. This late at night, we were easy pickings for cops to jam us.

"So whatup in the barrio?" I said.

"Rico's the chingón now, fool."

I stared at him. "You trippin me, right?"

"Chivas caught a case, a 187. He's in county, no bail. He's still calling the shots, but Rico's running the street."

So that hijo de fuckin puta Rico got in slick with the shotcaller, taking my place while I was doing *his* time. I kicked an empty can into some trash bins. Someone groaned. We pulled our fists out of our pockets. A drunk was propped up against the fence.

"Wanna roll him?"

"Nah, his ass ain't worth it," I said.

We walked on.

"Rico's stepping on us hard, bro. He's got the clica slinging day and night, collecting taxes in the park. The dudes with the fake IDs. Anybody parking their ass on the grass."

"That bullshit again?" I always hated that small-time crap, hitting on guys who made like ten bucks a day pushing ice cream carts. "I thought Chivas wanted to stick to big shit off the street."

"That was before life without parole was staring him down. That ain't all. He's stepping on Rico to find new territory we can move into. Rico wants us to hit this place where the maricones hook up."

I frowned. "Damn."

"Chivas ain't going with no P.D. so he's gotta pay for a lawyer." Blueboy rubbed his fingers and thumb together.

"So he knows he's going down on this murder."

"They got DNA on him. They found his blood on a body dumped in the desert, like a tiny speck of it. Case was cold til they tested the blood."

"He's right to get his own lawyer, that's for damn sure. All them P.D.s want you to do is cop a plea so they don't have to work the trial."

"Ain't that the truth."

Chivas was an O.G. back from when the Salvadorans got together in the eighties against the Mexicans, who didn't appreciate thousands of guanacos flooding into L.A., even though we were escaping a civil war.

He got his placa because he was always watching a Chivas de Guadalajara soccer game on TV with a bottle of Chivas Regal in his hand. He was respected in the barrio because he put in a lotta work over the years but always beat the raps. But now la ley finally caught up to him. Big time.

If he went down on this 187, he was behind the wall for thirty years, at least.

"So this is Rico's big chance to be shotcaller. He must really be getting off on that," I said.

"You know what he's like, homes."

"Yeah, I know that aight."

I'd been the one in the clica who Chivas trusted the most, his right-hand vato. That was why Rico set me up with a .38 with an armed robbery on it and got me sent down. With Chivas in lockup, it looked like Rico's play worked out better than he ever dreamed.

A lump rose in my throat.

We stepped out of the alley to go to the market on the corner. A whistle, low and long, sliced the air. An LAPD black-and-white rolled down the street real slow.

We ducked back in the alley, pressing ourselves flat as flip-flops against the wall in deep shadow. It seemed like forever til the patrol car crawled by. We slid down the wall to a squat in case it circled the block.

"I'm real glad you're back, Mags. The others gonna be real happy, too."

"It was a long haul this time."

"The homies weren't down with what happened. Wasn't right."

"No, it wasn't." I paused, then I figured I just had to come out with it. "I can't get involved again, Blue. I gotta stay straight."

A tick of silence passed. Blue shifted his weight like my words were too heavy for him.

I held my breath, waiting for his reaction. What I just said was like walking out of church while the priest was saying misa. Disrespect, with a capital D.

"You want out?"

"Yeah, I do."

"I feel you," he said finally. "This ain't no kinda life, watching your back all the damn time." He understood. I knew he would. He pitched a piece of gravel against the opposite wall. "But we chose it."

Maybe he didn't understand as much as I thought. I knew I was letting him down, but he hadn't just done twenty-six months on a setup.

"Maybe it kinda chose us."

"How you figurin on gettin out, exactly?"

"I just took a fuckin felony rap for the clica. And I did forty-five days in the hole over a beef with a 5150. Felt like a fuckin year."

"We heard about that. Chivas said you're a real loyal soldier."

"I just about lost my mind for that loyalty. I'm gonna ask Chivas to go on veterano status. I figure I put in the work, paid my dues."

"Ain't nobody gonna deny you're down for the clica, homes. But it ain't gonna be easy. Chivas is looking for soldiers to earn. He ain't gonna be waving bye-bye, and Rico's his man on the street. He won't do you no favors. You know that."

"Rico can be the fuckin shotcaller for all I care." The words corkscrewed on my tongue. There was a time when I couldn't have even imagined letting Rico win without a fight. Now I just admitted my defeat. It hung like a bad smell in the air. "I been thinking bout this a long time."

"Yeah, but that was in there. Now you're out here." He was right. Things did change when you were on the outside. "There's something else I gotta tell you, homes, bout your sister."

"Lissy?"

It had to be my older younger sister who always ran with trouble. Moms and Frank were real protective of Zully, my baby sis.

"She hooked up with a 5150."

"Fuuuuck." I rubbed my chin. "That's why she was so quiet at dinner, didn't hardly say a word to me the whole time. Does Rico know?"

He shook his head. "Flaco saw her with the 51 a few weeks back. Fool goes by Payaso. The only person he told was me. You might want to handle it before word gets out."

"How the fuck I'm gonna do that?"

Blueboy hoisted his left shoulder in his weird, one-sided shrug. "She's your sister."

Dealing with Lissy was like handling a live grenade. It figured that she'd pick a banger with the Cyco Lokos' sworn enemy. This was against code and could bring major repercussions against me and her. Fuck. I was only home for a few hours, and already the shit was piling up.

"Depends on how tight she is with him," Blueboy said.

"Yeah, maybe it's nothing."

"You want to go to Gato's and celebrate? He's always asking for you."

Gato moved stolen cars out of the port, shipping them to Colombia, where he was from. I used to be his top guy for jacking rides.

"I'm not ready yet. I'm gonna get me some candy bars and go on home." We stood. "Do me a solid. Don't tell Rico and the homies I'm back."

"I never saw you, homes, but they gonna find out soon enough."

"I just need some time. Get myself set up with a job, parole, all that shit."

He slapped me on the shoulder. "Come round and say hi to mi

mama."

I nodded. Doña Flor always treated me like another son. We clasped hands, pumping our joined fist against our chests. Blueboy jetted down the alley, and I rolled out into the street.

I made for the corner store, my head buzzing. This shit about Rico being the crew boss was throwing me. It should be me. I was Chivas's lieutenant. He always said I was the smartest of the crew. I could be trusted. I had follow-through. I had throwdown. What did that get me? Two years en el fuckin bote and somebody else moving into my slot. And I was gonna stand by like a punkass pussy.

A vein beat at my temple. But I couldn't let this fuck me up. I had to let it go. I took a deep breath and let it out slow, like they taught us in anger management. When I reached the bottom of my lungs, Rico was gone and Paloma was there. Man, it was happening all over again. I thought I had smothered it, killed it, but there it was. I wanted her, bad.

"Well, if it ain't mi amigo, Magdaleno Argueta."

I twisted. A face leered out of the shotgun window of the black-and-white that had crept up behind me. The panel of hairsprayed hair, the cheeks with an oatmeal complexion, the gold chain glinting in the hollow of his throat. Fuck.

"You paroled already? I thought I put you away for longer."

I hardened my jaw. "I did my time, Officer Morales."

"I don't think you learned your lesson, homeboy. You're still hanging out on street corners."

"Goin to the store. No law gainst that."

"If I catch you with your homies, I could run you in. You know that, don't you?"

"You see me with any homeboys?" I held my arms out and made a show of looking around.

Morales locked his eyes into mine and poked his finger in the air. "You get mouthy with me, sonny, and I'll violate you faster than you can sing ay-yai-yai."

The police radio squawked. "Two-eleven in progress. All units in the area respond to the jewelry store in the strip mall at Venice and Union. Code three."

The cop at the wheel picked up the handset.

"Sounds like you got an armed robbery to attend to, Officer," I said.

Morales' eyes stayed on mine. "Light em up, Yankevich."

The Crown Vic's light bar flared in red and blue flashes and it zoomed off with a low roar, siren yelping. It blasted through a red light and disappeared.

Cops. They thought they owned the world and in a way they did. They could do whatever they wanted and get away with it. Everyone listened to them because they had a badge and a uniform. No one listened to us, we were just cholos.

But sometimes they were wrong, and we were right—and then what?

I swung open the store door too hard and it crashed into the wall.

"Oiga, you break it, you pay for it," the pot-bellied mexicano called from behind the counter.

I heard the snap and hiss of a beer can tab as I walked in the door. Pops. Home from his night job cleaning offices. By day, he shoved boxes around a warehouse. I entered the kitchen. He stood at the stove, heating up the dinner Moms left him. A Colt 45 sat on the counter, by his elbow.

"Hola papá."

He didn't turn around. I fingered the candy bars in my pocket as he finished what he was doing and switched off the gas before facing me.

"Hijo." I hadn't seen him in two years and all I got were two syllables and a look that lasted less than a fuckin match strike. I couldn't deny that it hurt.

The table rocked as he set his plate on it. He bent to fix the wedge of cardboard that had worked loose from under its leg. He straightened himself, shook the table to make sure it was steady, then picked up his fork. I forced myself into the chair across from him.

In the old days, when I caught his vibe, I would've been out the door and on the street by now. But all those nights in lockup, as I lay on my cot, hands laced behind my head and staring at the cement ceiling, I promised God I was going to be a better son, be more like Frank, although I'd never admit that to Frank's face.

"You going to get a job now, vos?" Pops tore off a piece of

tortilla and curled it to scoop up his rice. He spoke into his plate like it was going to talk back.

"Sure am. I'll be able to help you and mamá out with the bills."

I suddenly caught sight of my hands on the table. The tattooed hands that he hated. They were inked with spots like a jaguar pelt and claws on each knuckle. The jaguar was the Cyco Lokos symbol, representing Central America. The spots and claws meant I'd earned my stripes for the clica. I was so fuckin proud of those tatts I put them where everybody could see them.

Now I buried my hands in my lap.

He didn't answer, just kept shoveling rice and beans into his mouth. He looked smaller than I remembered, as if all the years working two or three crap jobs at a time had worn him down. His shoulders were rounder, the wrinkles around his coffee-drip eyes deeper, his lips thin like scars. He wore the same faded gold and orange plaid shirt he'd worn for years with his white undershirt showing grey and frayed at the neck. His hair was still thick though, and black as a bad-luck cat.

"I got my high school diploma now, papá."

He still didn't answer.

"It's not a GED, it's a real diploma. I graduated. Had the top grades in my class."

At graduation, all the men slapped my back and shook my hand. Mr. Estevez, the English teacher, and the other teachers and counselors told me I should feel proud of myself. I tried to make that feeling real again, but it was like catching water.

"You going to stay out of trouble this time, vos?" Rice grains stuck to his mustache. He gulped his beer. When he lowered the can, the rice was gone.

I wanted to believe I heard a prick of hope in the question—that he hadn't given up on me totally. I couldn't blame him if he had. Still...

"Sure will." My voice sounded like one of his empty beer cans rolling on the floor. "That's the last time I'm going to el bote."

He burped and pushed back his chair, glancing at me as he picked up his plate. He placed it in the sink and grabbed the slice of chocolate cake Moms left for him—my welcome home cake. He sure welcomed my cake.

My insides quivered. On the street, I was hard as asphalt. I never stood down from stepping to a bluesuit, Rico, any motherfucker who dissed me. But my father had a way of turning me into Jello. And I hated him for it, just like he hated me for being a cholo.

"Buenas noches, papá." I pressed my fingers against my ears so I wouldn't hear his silence as I walked out of the kitchen.

A crack of light shone onto the hallway floor from under the door of the girls' room. Lissy was still up. I danced my fingers on the wood.

"Yeah?" she said.

She was lying on the bottom bunk, filing her nails. Zully was asleep on the top. When we were little, all four of us shared a room in two bunk beds. Then Moms moved Frank and me to the sofa bed in the living room and sold the extra bunk. I always thought the girls should share the sofa bed since they were smaller, but Moms said girls needed a room of their own more than boys.

I sat on the edge of the bed. Lissy put down her nail file and shifted her legs to make room. "Don't let him get to you, bro."

"How'd you know?"

"Cuz I know that look on your face."

"He ain't changed, huh? I don't know why I expected different. I just thought, maybe..." My voice tightened. I had to build my wall back up. Coming home had punched holes in it.

"He ain't ever gonna change. Just stay outta his way, like always."

Lissy and me were born exactly fourteen months apart. I was twenty-one, she was twenty. She was the one in my family I was closest to.

We were the middle kids, the ones without the special value of being the oldest or the youngest so we always stuck up for each other no matter what.

"Whatup with you, girl?" I had to talk to her about this 5150 shit but I didn't feel like tackling it right then.

She looked down and shrugged. She was hiding something. So, it was true. Puchica.

"What are you guys talking about?" Zully swung her head down from the top bunk. She'd really grown up since I'd been away. She was fourteen, and as baby of the family, spoiled.

I tweaked a strand of her hair hanging down. "You got school tomorrow."

"It's more interesting listening to you."

10

Lissy punched the mattress above her.

"You woke me up," Zully whined.

I stood. "Back to bed, girl. I gotta catch some zees, too. I'm gonna start looking for a job tomorrow." She lay back. I tucked the covers around her. A crowd of stuffed animals bordered the foot and wall. Minnie Mouse and Daisy Duck were her favorites. "You hardly got room to sleep with all them peluches," I said.

"They keep me company."

I smiled and said goodnight. Lissy didn't answer. She was filing her nails like she was sawing them. Yeah, something was definitely up.

In the living room, I moved the coffee table to one side, a pain in the ass since it only had three legs. The fourth was a pile of old books. Pops had kicked out the leg during one of his borracheras. After pulling out the sofa bed, I stripped to my boxers and got in, plucking an Almond Joy from a jeans pocket. Trying not to feel the springs jutting into my back, I sucked the sweetness from the coconut on my tongue and stared at the greenish light from the glow-in-the-dark rosary around my neck. I went to pull it over my head, but I couldn't.

Moms brought me the rosary, along with some socks, the one time she and the girls visited me not long after I got sent down. They came on a free bus organized by some church to take family members to visit inmates. They never visited again, even though I always wrote and told them when a bus was scheduled from LA to my facility. It wasn't that far, as prisons go, two hours southeast from the city. Some guys got sent way north or to central California, a day's drive away, but I guess it was far enough for my family to forget about me.

So inside, I never took off that rosary. The glow made me feel like I was alive, still connected to mi familia and not melted into black nothingness. Now that I was home, I figured I'd quit wearing it, but somehow, I couldn't bring myself to take it off, not yet anyway. I guess I still needed to something solid to feel connected.

TWO

The apartment was quiet when I woke with a vision of Paloma in my head and wood in my shorts. It took me a moment to realize where I was in that haze of re-entering the world. I looked around.

Pops' armchair still had a big hollow in the cushion, the black velvet picture with the neon-colored outline of the San Salvador volcanos was still on the wall next to the glued-together plate saying "El Salvador," another victim of Pops' drunken rages.

The TV stand was new, new picked up from a Westside alley, that is. Frank's fire academy graduation photo stood next to his high school graduation picture on top of the TV with the rabbit-ears. The arm-size statue of the Virgin that stood on a plastic lace mat on a corner stand was gone. I guessed she suffered the same fate as the plate and the coffee table.

I got up and went to the postage-stamp sized bathroom. A bottle of Polo sat on the shelf. I picked it up as my piss thundered into the toilet. It was the real stuff, not the knockoffs they sold out of trucks down by MacArthur Park. Frank's, no doubt.

Now he was a firefighter, he had money to burn. He was prolly getting more pussy, too.

I came out, scratching my head. The new growth of hair was itching. I had shaved my head for years, but I had decided I was going to grow my hair in as part of my new life.

Nobody was around. I must've slept through the morning rush

for work and school. I pushed open the door to Moms and Pops' room. It smelled musty, like unwashed bedsheets. One of those furry, fringed blankets they sold on sidewalks was pulled over the bed. This one had a lion on it. The crucifix that Moms brought from El Salvador hung on the wall.

We left when I was four. My only memory of my country was being in a room with Frank and Lissy. Lissy was crying and I was trying real hard not to. Frank held us tight and kept telling us that mami was coming soon.

My parents never talked about El Salvador. All I knew was that my dad had been a guerrilla fighting the government to make things better for poor people, who were most of the population. People disappeared in the middle of the night, got blown up by land mines. There were no jobs. Tens of thousands of salvadoreños headed north. Us included.

I saw the time on the clock on the bedside table. Shit, I had to move.

Angel leaned back in his chair and knotted his hands behind his head, exposing blooms of sweat in his pits.

"You know what's weird about being a parole agent, Magdaleno. The guys I really like, I really hope I'll never see again. And you're one of them, but you keep coming back."

He sprang forward, lowering his arms gracias a Dios, and flipped open the folder labeled "Magdaleno Jesús Argueta" on his desk.

"You don't have much parole time anyway, since you almost maxed out your sentence because of that fight. Looks like you did real good except for that. Is that where you got that scar on your face? I don't remember that."

He compared the real me to the photo in the file. I smoothed the raised line on my jaw that he was staring at. The cut had healed into what the doctor called a keloid scar—a puffy, red, angry slash, which I kind of liked at the time because it suited my mood. It had since faded into a fleshy pink. Just as well.

"This fool shanked me. The doc said I was lucky he didn't get some big artery in my neck."

"The carotid."

"Yeah, that."

"Says here you were the instigator, that you stabbed him in the kidney with a sharpened toothbrush."

I nodded. "True that."

"What happened?"

"Some 5150 was running his mouth all over the yard bout how the Cycos ain't shit and how the 5150s were crushing us on the street. I had to represent. If I didn't, I'd get shanked for being a pussy." It earned me twenty-three hours a day alone inside a cement box. It also earned me respect. Nobody fucked with me after that.

Angel gave a weighty sigh and loosened the top button on his shirt. He'd gotten fat since I last saw him. A bicycle tire of flesh oozed over his collar. His mustache needed trimming. He also needed to iron his shirt, which had a nasty stain like egg yolk on the cuff.

My years in the clica made me extra fussy about appearance. We wore starched out, ironed-to-a-crease pants. White shirts had to dazzle. Any stain, they got thrown out. The way we saw it, even if you were poor, you didn't have to look it.

"Lemme see that picture," I said. He handed it to me.

I was naked from the waist up to record my tatts. A jaguar tail curling around my collarbone, "Mamá" written in cursive script on my right pec with a weeping Madonna under it, a dagger on my shoulder, a cross draped with a rosary on my stomach. I wasn't going to tell Angel I'd gotten a new tatt since that picture.

My eyes were the same, dark as Coca-Cola, but I had a younger, softer look to my face, though I sure didn't think that at the time. My skin was a sunny brown, my cheeks were filled out. Now my complexion was sallow, my cheekbones were doorknobs. I had an edge to my face like someone took a chisel to it. That was what the pen did to you.

I tossed the picture back into the open folder. "It got in there that I got my high school diploma, top of the class?"

"Yeah, it's here. I always said you were smart. You just didn't apply yourself."

I sure heard that a lot over the years. "I did apply myself, just not to the shit everybody wanted me to apply to."

Angel ignored my remark. "That's what we like to see: rehabilitation."

"There ain't a lot of that inside." I rocked back on my chair. "It's more like a school to make hard bangers."

He ignored that too.

"You know the drill, but I'll tell you again. While you're on parole, the cops can search you without a warrant. They find anything on you, you'll be in violation. Random piss tests. You inhale a blunt even one time, it'll show right up. Violation. Cops need you to help them on something, you help them or violation. And you get violated, you're back inside."

I nodded.

"Truth be told, I'm getting out of the life. I'm sick of all the bullshit."

Angel made a yeah-right face. "You know how many times I heard that? The life's not going to let you go so easy. It's going to take all you got to stay away. You need to get a job, make new friends, get a girlfriend out of the neighborhood, stay busy."

"Thanks for the vote of confidence."

He stared at my head. "You going to grow your hair in?" He looked around the corner of his desk at my lower half. "Wear jeans that fit?"

"I just got out, man. My hair's gonna take a while and these are the only threads I got."

He pointed to my hands. "How about getting that ink off? I can get you free tattoo removal."

"I get your point, but I'm serious."

"I'm rooting for you, Magdaleno. If anyone can do it, you can. It's all down to you. You know what you gotta do. Now get out of here. See you next month."

He didn't think I was serious, but I was.

For the next six hours, I hiked all over downtown LA looking for help wanted signs. There weren't any. I went inside the stores and restaurants and asked if they had any jobs—bus boy, dishwasher, stock boy, cleaner. People shook their heads.

Sorry. Try at the corner. Come back next week.

I walked and walked til I found the library on Fifth Street. The library was my place in lockup. I chilled in there for hours, reading all kinds of shit. History and James Bond were my favorites. After seeing me in there all the time, the librarian gave me a job, checking books in and out, shelving them. Maybe I could get a job like that. I had experience.

The place was huge. There were too many books, if there could be such a thing. My sneakers squeaked real loud on the floor, and I kept waiting for someone to kick me out. But they didn't.

A lady gave me an application and a pen. That was the furthest I had gotten so far so I was pretty happy, but when I saw the questions, I knew it was all over.

Work experience. List, starting with most recent employment. Library assistant, California State Youth Correctional Institute. Jacking rides, Cyco Lokos.

Supervisor, name and title. Chivas, Shotcaller.

Have you ever been convicted of a felony? Check. *If yes, please explain.* Possession of a firearm (It wasn't mine).

Personal References. Name and relationship to you. Blueboy, Jackie Chan, Tweety, Flaco, Cojo, homeboys.

Shit, even the name of the school on my diploma—New Horizons Academy—sounded like one of those continuation schools for dropouts and troublemakers. I wouldn't even hire me. I crumpled up the application and tossed it in the trash. My chair screeched on the floor as I pushed back from the table. Heads turned. I held up my chin on the way out.

Fuck the job search. I marched across the Sixth Street overpass back into my hood, Pico Union. Paloma popped into my head. That look she gave me, the way she said my name.

Shit. I didn't even know if she had a man. Why wouldn't she? All I knew was I had to see her.

I'd known Paloma since she wore her hair in braids and her face bunched into chipmunk cheeks when she giggled. She was three years younger than Blue and me. Since I had two little sisters already, I had no time for another one. I never even noticed her until a couple months before I got locked up this last time.

I was coming outta a 7-Eleven, unwrapping a Reese's. She was wearing those skinny jeans, so tight they were practically painted on her legs, leaning against a car talking to a guy in a wifebeater. He was rapping her heavy, his arm stretched out on the roof of the car and her under it. My eyes fused with hers like we were seeing each other for the first time. A minute later, she was by my side and the dude's car was peeling out of the parking lot.

"Walk me home, Mags?" she asked real innocent, giving me a shy smile.

I purposely took the long way by MacArthur Park and after I bought her a Creamsicle from a viejo pushing an ice cream cart, we sat on the ground by the lake, talking as we tweezed blades of brown grass.

As I walked her home two hours later, she switched her purse to her shoulder farthest from me, leaving the near arm free. Our hands kept brushing, shooting me with electric tingles, but I didn't do anything. She was Blueboy's sister. I couldn't. I resisted for twenty-four hours, then I caved and went to see her when I knew Blue wasn't home and her mom would be working. That time there was no fuckin way we could leave it at touching hands.

I saw her every day I could after that, pure stealth all the way. Homeboys' sisters were off-limits. Too much could go wrong with women, and personal shit created bad blood, divide loyalties, Chivas said. We had to stay laced up tight as a combat boot. Not to mention, Blueboy and me basically considered ourselves brothers, which kinda sorta made Paloma my sister. He wouldn't be down with this at all.

After I took the plea deal and knew I was getting sent down, Paloma came to visit me in county like she always did. We sat at the table and all the chatter noise dropped away. It seemed like we were the only ones in that crowded visiting room. As we sneaked a handhold when the guard was looking in the other direction, I steeled my eyes to look into hers and told her I didn't want to see her again. I had to forget her, she had to forget me. Like we never happened.

Her eyes clouded and her lower lip trembled. I had to get the fuck out of there. I practically ran out of the visiting room, leaving my heart ripped out and bleeding on the floor. But it was easier that way.

Easier til now.

The pitbulls next door to Blueboy's house announced my arrival. I knocked. Seconds dripped by, I bounced on the balls of my feet. Then the blinds rustled, and the door opened, and I was looking into eyes deep and soft as a lake.

"Magdaleno."

For a moment I forgot to talk, then I remembered I had to say something.

"Hey, nena."

"Blueboy ain't here."

"Y la doña Flor?"

"She went to work already. You just missed her."

There was an awkward pause. I swallowed. "I was thinking maybe ... we could talk."

She didn't answer right away, and I thought I had to be the biggest fuckin fool alive. She was gonna slam the door in my face. Then she stepped back, leaving me room to enter. We sat on the couch. She tucked a leg underneath her nalgas, like she always did, and wagged a bare foot with Halloween-orange toenails. She was wearing short cutoffs, very short cutoffs.

"So how you been, Mags?"

"Getting adjusted and all that. Started lookin for a job today, met with my parole agent."

"That's good."

She frowned and leaned forward to trace the scar on my jaw with her forefinger. I could feel her breath on my chin.

"A fight in lockup." I fingered a splinter of her hair. Chestnut-colored satin. "You did something to your hair."

"I put a rinse in it, lighten it up. Got tired of the same old, same old. Like it?"

"Looks fine. But you always looked real fine." I inhaled the angles of her cheekbones, the bluntness of her nose, the peak of her eyebrows. "So how you been?"

"Working, El Capitán over on Alvarado and Ninth."

Her thumb brushed my cheek like a feather. Ripples waved through me, from skull to sole. "I know that place. I'll come in and ask for your table."

"I mostly work in the kitchen, doing prep for the chefs. Sometimes they let me work the tables, like this week. I'm doing the early shift. I like that better cuz of the tips."

"I got my diploma, not a GED, a real diploma, top score in the class."

"That's good, Mags, real good."

Silence fell as we searched each other's eyes for any spark of what we once had. The moment swelled like an inflating balloon, then it burst. I grabbed her hand and buried my lips in her doll's palm. She slid her arms around my neck, and I wrapped mine around her waist and the world disappeared.

It reappeared in her room in a tangle of skin, sweat, sheets. And a panic attack. "What about Blueboy, your moms?"

"Chill, they won't be home for a while." Her head lay on my chest. I strummed her shoulder with my hand. It was late afternoon. Golden light streamed through the blinds, striping her back with shadows.

"Hey, you got a new tatt. I didn't even notice." She propped herself on an elbow to look at it.

"Yeah, I meant to show you." I suddenly felt embarrassed.

"A dove, right over your heart?" Her face creased into a knowing smile.

"Yeah, una paloma de paz." That was her full name. Dove of Peace. Her mom named her that because she said children were the hope for peace in El Salvador, a new generation without war.

She grabbed me so hard it took my breath away.

"I missed you, nena," I whispered in her ear. "You have no idea how much. I prayed every night you would be here for me. I didn't think you would be. I know I don't deserve you."

"It really hurt me, what you said on that last visit, but then I understood. You were just tryna make it easier on me. I tried to let you go, but you were always there in my mind."

Something eased in me when she said that. "Me, too."

Our lungs moved in unison, in and out. "I want to tell Blueboy this time," she said. "I want this to be real."

"I'll break it to him. Just give me some time so it don't seem so sudden."

"I don't know why this has to be against code. I mean, it's dumb."

"I'm getting outta all that now, so I won't have to go by no code."

"You mean it? For real?"

"I'm tired, nena. I just want a normal, peaceful life."

She rolled on top of me, hunting the truth in my eyes. I wanted to stay like that forever, meshing her heartbeat into mine.

"What made you change?"

"I did forty-five days in the SHU for a fight. You know what I did all that time? Rub the tatts on my hands. I rubbed them so hard, they were bleeding, and I had to get bandaged up. When the bandages came off, the ink was still there. And I got real depressed. When I got outta the hole, I realized what I was tryna do—rub the tatts off. Deep down, I knew I didn't want to be in the life no more."

"That's heavy shit, Mags."

"That's what lockup does to you. You get to thinking about things. I thought a lot about you, about how it could be if I wasn't in the clica. I got so tired of thinking, I banged my head against the wall to make the thoughts stop." I tidied her hair into a waterfall on one side of her neck. "But I don't know how Blue's gonna take it, you and me."

"He'll get used to it. He's gonna have to."

I caressed the landscape of her body as she lay on top of me. Round, smooth hills of her buttocks. The valley of her waist. The wavy sea of her ribs. The cliffs of her shoulder blades.

"He ever say anything to you? Like he suspected about us?" I said.

"Uh-uh. It's getting late. We gotta roll."

"Just five more minutes."

I pressed my mouth to hers. It was more than five minutes.

THREE

I floated home in the twilight full to bursting until I saw an electric blue Caprice Classic, tricked out in chrome hubs and fat tires on a jacked up suspension, parked in front of the apartment building. My brother was polishing the hood. He was geed up in an orange and black Hawaiian shirt, hair gelled back and shiny, skin bronzed. A fuckin walking tropical vacation.

"Yo Frank."

"¡Hermano!" He threw his arms around me and slapped me on the back. I caught a noseful of that designer cologne. "You made it home, bro."

"Here I am."

"Sorry I couldn't make it to your welcome home dinner. I was on duty."

Frank was twenty-five, but he'd been acting like he was forty-five since he was a little kid.

With Pops either drunk or in a depression, Moms relied on Frank to be the man of the house.

It was Frank who threatened the landlord with filing a complaint with the city about the broken heat when he was twelve. It was Frank who went to the police station and the emergency room to find Pops when he didn't come home. It was Frank who made the payments on the corner store tab.

I always wanted to help out, but whenever Moms asked me to go to the store or take Zully to school, Frank would butt in and say he'd do it, or he'd come home early with the groceries and show me up. As he got older, he started ordering me and Lissy around, telling us to clean the house, be home by ten. He'd even go to the parent-teacher meetings Moms was always getting called to. That's when we really hit the streets, to show him we weren't letting him be the boss of us.

Frank gestured to the Caprice.

"So whadda ya think, vos? This is my baby."

"Vergón, real tight." I stroked the hood. It was a sweet paint job. I checked out the interior. The steering wheel was one of those chrome chain link jobs.

"She cost me, but she been worth it." Frank propped open the hood and slipped behind the wheel to switch on the ignition. "Nothing like these bench seats on a date." He laughed, showing teeth that looked like kernels of white corn. "Check this out."

The engine growled right away. He pressed the gas, and it answered with a throaty rumble that dropped into a deep purr. I peered inside the hood.

"Smooth, huh?" he called out.

"Real clean, vos. You done a good job on it. What year is it—eighty-three, eighty-four?"

"Eighty-two. Wanna go for a ride before I go pick up my girl, Glenda? She's coming over for dinner tonight. Come on, jump in."

I shut the hood and got in. I was envious as hell, but I did want to see how the car drove. Frank slid on a pair of Ray Bans and pulled out, right hand on the wheel, left elbow resting on the window ledge with his fingers holding the roof. The Man.

"I'm off these next three days. I do three on, four off. So, you get the bed to yourself half the time. More when I can swing it. Glenda tells her parents she's sleeping over a friend's and one of my buddies lets me use his place when he's at the station. Anyway, I can help you look for a job, or whatever." He glanced over at me.

"I got it under control." Last thing I wanted to do was give Frank permission to run my life. It was going to be enough trouble keeping his ass out of it anyway. "Thanks all the same," I added, just to show I didn't mean nothing negative by it.

We hit the shopping area around MacArthur Park, and I read the signs on the stores to myself. *Envíos a Guatemala y El Salvador. Llamadas a México. Casa de Empeño. Pupusería.* The sidewalks were crammed like a giant flea market—people selling jeans, pots

22

and pans, plastic bags of mango slices, anything they could find to make a few bucks. Everything looked familiar and strange, old and new, I belonged and I didn't.

Frank kept running his mouth. "You were always real good at fixing rides and shit. You should get a job as a mechanic."

"Yeah, maybe."

I stuck my nose out the window to smell the bacon-wrapped sausages cooking on carts with propane gas tanks. Three big jaguar spots were spray painted in black on a wall. The Cyco Lokos sign. This was our turf.

Frank noticed me looking at the tag.

"You ain't going back banging, vos." I guessed it was a question, but he didn't say it like he was asking.

"Nah, man, that's all behind me. Don't trip."

"I hope so. You make sure you stay away from those homeboys, nothing but trouble. Get you right back where you came from."

I let the urge to grab him by his shirt collar fly out the window and changed the subject. "You working a lotta fires?"

"I'm out in the Northeast Valley. It's fuckin hot out there. Summer's gonna be a bitch. We're getting ready for wildfire season."

Frank had wanted to be a firefighter since he was a little kid. After squeaking by in school, he put his name on the FD list, which was so long it took five years for him to be called. But he waited it out. He went to the academy, passed all the tests and now he was a rookie firefighter—the hotshit hero.

We were back in front of our building. "Good to have you home, have the family all together again."

I couldn't help but glare at him, but I swallowed the words jumping to get out of my throat. *If you're so big on family, why didn't you ever come see me in lockup?*

"Felicidades on the ride, 'mano."

I remembered what Mr. Estevez said to me after reading an essay I wrote about my family, which won first prize in a writing contest. "So, your brother's a firefighter and you're a gangster."

I was straddling a chair at his desk, resting my arms on the back. "Don't be tripping me with that shit."

"Maybe you're more alike than you think."

I smushed my lips into a "yeah, right" face.

"Seriously. I'd say you're both good at what you chose to do," he said.

Nobody had ever compared me to Frank in that way. It was always him as the plus and me as the minus. Watching the Caprice roll down the street, I still couldn't figure how Frank and me were alike.

Moms went all out for Glenda's visit and made carne asada, yuca con ajo, arroz y plátanos maduros. It was a way better dinner than my welcome home arroz con pollo y frijoles. At least I got a cake.

I had to admit Glenda was fine. Classy. Spine book-straight, fingernails painted cherry- Popsicle red matching her lipstick. Setting the fork on her plate like it was silverware on fine china instead of aluminum on hard plastic.

She worked in the fire department's benefits office as a claims assistant. That was how she met Frank. "It was like love at first sight," she said, casting a saccharine smile at him. Frank looked as serene as a puppy sucking a teat.

Glenda handed around the basket of tortillas and asked polite little questions of Lissy and Zully. All eyes were on her. She was the star of the table.

I had been gone for almost two years, but after just two days I was scenery already. Nothing had changed.

"That was riquísimo, Doña Esperanza," Glenda said at the end of the meal.

Moms smiled a sunray, and I felt a pinch inside. I wanted some of that shine, like the time when I was eight years-old and played one of the Three Kings in the Nativity pageant at church. I fluttered my fingers at mi mamá in the audience, keeping my hand at my side so the teacher wouldn't see. Mi mamá's eyes fixed on me and she beamed.

"Yeah, best I ever tasted, mamá." I won a warmed over smile.

Glenda offered to help with the washing up as soon as Moms got to her feet with plates in her hand.

"No, no," Moms fussed. "You sit with Frank in the living room."

"I'll help." I grabbed some plates, but my effort was lost in the glow of Frank and Glenda.

"Isn't she pretty?" Mom said as we crowded the sink. "I'm hoping this works out with her and Frank. I want to see him settle down with a nice girl and start a family."

Frank and Glenda were pretending to watch some game show on a Spanish channel. Frank hated Spanish TV, but he was playing along with the game on Glenda's thigh, pressing an imaginary buzzer, and she was giving him knowing smiles. They didn't stay long after I plonked my ass down and switched the channel to the new novela, "Pasión del Milenio." I got hooked on telenovelas in lockup and finally realized why they were so damn popular. They made you forget about your own sorry life for just a little while.

I wanted to bring Paloma over. I wanted mi mamá to say my girl was nice, that she wanted me to settle down and have a family. My fingers found a hole in the arm of the couch. I pinched the foam underneath and pulled out a tuft. I kept yanking it as I remembered how I basked in Mom's gaze at the Nativity pageant so long I forgot to say my lines, and the other two kings jabbed me with their elbows. Everybody snickered, and my mamá's smile collapsed.

I wondered what my homies were doing. I missed them, and I missed how I felt around them—like I mattered.

Angel was right. It was going to be hard to stay away from them. I had to keep busy. Paloma was working the late shift, but maybe I could catch her on her break. I stood up and said I'd be back soon.

The next day Zully smirked at me when I came in the door after another day of a no-luck job hunt. She was watching TV with the balls of her feet resting on the coffee table with her friend Belinda, whose teeth were as crooked as the edge of a tin can. Belinda never talked, just giggled.

"What?" I said to Zully.

"Mi mamá is so pissed at you." She pointed to the arm of the couch. There was a huge crater in it where I had dug out the foam. Fuck.

"I'll buy her a new chair."

"How you gonna do that seeing as you don't got a job?"

I smacked her toes. "Get your feet off the damn table, girl."

FOUR

I chewed on a Twix and strolled down Broadway, wondering what the fuck I was going to do. It was my third day of job hunting. I had just gone around the seafood warehouses near Skid Row, but nobody wanted a tatted down, scarred up gangbanger. Everybody took one look at me and made up their minds without even asking about a criminal record, work experience, nothing. They didn't even give me a chance. I was fast sinking to the point of asking Pops if he could get me on at either of his jobs, but I always swore to myself I wouldn't go there.

When I was twelve, I went with him one week to his night job cleaning offices after he hurt his back at the warehouse. If he didn't go to the cleaning job, he didn't get paid. I came out of the women's bathroom holding a bag of bloody Kotex when I heard yelling. I ran down the hall.

A small, brown man stood in the middle of a big office, holding the vacuum handle in one hand, the cord looped in the other, staring wide-eyed at a woman behind a desk littered with Chinese takeout boxes. She looked at me.

"Do you speak English?" she barked.

"Yes."

She waved a flabby white arm at the small brown man—my father. "This man doesn't speak a word of English! I've asked him several times to come back later. I have a very important contract to write and he is disturbing me. Tell him he has to wait until I finish."

I wanted to sink into the floor. Pops looked at me, waiting for me to translate. Neither of my parents spoke a lot of English. I told him we'd have to come back later.

"Sorry, sorry, sorry," he told the woman, bobbing his head like a dashboard dog.

My father had been a guerrilla fighter in the mountains of El Salvador. I didn't know who I was more pissed at—him or the gabacha bitch.

"Stop it, papá. Let's just go." I tugged his arm.

"Is this man your father?" she asked.

"Yes," I whispered.

"We have laws against child labor in this country. I have a good mind to report him. You tell him that!"

She sat down at her computer, and I closed the door quietly.

We finished all the offices, and the bitch was still working. We waited almost an hour, falling asleep, til she left and we could go in to do her office.

Afterward, I sneaked back and dumped the Kotex bag on her floor. But Pops caught me and yelled at me that a stunt like that would cost him his job.

As I scooped up the mess, I vowed I would never become that small brown man.

Not long after that, I started running errands for Chivas.

I didn't want to ask mi mamá for a job, either. She sewed sequins and appliqués onto T-shirts and baseball caps at a factory.

I really wanted to prove to mis viejos —and to myself—that I was capable of doing something right, but I was running out of options.

I'd given a chunk of my gate money to Moms and I didn't have much pisto left in my pocket.

I walked past two huge speakers outside a store blaring Mexican banda music, the racks of Spanish magazines on the newsstands, the discount stores with kids' tricycles and bicycles chained up in a row on the sidewalk with a sign yelling *¡Rebaja!*

Then I saw it. "Help wanted."

The sign was stuck in a dusty storefront window displaying quinceañera dresses that looked like neon-colored lampshades with ruffles and bows.

I tossed my Twix wrapper into an overflowing box of trash on the curb and entered.

The storeowner had a receding hairline, a sagging jowl and a heavy Asian accent. "Yes, I got job for you. Start right now," he said. His name was Mr. Choi.

My spirit soared. From behind the counter, he dug out two giant orange arrows joined with two strings, a yellow curly wig and a red clown nose. My high flying moment was just that —a moment. He wanted me to stand on the corner wearing the outfit and the "Quinces! Cheap!" arrow over my shoulders, handing out sale fliers.

"How bout we ditch the arrow and the wig, and I just hand out the fliers?"

"No, you put sign and wig."

He wasn't checking my record or my tatts. He was paying cash. I jammed the wig on my head, the red ball on my nose, threw on the arrows and swiped the pile of fliers out of his hand.

"I got a job!" I sang as I walked through the front door.

Zully was chewing a pen cap at the kitchen table, an algebra textbook open in front of her.

"You mean a real job?"

"Yeah, a real job. Is that so hard to believe?"

"Kinda."

I scowled at her. "Where's mi mamá at?"

"Not home yet." Zully's eyes stayed on me as she toyed with her tip of her ponytail.

"Lissy?"

"In the bedroom. She's not feeling so good."

"Who's this fool I'm hearing she's with?"

"Benny?" Zully looked down at her math book. "I don't know."

I went to the girls' room and peeked through the half open door. Lissy was lying on her bunk. "Whatup, girl?"

She turned her head, her eyelids droopy. Her hair was a frizz of orange and black. She'd put some kind of streaks in it. I don't know why girls thought that made them look prettier. I sat next to her and wiped a trail of drool that crept from the corner of her mouth with my thumb.

"I feel like shit."

"What you got?"

"No sé. It's like I can't make my body do nothing. I had to come home early from work."

"Maybe you got the flu or something."

"Maybe."

"So when you gonna go to beauty school, sis? Get your own salon?"

She looked at the wall. "That's just a dream, Mags. Dreams don't really happen, don't you know that by now? They're just pictures to have in your head."

I felt a stone the size of a cherry at the bottom of my stomach. That little stone that comes when someone says a truth you don't want to hear. But I couldn't admit she was right, for me or for her. I pumped up my voice. "I'm gonna grow my hair out so I can be your first customer. But I don't know about a manicure."

She gave me an imitation of her old million-watt smile.

"Tell me, who's this dude you hooked up with?"

Her smile disappeared. "Un muchacho." She picked a piece of fluff from the blanket. "Who told you?"

I ignored the question. "He treating you good?"

She nodded, still concentrating on the fluff. I couldn't come down on her. What about me and Paloma? That was against code, too. These rules were stupid. If my sister was happy, if I was happy ... but I knew that didn't matter in the end.

"The real deal, huh?" I said. "Well, if he gives you any shit, I'll give him even more shit. You know I been down that road before." She found her smile. I stood. "By the way, I got me a jale."

I was stuffing my face with bread and cheese in the kitchen when Moms walked in.

"I got a job," I said, struggling to get the lump of bread off the roof of my mouth. "At a store downtown."

"Congratulations, m'ijo." She hugged me. She was soft and firm at the same time, like a ripe peach. Her head came up to my nose, and I could smell her strawberry shampoo. I tugged on the greying braid dropping like a bell-rope down her spine, my game with her since I was a kid.

"It's not much, handing out fliers, but it's something."

"It's honest work. If you keep eating, you'll spoil your dinner." She was already tying the faded yellow apron with white ruffles around her waist. Every salvadoreña had a frilly apron like that. I kissed her forehead, furrowed like a piece of corrugated metal. I wished I could wipe off the lines I gave her. Mi mamá was the glue that held the family together. Without her, I didn't know where we'd be. But it always seemed like there was never enough of her to go round. She always had some more pressing need than me. Mainly Pops. She was always taking care of him, cleaning up after him. Like he was the kid, not us.

"Mamá, I gotta go to Belinda's and drop off a book. I'll be right back," Zully said. "Bendición." She bowed her head so Moms could kiss her hairline.

"Dios te bendiga, m'hija. Don't be long. Dinner's coming up."

Something unexpected pricked inside me, seeing Zully ask Moms for her blessing. I stopped asking for her blessing years ago, bout the time I joined the clica. I figured I didn't need my parents' blessings, and who were they to bless me anyway? They weren't blessed. We sure as shit didn't have blessed lives.

Frank said it was a sign of respect, but it made me mad seeing my brother and sisters, even Lissy, bow their heads and ask for bendición like Moms and Pops were all that, but this time I realized it wasn't anger I felt. It was envy. I wanted to see my parents the way my sisters and brother did, to be able to ask for their blessing. I just didn't know if I could.

FIVE

The fuck you think you're doing?"

I straightened. I was getting the arrow and the wig from behind the counter. Some jaina with bouncy curls in her hair and her hands jug-handled on her hips filled the doorway to the back room.

"I'm getting ready to work, that's what the fuck I'm doing."

"Oh, you doing the sign?"

"Yeah, I'm doing the sign."

She disappeared and a flash later handed me a huge pile of fliers. "Mr. Choi wants you to hand these out today, coupons." I snatched the pile. "Chill out," she said.

She continued standing there, eyeballing me with her arms folded.

"¿Qué?" I said.

"Just doing my job, watching the store."

"Like I'm gonna gaffle a grip of quince dresses? That's what you're saying?"

"Well, I don't know you for shit."

"Magdaleno. Now you know me."

Her face softened a shade. "Yvette."

"Just so's you know, I get a bathroom break in two hours, in case you think I'm slacking off," I told her.

When I came in for my break, she was leaning on the counter, flipping the pages of a Spanish celebrity magazine. She glanced at me and kept on flipping as I passed her. I went to the back room, my knees cracking as I sat in a chair and ate the hot dog I bought in the street. I felt her staring at me and looked up. She was leaning against the doorway, looking at my hands.

"You always stare at people?" I said.

"Just wondering why a homeboy is doing a job like this."

This girl had the personality of fuckin sandpaper. I ignored her and finished my hot dog, which now tasted like cardboard.

"You got another break coming up?" she asked as I pushed past her to go back to work.

"Nope."

I shoulda known then the day was going to shit.

I was sweating hard under the stupidass wig and trying to ignore the red lump on my nose. People kept banging into the damn arrow and refusing to take a fuckin flier about the First Communion dress sale. Most of the fliers people did take ended up on the sidewalk, and I had to pick them up. Mr. Choi said the city would be on him if his fliers littered the "public right of way." Most of the other fliers ended up in an overstuffed trash can on the other side of the crosswalk. What was the fuckin point of this? I wondered if I should trash the fliers and tell Mr. Choi I handed them all out. But I reminded myself, I was getting paid by the hour. So, I recycled the clean fliers from the sidewalk and the trash and kept going.

Paloma's body was basically the only thing I thought about all day long. We dry humped in a doorway in the alley behind the restaurant on her break last night, and I was kinda hoping to do the same, or more, that night. Lucky for me, the arrow covered me from belly button to knees.

"Ay yo, homes!" A familiar voice sliced through the bustle. "Mags!"

I twirled faster than a ballet dancer, my stomach clenching. Fuck. It was him. Rico. Slashing across the street aiming the shopping bag in his hand at me. His shorts slung so low the waistband of his boxers showed. Socks, white as fluorescent light, pulled neatly to his knees. Ink flowing out of the arms and neck of his plaid shirt. Exactly how he looked the last time I saw him.

The memory of that day bore down on me. We were kicking it at a street corner, and Rico was bragging about how he shot a .38 into the ceiling of a liquor store he was jacking, and the storeowner pissed his pants. As he was talking, he took the .38 out of his waistband in a live re-enactment, and I just had to take the piece, feeling its cold weight in my hand for just a second or two before handing it back to Rico. That second or two cost me twenty-six months of my freedom.

When Tweety yelled, "Five-o!" Rico took off like an Olympic sprinter. I never even saw him throw down the gat. I had no reason to run.

As Morales was giving me his routine hassle, he kicked the edge of a bush behind me. Then he crouched. When he straightened, he was dangling the piece with a pen hooked through its trigger guard. He busted me on possession of a firearm. It got worse. The gun had a fuckin robbery on it. They matched the piece to the bullet fuckin Rico fired into the ceiling during the holdup, and my prints were the only clear ones. They hit me with a first-degree robbery charge and assault with a deadly weapon, which they tacked on since "I" waved the piece around and shot it during the robbery, like I would ever pull such a dumbass move, plus possession. I was looking at twenty years.

They had no evidence on me besides the .38. The storeowner didn't ID me in a lineup and none of my prints were found in the store, but I had no alibi.

The fact was, I was doing a drop with Chivas to the big jefe that night. Lissy signed a statement saying I was watching TV with her at home that night, but nobody believed her, seeing as she had said that before when I got busted. I couldn't drop the dime on Rico, or I'd have a shank between my ribs within twenty-four hours.

Still, I wanted to fight it, go to trial, but my public defender, a white vieja who huffed and puffed like one of the three cochinitos every time she walked, told me to plead out.

"You're not going to get a better deal," she said in between wheezes.

Since the DA knew their case for the robbery and ADW was weak, they'd drop those charges if I pleaded to possession. So I did. I was guilty of none of it.

Now Rico was throwing his arm around my shoulders like I was his compa. A thick gold chain glinted around his neck. I had a cord with an orange arrow slung around mine.

"Ese." My voice had as much life as a three-day-old soda.

I never knew if he dropped that .38 by accident, as he said, or if he saw his chance to set me up. I kinda figured the latter. Someday, somehow, I'd get him to admit the truth to me.

"I thought that was you. But I said to myself, 'Mags, in that fuckin pendejada? Couldn't be.' But I looked again and it sure as shit was you. Whatup with this?" He flicked the red nose ball. I caught his wrist in midair and stared him down in his swamp eyes. "Easy, homie," he said.

I dropped his wrist. "Just making a few bones."

"I heard you were back. We been waiting for you at the garaje, but you ain't showed up." Rico drilled my eyes. "You avoiding your homies or what?"

The ball was itching my nose like an oversized mosquito bite. "I got parole and all that. I just wanted to get set up first."

"I figured you needed a couple days to get readjusted, grab some pussy." He shook his head. "But damn, this shit?" He shook his head. "You ready to get crazy again?"

"Keeping it lo pro, Rico."

Rico studied me. I suddenly glimpsed myself in his eyes. I had become a small brown man.

He perked up. "Hey, I just had a kid. A boy. I'm buying some bottles and blankets and shit."

"Felicidades."

"With Maribel. But I got my side action, feel me?"

"You were always real slick with the jainas." I knew a little flattery would soften the rough edges of the meet. He smiled big.

"Tell you what, I'll give you some lessons, make you real smooth."

"Yeah, I'm out of practice now." I tried to laugh.

"A lot of changes gone down in the barrio. We need to catch you up." His arm hooked my neck in a chokehold. "You our firme homeboy, man, you'll always be part of la familia. We need you." He squeezed a little too hard. "You come by the garaje. We got a jump in day after tomorrow. We'll be waiting. We'll hook you up again, then you can dump this shit." He pointed his forefinger at me with a barbed wire smile. "Missed you, Mags."

I watched him vanish into the crowd of shoppers and spat on the ground to get rid of the bad taste that had flooded my mouth.

I lay in bed stewing about Rico that night. Running into him had put me in a funk Paloma couldn't even get me out of. No fuckin way he just bumped into me. Somebody saw me in that stupidass outfit, told Rico and he came over to humiliate me. That was how he operated— pulling strings from the shadows. I should have gone to the garaje right when I came home, then everything would've been on my terms. Now I'd let Rico get an edge on me. I had fucked up. I was a dumbass to think I could avoid him or the homeboys.

Being a loner inside had dulled my blade. After I got out of the SHU and back in gen pop, I got the job at the library and enrolled in school. I kept my head down, didn't want nothing with nobody. I was shelving books one day and noticed the tatts on my hands. It was like they belonged to somebody else. I had forgotten about them.

It was then I knew I was more than the skin of my tattoos. They were a part of me, but not the whole of me. But like Blueboy said, that was in there and this was out here. I was back to being my tatts. The black ink was soaked deep into my pores.

I had to get sharper, get back on my game. I had to think like the street again, constantly striving to be one step ahead but always checking my back at the same time. Someone was always ready to stick you between the shoulder blades over power, money, girls. Could be one of your own homeboys or a rival, buyers or suppliers, or the po-po. It was fuckin exhausting.

That's why loyalty was the backbone of the barrio, along with respect. But what did I get for my loyalty?

I lost my freedom and almost my mind while someone else took my place, not because he earned it, but because he played the game better than me.

Still, Rico had to respect me. I had status for taking the possession rap and hitting that 5150 inside—and I knew that would give me some wriggle room. The question was how much. Would it be enough to get me veteran status?

Judging by Rico's attitude on the street, it might not be. It was going to take more than wishful thinking.

Blueboy was right. I had to come up with a play. In the meantime, I'd have to go to the jump in or the homies would come looking for me.

Pops came in. I hadn't told him about my job yet. He had to give me recognition for that, seeing as how that was all he ever bugged me about. He passed through to the kitchen. The fridge door thunked, and the gas whumped as the stove ring lit.

I waited til I heard him sit down, then I went into the kitchen. I watched him suck down rice and beans and beer for a second, hoping he'd look up, but he didn't.

I spoke. "Papá. I got some good news." He swallowed some beer and stuck another forkful of rice into his mouth. "I got a job. Downtown." I paused. He kept eating. "Now I can help you and mamá out."

After scraping the last grain of rice from his plate, he got up and fetched another beer from the fridge. He glugged it down, his back to me. I snapped. "And you know what? It's not cleaning fuckin toilets!"

He turned around real slow, eyes black as flies. "You think you're some kind of king?" He clunked down his can and walked out.

My hands curled into fists. I wanted to destroy everything in that fuckin apartment. Why did I ever want to come home? I turned into the living room and grabbed my pants. I was going to hit the street. The front door opened.

"Going somewhere, vos?"

Frank. He'd accuse me of banging if I went out. I stepped out of the jeans and flung them onto the floor. I got into bed and turned my back to the room. I heard him go into the bathroom. A piss waterfall, a flush. The floorboard creaked. His shoes thunked onto the floor, belt buckle jangled. The light switch clicked and finally, the mattress sagged with his weight.

"Man, I'm beat," he said. I said nothing. "You okay, bro?"

I wasn't going to answer but the words shot out. "What the fuck is wrong with Pops? Why is he so fuckin mad all the time?"

"Who the fuck knows? I think it goes back to the war in Salvador."

I rolled onto my back. "What's the big fuckin secret? I tried asking mi mamá, but she always waves me off."

"They never told me either."

"So that's why he drinks all the time?"

"I guess it helps him forget. I figure he has PTSD or some shit."

"Remember those nightmares he had? He'd wake up

36

screaming."

"He ain't had them in a while. You gotta let him slide off you."

Easy for him to say. Pops always treated Frank nicer than me. "You know the best thing he did for us?" I said.

"What?"

"He got us citizenship."

"You're lucky he did that. They're taking away green cards and deporting anyone with any kind of conviction now, even petty shit," Frank said.

"Yeah, I knew some of them fools in lockup. After they do their time, they get sent to immigration detention and then they're shipped out."

"Pops started drinking real heavy after that lawyer ripped us off, remember?" Frank said.

A few years after we arrived in LA, some lawyer told him that political asylum was the easiest way to get papers, and he and mamá had a good case. The lawyer charged five thousand dollars up front. Pops borrowed money, and Moms pawned two gold rings her mother had gave her. They, and Frank, sold roses at the bottom of freeway exit ramps every spare minute they had. I stayed home to take care of the girls and the landlord banging on the door. After they paid the lawyer, they never saw him again. We got our green cards through an amnesty program, and as soon as we qualified, Pops got us all citizenship. He said he wasn't going to be at the mercy of a weasel lawyer ever again.

Frank rolled on his side, ready to go to sleep, but I wanted to keep talking.

"You remember anything about Salvador, Paco?" That was Frank's nickname when he was a kid, Paco being short for Francisco. He was named for a guerrillero compa of Pops' who was killed in an ambush. But since the age of thirteen, he made everyone call him "Frank."

"Not much, a couple things," he mumbled.

"Like what exactly?"

"I remember when you were born. I went to stay with tío Salomón and his wife. They were real nice. They took me to abuela's, and I chased the chickens in her yard. Pops was up in the mountains back then, so he didn't see you for a while."

"That's Pops' youngest brother, the one he likes, right?"

"He's good people. He's the only one Pops still talks to now and then."

"I wish I remembered more. I guess I was too little."

Frank answered with the deep, rhythmic breathing of sleep. I was Salvadoran by blood and birth, but I really didn't know shit about the country. I only knew it from other people's memories. I didn't really feel Salvadoran, but I didn't feel American either, even though I had pieces of paper that said I was both. I was from the streets of LA. That was all I knew.

SIX

Paloma and me were always trying to figure things so we could see each other without anybody seeing us. Her mom worked nights at the hospital and Blueboy was usually out kicking it at night, so most of the time I could go over to her place but sometimes Paloma had to work the late shift. On those nights, we had to settle for seeing each other on her break in the alley behind the restaurant.

The night I had to go to the clica meeting she was working, but I was uptight and wanted to see her. She always calmed me down. It was too early for her break, so Paloma told the boss she had cramps and needed to run to the drugstore. The day's final light was a grey veil floating over us as we crouched in a doorway down the block from the restaurant and kissed long and deep. I took her hand in mine. It felt delicate as a piece of lace.

"You nervous about the meeting, baby?" she asked.

"How can you tell?"

"You're holding my hand real tight." I loosened my grip, and she caressed my face. I leaned my cheek into the palm of her hand. "You gonna tell Rico you want out of the clica?"

"I don't know. I gotta see his mood. It might be better to wait a while, or talk to him alone, or see if I can talk to Chivas directly."

"You stood up to him before, lots of times. The sooner you do it, the better."

"Yeah, but now he's the boss. When he sees I want something from him, he's gonna use it against me. I know him."

"Don't forget what you did for him and the Cycos. You gotta make sure he don't forget. You deserve something in return. ¿Sí o sí?"

I smiled. "Sí."

"Eso. Now I better get back or they'll be firing my ass." We stood. "You gonna meet Blue?"

"Yeah." I drew her to me for a last kiss before we headed opposite ways down the alley.

Night dropped as I walked. Telling Rico I deserved to leave the clica in return for taking the hit on the .38 wasn't going to be as simple as she thought. That wasn't how the clica operated. It owned you. You were expected to take hits. You served until they told you different. Punto.

It was dark along the blocks. Kids must've smashed the streetlights. I used to be real good at that. Me and Blueboy had contests to see how many we could hit. That was how we got in with the Cycos.

Chivas paid us to throw rocks at the lights on the corners where they were slinging, or outside some store they were going to jack, then I got busted one night outside a liquor place with a rock in my hand. Blueboy escaped and warned Chivas to stay away from the store. I told the cops I was smashing streetlights for kicks. I didn't say anything about the Cycos. I got probation and the belt from Pops. I didn't care.

I earned big points with Chivas. He put Blueboy and me on the official track to be jumped in as members.

We met another buster wanting to be jumped in, too—Rico. He made it a race to see who would be jumped in first. I won. Then Rico wanted to be my carnal, hanging around me all the time, but I already had Blueboy.

After I distanced myself from Rico, he turned everything into a contest between him and me. I didn't want it that way, he did.

I bought a Milky Way and headed to the abandoned house where Blueboy would go to chill.

I crawled through a hole in the chain-link fence and whistled low.

A whistle answered from the back, along with the scent of mota on the air.

I trudged through the tall weeds, kicking empty bottles, wadded up diapers and food containers out of the way.

My eyes adjusted to the darkness and made out a figure hunched on the back step. I sat next to him, detecting a stench as a breeze rustled the grasses.

"¡Puta! The fuck is that stink, man?"

"A dead mutt in a box over there. You only smell it when the wind blows."

"And you gotta sit here?" I pulled up my T-shirt over my nose and mouth.

"I get the place to myself."

"That's for sure. So how you think I gotta play this with Rico?"

"You gotta kiss his ass. That's the only way he's gonna do anything like go to Chivas for you."

"Fuck that, fool. I already kissed his ass—for twenty-six fuckin months."

"He ain't gonna see it like that. You know like I know, you gotta take a hit for the clica if you got to and then be ready to take another one. That's the code."

"Me getting sent down wasn't about no code. That was about Rico and me. You know like I know."

"Yeah, Rico's always got that beef with you, but he's in charge now. You gotta go through him to get to Chivas and, like I told you, Chivas is looking for everyone to earn right now."

"I gotta find a way to get to Chivas directly."

"What makes you so damn sure Chivas is gonna put you on inactive just like that?" Blueboy's voice rose.

I stared at him. It hit me that he wasn't down with me leaving the clica. I thought he'd be on my side.

"I figure I got a fifty-fifty chance."

"You know why he ain't gonna want to let you go? You know too much about his business."

The red ember of his blunt flared as he toked. I did know too much. I took out my Milky Way and bit off a chunk.

"I ain't no fuckin rat, if that what's you're saying."

"I know. But you gotta see it like they see it. You been away for a while and nobody knows what went down with you, who you been talking to and shit."

I felt a rise of anger.

"I tell you who I been talking to—no fuckin body. You know what the hole does to your mind, fool? It turns you inside out. When I got out, every little noise was a crash inside my head. I couldn't stand being round people, couldn't talk to them, even if I wanted. It took a long time for me to get back to myself."

I didn't tell him how I cried in the night for mi mamá like a fuckin mocoso kid, how I humped the mattress and imagined Paloma's skin and flesh on mine. When I opened my eyes, I couldn't believe she wasn't there. I stopped doing it because it just made the time worse.

"Why you being so negative, homes?" I said.

Blueboy spoke in his tight inhaled voice. "I ain't being negative. I'm being real."

"You don't want me to get out."

Blueboy exhaled a lungful of smoke. "You and me been through a lotta crazy shit," he said quietly.

"True that."

"You're the brother I never had. We signed up for this together, 'member when we got jumped in?"

"Like I'm gonna forget? Longest beatdown of my life."

"You got off better 'n me. I got two broke ribs."

"I got kicked in the back of the head, and it hurt like a motherfucker for three days straight."

That night, Blueboy and me walked home real slow. We were both pretending like nothing hurt, like we were big tough locos.

Blueboy was breathing heavy, his face the color of cigarette ash. Every footstep sent pain racking through my body. My head felt like it'd been chopped with an axe.

Then Blueboy stopped. "Gotta tie my shoelaces," he said.

We sat on the curb, trying not to let the pain show. Blueboy didn't even pretend to tie his laces. He knew I knew it was an excuse to rest.

After a couple minutes, we got up and walked on.

"We got a history, a lot of good times with all the homeboys," Blueboy said. "Hey, 'member that time we got wet and went around lifting the front ends of rides?"

I chuckled. "Yeah, I got you. I lifted that pickup about three inches."

"You beat me by half an inch, dog. I thought you were having a heart attack, your face got so red. We did a lot of stupid shit back then."

"Yeah, we did."

"You gonna throw away all that?"

"I ain't throwing it away, just seems like it was different back then." I screwed up the candy wrapper into a ball and tossed it into the grass. "Why don't we go out together, like we came in?"

Blueboy shrugged with one shoulder. "What else I'm gonna do, Mags? For real?"

"We'll figure something out. We could go somewhere else, away from here."

He was thoughtful for a moment. "You ever think about going to Salvador?"

"What I wanna go there for?"

"I don't know. See where you came from, shit like that."

"Never really thought about it. You thinking bout going?"

"Know what I want to do? Find my viejo and make him recognize me, just once, make him say, 'You are my son.' That's the only thing I want to do before I die."

I thought back to what Blueboy told me years ago, when we were sitting on the roof of my building, drinking Pops' beer I stole from the fridge. We were looking out at the bony mountain ridge, a serrated edge along the sky. I paid for that beer with a beating later but I didn't care—it was for Blueboy.

His mom, Flor de María, was the cook for the workers on a coffee estate called Finca Tres Lunas, up in the mountains of San Miguel. It was owned by the Mannheims, a rich family who came from Germany like a hundred years ago. Flor de María was nineteen with long eyelashes that fluttered like hummingbird wings—Blueboy's words, I was impressed.

When the owner's family cook got sick and went back to her pueblo, they called Flor de María up to the casa grande to cook for them. The boss's son, Enrique, noticed her right away. He wasn't much older than her. He started coming round the kitchen when she was alone cleaning up at night. She couldn't say no, she was afraid she'd get fired. Besides, he was handsome, with light hair and skin and eyes, and brought her little gifts, treated her nicer than anyone ever had. She fell in love with him and thought he loved her, that's what he said, anyway. When she got a belly on her, Enrique stopped coming round. They got a new cook and sent her back to the workers' kitchen.

Flor de María knew Enrique would never marry her, but she hoped he'd recognize his kid, give him his surname. After the baby was born, Enrique came and looked at his son. The baby looked just like his viejo, too much like him, blanquito with eyes as blue as the Virgin's robe. The next day the foreman called her into his office, handed her an envelope of dollars and a suitcase. She wrapped Blueboy in a blanket tight as a sausage and paid a coyote to go to el norte.

"Know what?" I said. "I'll go with you to Salvador. We'll find your viejo and make him fuckin recognize you." I held up my arm, elbow on my knee. Blueboy clasped my hand.

"Hecho," he said and exhaled a stream of smoke. "You say anything yet to Lissy?"

"She ain't been feeling so good so I ain't had the heart to say anything."

"It's the code, Mags," he said flatly. He took me aback. Blueboy was never such a hardass before. Or maybe he was, and I never realized it. "You really gonna keep working that job? I mean, a fuckin clown suit?"

"It's for fuckin parole, man, and it's just the wig and the nose." My voice was sharp.

"Hey, I'm gonna tell all the homeboys where to go see you if you don't give me the rest of your candy stash." Mischief crept into his voice like a little kid. That was the Blueboy I remembered. He knew his attitude was pissing me off, so he switched up.

"What if I already ate it all?"

He fell on my shoulders and bagged up like that was the funniest thing he'd ever heard. His laugh was like a donkey heehawing. I cracked up, like I always did when he laughed.

"I missed the fuck out of that burro honk, bro," I said when I got my breath back. Blueboy was still chuckling, leaning on my shoulder limp and heavy. I pushed him off me. "Let's get the fuck outta here."

We zig-zagged through alleys and rolled over fences in a fluid, wordless rhythm, eyes and ears pricked, just like we used to. I felt the edge coming back. Suddenly, I couldn't wait to see my homeboys. We stopped at a bunch of bushes in an alley and dove in, crawling through a hole in a cement block wall. I stood up in the garage behind an apartment building—the Cyco Lokos safehouse.

The air smelled of stale cigarette smoke. The same old ripped up couches and odd armchairs sat around a piece of dirty beige carpet. Burned down candles in jars with pictures of the Virgin and saints sat on upturned crates.

"Look who I found," Blueboy said.

"Mags!"

"¡Ese!"

One by one, the homies hugged me and clapped me on the back. "Whatup, Mags?" "We missed you, dog."

I looked for my firme homeboys. Cojo, Tweety, Flaco, Jackie Chan. They were smiling, waiting with arms folded til the other homies finished greeting me. Then one by one, they came up.

Cojo was first. He was called "gimpy" on account of his left foot turning in on itself. A club foot, they called it. Doctors said it could have been fixed when he was a baby, but Cojo was born in a village in Salvador where they didn't know nothing about nothing, so they left him like that. People in the village told his mom she must've sinned to give birth to a disabled kid. It made me mad. The unfairness of where you were born determining your body, your whole life outcome.

But what Cojo lacked in his lower limb, he made up for in his upper ones. His shoulders practically filled a doorway, and nobody could ever beat him in arm wrestling. He was always looking for a match.

"I'm gonna take you on soon. I been working out bigtime," I said.

He grinned. "Whenever you ready, homes."

Flaco was skinny as a palm tree with hunch in his shoulders and an Adam's apple that looked like a mango stone stuck sideways in his throat. He was Guatemalan and had the Mayan pyramid of Tikal and a quetzal bird tatted on his shoulders. If you wanted to get the score on anything going down in the barrio, Flaco was the vato who got the 411.

"How's the lil homie doing?" I asked him.

"Real good." His little brother had Down syndrome. Flaco was real protective of him. We all were. Andrés was a honorary homie.

"I'll come by and see him."

Flaco smiled. "He'd like that, homes. He's always asking for you."

Jackie Chan loped up next. His vieja was Chinese-Salvadoran so Jackie had kind of a chino look. That's why he was called Jackie Chan. His dad was a hardcore junkie, in and out of jail, promising to get clean and then disappearing, showing up when he needed money or food, or when he was beat up. Jackie always tried to rescue him. I spent many nights with Jackie looking for his pops. One night we found him curled up on the grass in MacArthur Park, nodded out, arms black and blued, feet bare and crusted with grime. Jackie stared at him, then turned and left. He never mentioned him again.

I grabbed the back of his neck and hugged him to me. "You aight?"

He held on to me for that extra second. "Good to have you back, Mags." I knew he meant it.

Tweety boxed the air as he bounced up to me. Everybody bagged up. He was an amateur bantamweight boxer, small, but built like a piece of wire. He spoke in a squeak, which is why he learned to fight so he could beat down bullies. He wanted to turn pro and go for a belt.

"You better come to my next fight, homes," he said.

"And if I don't?"

"Then you'll be my KO number eleven, homes."

I laughed and air-boxed him back. "I missed you clowning around. I sure coulda used some a that inside."

"I'm gonna make DVDs of myself. Next time somebody gets sent down, they can take one with em."

I felt someone grab the back of my neck like they were picking up a dog. I jumped and wheeled at the same time. Rico. I should've guessed.

"Welcome home, Mags." I wrenched his arm off me. "Sorry, homes. I shoulda remembered you must be sensitive to people coming up from behind. A lotta shit in the pen happens from the rear, I hear," he said. Someone snorted a laugh.

I stared him down. "The fuck you say?"

He held up his hands in surrender. "I'm fuckin with you. Don't mean no disrespect, Mags. My bad." He turned to face the homeboys. "I got a few words from Chivas to pass on. Mags here is an honorable soldier. He showed the loyalty Cyco Loko homeboys gotta have. He took this rap, and then he represented us against a fuckin 5150 dissing us inside and took that rap. We're real happy to have him back."

Everybody nodded. I crossed my arms and eyeballed the floor. I wasn't used to all the attention. I wondered if Chivas was going to make me his lieutenant after all.

"Aight, we got some business to attend to, then we can party. Where you at, Mouse?" Rico said.

A peewee stepped out of the crowd. I could see how he earned his placa. His eyes were close to a pointy nose and his ears stuck out like handles. The charcoal smudge of a first-time mustache added to the effect.

He folded his arms and set his feet apart in the banger stance. He aimed his eyes straight ahead, trying not to look scared but he wasn't fooling anybody. We'd all been in that same spot.

"Let's start the fiesta," Rico said.

We moved into a circle around the kid. He licked his lips. I shook my arms loose.

"Mags, in honor of your homecoming," Rico said.

He was sure into playing the boss. Fuckin cabrón. It should be me giving the orders, not him. It should have been him that got sent down, not me.

I flexed my fists as I moved in front of the kid. His eyes flicked at me then away. Fuckin Rico. I no longer saw the kid. It was Rico's face swimming in front of me.

"We go for sixty seconds, and ¡dale!" Rico yelled.

My right arm whammed the kid's solar plexus with an uppercut. Grunting, he jackknifed, eyes wide, jaw gulping for air.

The homeboys surged, raining blows on the kid. Power ran through my veins.

I unleashed punches, hard as I could make them. He tumbled to the floor and balled himself up. A hurricane of feet attacked him.

I kicked him anywhere I could find a space.

"¡Ya!" Rico yelled.

Everyone pulled back. I booted him in the kidney. Again, again, again. I couldn't stop.

Hands yanked me back. I heaved ragged breaths, the only sound in the shocked silence.

"The fuck wrong with you?" Rico's glare could've cracked cement. I rubbed my nose, embarrassed. What I'd done was way out of line.

The peewee's face was bloody and already puffing. He dragged himself to his hands and knees. He brought one foot up, then the other. He stood, swaying and swabbing the dribbles of blood from his mouth with his arm.

Rico clapped him on the back. "Bienvenido a la familia." The air cleared. The homeboys pumped fists with Mouse as he smiled in a daze.

Blueboy steered me to the side.

"The fuck you trippin for?"

All I could do was shake my head. Beer and bottles appeared. The sweet scent of mota kissed the air. I went over to Mouse and stuck out my hand as my apology. We pumped fists.

I sat with my homies. Jackie Chan told dirty jokes. Flaco farted. Blueboy was running away from some girl. Cojo was running after another. Tweety cracked us up. It felt seamless, like I'd never been away.

Rico, king of the clica, pulled up a chair—his throne. "We're gonna move on Elysian Park, sooner the better."

Sourness crept up the back of my throat. I knew right then I couldn't let Rico get away with setting me up to go down on that piece.

If I asked him to go on inactive status, it would be giving him more power over my life, and I was done with that. I had to get payback and then I could get out. I opened my mouth.

"You sure that's open turf? Don't the 5150s got some action up there?"

Rico's face tightened. "This came down from Chivas."

Flaco spoke. "That's 5150 turf, but they ain't been collecting since a grip of their fools got busted in a takedown."

"There's gotta be a reason why they ain't collecting up there. They ain't gonna leave money on the street like that," I said.

"You heard Flaco, they ain't got the ranks. It's a perfect time to move in. And if the 5150s do hassle us, we take em on and take em out," Rico said.

"Taxing maricón putas is petty shit. We need to make real feria," I said.

Rico eyeballed me. "You been gone for a while, Mags, things have changed up."

I made a show of shrugging. "Whatever you say, homes."

I went outside to take a piss. The moon hung like a giant comma in the sky. Footsteps shuffled next to me. The sound of unzipping sawed the darkness.

"You better show respect, Mags." Rico's voice landed on the back of my neck. "I'm calling the shots now. I know you don't like it, but that's how it is."

My arms tensed, but I held them. Now wasn't the time. He zipped up and went back to the party. I took a deep breath and followed him.

I watched Rico telling jokes, slapping his knee, getting high. When he let himself be a regular guy, he was okay. But sooner or later, he'd put up a wall to see who could jump highest, fastest. He had always tried to impress Chivas, talking him up to other people when Chivas was there to hear him do it, giving him presents of Chivas Regal, siding with him on everything, inviting him to his tio's cockfights.

On the street, he'd use Chivas's name, bragging that he was close to him so he could get pussy and favors. A couple times that got back to Chivas and he'd lay into Rico for it. Chivas saw through Rico, or so I thought. He'd use him to wax his car, buy his booze, run errands for Esme, his main lady, and his rucas on the side. But it was me who he'd take to pay the tributes to the higherups, do the dope pickups, deliver feria to Esme. I did the important stuff because he trusted me.

I was sure it was the day the cops chased us that pushed Rico to set me up. Cojo, Rico and me were jacking a ride. La ley swooped in, tires screeching as they braked. "Five-o!" Rico yelled. We booked, throwing the screwdrivers and slim jims down a street drain. We were way ahead of them, almost at the end of the block by the time they barreled out of the squad car. But Cojo, with his gimpy leg, fell behind. I looked round and saw the panic on his face as he tried to make that damn leg work, but it wouldn't.

The cops were gaining on him, but they were old-timers, bellies hanging over their belts from too many doughnuts. I ran back, picked up Cojo and slung him over my shoulder like a sack of rice. Rico was long gone. I sprinted as fast as I could with the extra weight, but I knew I wouldn't make it. We ducked into an alley. I tossed Cojo into an open Dumpster, then threw myself in. We covered ourselves with garbage, holding our T-shirts over our noses.

Something furry brushed my cheek, and I almost yelled. Cojo kicked. He'd felt one, too. I closed my eyes and steeled every muscle in my body against the rats.

I could hear panting. The cop must've been right outside the Dumpster. "Lost visual on suspects. Ending foot pursuit." The radio crackled. "Ten-four." Feet scraped on asphalt, then quiet.

We waited a little while longer then climbed out, brushing off potato peels and baby shit. Cojo was real embarrassed. He hated being reminded of his leg. I promised him I wouldn't tell anybody, but he went and told Jackie Chan, who told Chivas. Chivas held me up as a loyal homeboy. After that, he had me tag along with him practically 24/7, and even pass on his orders to Rico. Not long after that, I very conveniently got sent down.

Rico was waving a bottle of mescal by the neck, holding it up to show the worm. "Got this special for tonight," he slurred. "I knew Mouse would need it. Take the pain right off, homeboy."

He passed it to Mouse, who took a big swig, then coughed and shook his head. Everybody laughed. He handed the bottle to Flaco.

"Damn!" Flaco said after his shot. The bottle made its way round the circle. When it got to me, I hesitated for a split-second. It was going to hit me hard since I hadn't drunk a drop of alcohol in two years. I steered clear of that prison pruno they made from whatever shit they could scrape up from the kitchen.

Rico zeroed right in. "Clowns can't take mescal?"

Staring him down, I took two huge gulps. My stomach lurched as the liquid flames hit it, but I hardened my face. I lowered the bottle and wiped my mouth with the back of my hand.

"The fuck you saying about clowns?" I handed the bottle to Cojo.

Rico smiled like he had a big secret. When the bottle got to him, there was only an inch or so of mescal left. He drained it and pulled back his lips to display the worm caught between his teeth. He closed his mouth and chewed, grinning.

After the meeting, I rolled home with Blueboy. "Why the fuck you challenge Rico like that?" he said.

"Just seeing that cabrón, listening to him. I couldn't take it."

"You ain't gonna get nothing from him acting like that."

"Remember when he waxed Chivas's ride and I had to make him do it over cuz it didn't have the showroom shine Chivas wanted?" I didn't like coming down on another homeboy, but Chivas said it was leadership training, yeah, training right into el bote. Chivas, I realized, had used me too, to do his dirty work, to test my loyalty.

"Rico was so pissed steam was practically coming outta his nostrils. He'll prolly make you wax his truck now." Blueboy chuckled.

"He's got a truck?"

"Brand new."

Was there anything Rico didn't get while I was doing his time? "He deserves payback, Blue. I don't think I can let this shit slide."

"Just watch your back, homes. Rico don't play."

He turned off to go visit one of his rucas, and I continued on home. Apart from Rico, it had been a good night. I loved my homeboys. Leaving the clica would mean being on my own. I had never really thought about that part. I'd have Paloma, sure, but girls weren't the same. Blueboy was right. We had a combat history together.

The time Flaco got shot in the back and the doctors gave him a fifty-fifty chance. We went to Santa Cecilia's and lit candles—Rico's idea, and Flaco pulled through. The time when a coyote brought Cojo's cousin across the border, raped and robbed her, then threw her out in the desert. We hunted him down like a pack of wolves til we found him in a bar in a nearby town. We left him barely breathing. We'd shared some heavy shit. I'd never find homies like that again.

SEVEN

Mr. Choi had a special on wedding gowns, so he wanted me to stand on the corner wearing one with the arrow.

"No fuckin way, man."

"You'll get lot of attention."

"Attention for being a jackass. Forget it. I quit before I do that."

We went back and forth til we finally settled on me wearing a veil on the stupid orange wig. Yvette smothered a laugh as I walked out of the store. I flipped her the finger.

Even Mr. Choi cracked a smile. "Looks goooood."

I put sunglasses on so I could hide behind something as I thrust fliers at people. I felt ridiculous.

I kept telling myself that it was only a job, money in my pocket. I was doing what I had to.

A couple hours later, Yvette came up to me on the sidewalk, smirking. "Just thought I'd come by and see how you were doing." I glared at her. "I know a party going down this weekend."

"That's good. Scuse me." I shoved a flier at a lady.

"So, you wanna go or what?"

"I'm busy."

"You gotta girl?"

"What's it to you?"

"Just asking."

I shook my fliers at her, signaling I had work to do. She crossed the street and entered a botánica, a narrow storefront with a grimy window jammed with statues of saints, candles, multicolored beads and a sign that promised help with money, love and health.

So, she was into that hocus pocus shit, a giant ripoff of poor people, if you asked me.

I remembered there was one of those quickie wedding places up the block. That was the logical place to sell cheap wedding dresses. I wandered up the street, trying not to catch my reflection in store windows, and found the Romeo & Juliet Wedding Chapel. "*Matrimonios $1.50,*" said the window sign on one side of the door. "*Divorcios $500*" said the sign on the other side. Marriage seemed to be like the clica—a lot easier getting in than out.

I was outside the place for maybe fifteen minutes when a dude with a bad combover and dressed in a suit rushed out the front door.

"Hey, you have to move down the street," he said to me in Spanish.

"The fuck you talking about? This is a sidewalk."

"Nonono. You're ruining my business. You have to move."

He shooed me with his hand like I was a fly. I wasn't having none of that.

"What? I ain't moving."

"Who do you work for?" He read the flier. "Choi!" He ran inside.

Five minutes later, Mr. Choi panted up the sidewalk and the suit came out again.

"I did not tell you come here," Mr. Choi told me.

"You want to sell wedding dresses, right? People come here to get married."

"No. You see sign?" He pointed to the window. Then I saw the smaller print on the marriages sign. "Gown, tux rental. Receptions." "You make problem for me with other business."

The suit stood there with his mouth pursed.

Choi looked at him.

"So sorry. Employee." He hit the heel of his hand against his head and then shrugged with his palm up, like what he was he to do with this stupidass employee, and the suit knows how it is, dealing with idiot workers, them being both big businessmen and all. The memory of that bitch yelling at Pops and him standing there, taking it, flashed in my head. Not me, man, not me.

I grabbed Mr. Choi's shirt and shoved the fliers down it, then I ripped off the wig and slapped it on his head. His eyes bulged with fright.

"You're lucky I don't shove this up your ass, bozo." I hurled the arrow on the ground and walked.

"You fi-er!" he called after me.

I turned and hit the heel of my hand on the side of my head. "You stupid or something? I just quit, asshole."

I kicked every can, stone, bottle I saw on the sidewalk as I walked home. Every time my foot connected with an object, I thought of Mr. Choi and his shit job. Why did everybody have to treat me like a damn burro, like I didn't matter? Then I had nothing to kick for a block and I realized it was on me. My temper just dug me into another hole. Now what the fuck was I going to do?

I crossed the freeway bridge and slung into the barrio, looking for a store to buy a Snickers. I needed to see Paloma. She'd be at home but so would her Moms. I'd have to wait. I walked by a señora who had hooked up her own store on the sidewalk. She'd strung up bags of potato chips on an iron railing outside an apartment building, and put bottles of water, single pieces of gum and loose cigarettes on one of them folding tables.

She sat on a stool, hands under her thighs, swinging her legs, waiting for customers. How much money was she going to make by reselling bags of chips she bought at Costco? A quarter each? That was small brown thinking. That's all there was in this fuckin place— small brown people thinking small brown thoughts.

I always said I'd rather die than live like a small brown man, making shit money in a shit job taking shit orders like mis viejos. But that was my future. I saw it real clear in front of me, like a damn wall.

I got to the stores down by Alvarado where the sidewalks were full of people selling shit.

A girl roasting ears of corn on a charcoal barbecue smiled at me with her eyebrows raised in a question. She was pretty, so I bought a corn on a stick instead of a candy. She smothered it with mayonnaise and grated cheese.

As I chowed my corn, I studied the bootleg porn DVDs a dude was selling on a sheet spread on the sidewalk. Nothing like T&A to get your mind off your troubles.

"¡Policía!" Someone yelled.

The sellers gathered the corners of their sheets with their merchandise and booked with their bundles bobbing over their shoulders, like cartoon robbers.

A black-and-white rolled down the street. "All items must be removed from the sidewalk immediately or you will receive a $200 ticket," the car boomed in Spanish. Morales was holding the handset of the PA system. Who else?

I remembered sitting in that car with my hands cuffed behind my back, and Morales playing his "screen test" game. He'd hit the brakes hard and without my arms to brace myself, my head bashed into the screen dividing the front and back seats. He'd grin at me in the rearview mirror, then do it again.

When we arrived at the station, he said to his partner, "Think homeboy here passed the screen test?" and snapped his gum.

"Homeboy's gonna be the lockup star," the other pendejo said.

Morales kept running his mouth as he cuffed me to a wooden bench.

"Man, I hate cholos. My father was killed by one of you. He came from Mexico for a better life and he ended up with a chest full of lead from a pinche cabrón tagging gang signs on a wall. You know why? Because my father told him to stop vandalizing the neighborhood. That's why I became a cop, to get all the cholos off the streets that I can. You're a disgrace to la raza, nothing but vermin."

He stuck his face into mine as he said the last bit. I could smell onion on his breath under the spearmint of his gum. I turned my head and held my breath until he left. Later, as he sat down to write his report or whatever, he made a big show of surprise. "You got a purple pitcher's mound coming up on your forehead, homeboy. How'd you get that?"

I had to stay the fuck out of Morales' way. I disappeared into the crowd and headed for home.

I heard screams coming from the girls' room as soon as I entered the apartment. I was through their door in half a second. Lissy had Zully by the hair. Zully was sinking her nails into Lissy's arm.

I yanked them apart. "Cut it out! Come on!"

Lissy had a big scratch on her arm, Zully a red welt on her neck. She was crying.

"The fuck?"

"She started it." Zully sniffed. "I wasn't doing anything."

"You told him. You can't keep your fuckin mouth shut!"

"Told who what?"

Lissy glared at me. "Told you. About Benny."

"Zully didn't tell me. Flaco saw you with him on the street."

Zully broke into the winner's smile. Lissy grabbed her purse and marched out. A second later, the front door slammed.

"It's okay, Zully." I hugged her and rubbed her shoulder.

"She practically choked me."

"You're all right now. I better go after her."

"Yeah, go after her. She's the only one you care about!" Her words lashed me.

"That's not true. I care about you, lil sis."

"Not like you care about Lissy. Sometimes I wish I had another brother, one I could have to myself."

I groped for words. "You got Frank."

"Not the same."

"It's just ... me and Lissy are like the black sheep of the family."

"Not to me."

It took a second for that to sink in. I guessed I'd never paid much attention to her, never thought how that made her feel. I just figured she liked Frank more than me.

"You know I'd never let anything happen to you. You're mi hermanita."

I hugged her and kissed the top of her head. She squeezed me back then pulled apart.

"You better go check on Lissy. She's pretty upset."

"You come to me about anything, aight?"

I brushed the tip of her nose with a finger. She nodded and smiled.

Lissy was already two blocks down the street, her long hair flapping like batwings with the power of her stride. I jogged to catch up.

"Lissy, wait up."

"The fuck you want?"

"Talk to you, girl."

"I know you know he's a 5150, and I don't need no shit from you about it."

"If I was gonna get on your case about it, I woulda gone and done that already. If he's a 5150 or a Martian, same difference to me."

"Yeah, right."

"Long as he treats you good."

"You don't mean that."

"Yeah, I mean that. Come on, let's get off the street."

We turned into an alley. It was kind of a street living room with some wrecked kitchen chairs pulled in a circle. Empty bottles and cigarette butts littered the ground. We sat.

Lissy checked her arm. A few drops of blood oozed bright on the scratch. "*Ay Dios*, this stings."

"You should put that orange stuff on it."

"Yeah."

"I quit my job today." I told her what happened.

"Fuck that chino," she said. "You can't let people diss you like that. You'll find something else."

"I don't know, sis. I already looked." I felt my mood sliding. I had to switch the subject. "So Benny, huh?"

Her face turned down. "He's in county, just got busted."

"For what?"

Her hands twisted. "Crystal."

Relief oozed through my body. Finally something had gone my way. If the fool was in jail, that basically resolved the situation, or at least bought some time. Hopefully, she'd forget about him. "He's a tweaker?"

"Noooo." She looked at the sky. "Well, yeah, he is. So what?"

"And you love him."

She nodded. I sighed. No matter how many times I told her to find a guy with a good job, school, no tatts, she always went for the knuckleheads. The real messed up ones, too. "He don't hit you or nothing?"

"Nah, I'm over all that." Her guy before I got sent down was slapping her around. After I saw her limping one night, she broke down crying and showed me the bruises on her back and thighs. She said he hit her there so the black-and-blues wouldn't show. Me and the homies took care of him—and we didn't care if it showed. Fools who lay hands on women were nothing but cobardes, cowards. No jaina was a fair match for a man.

"I got my own problem to worry about. I guess I can tell you.

Blueboy's sister Paloma and me, we're together."

Her eyes widened. "Blueboy know?"

"Nobody knows. We hooked up before I got locked up. I gotta tell Blueboy. I just don't know how."

"Damn, bro. You're really skating the edge. But you and her go good together." I smiled.

"So, we're the same then," Lissy said. "That's why you ain't been coming down on me about Benny. I thought you were taking it kinda chill. Stupidass barrio rules. Like we don't got enough rules to live by already."

"Lissy, you gotta figure out if he's worth it, him being a crankhead. Now he's locked up, you can really think about it. I want better for you, girl, I really do." Her face crumpled and tears leaked down her cheeks. "¿Qué pasó?" I said in surprise.

"I'm pregnant."

I felt a gut punch. "Fuck, Lissy. You sure? You get one of those tests at the drugstore?"

"I ain't had la regla in two months and I feel sick all the time. I'm pretty sure."

"How did that happen? You ain't been taking care of yourself?"

"I kept forgetting to take the pill."

One summer when we were little kids, we went for free swimming lessons. It was some city program. Everything was cool til the final test for the certificate. Lissy swam half the distance, then clung to the side of the pool and said she couldn't do anymore.

I swam over and told her to keep going, I knew she could do it. I tried to pull her hands off the side, but she wouldn't budge. She started crying and the instructor yelled at me. I felt bad, but I swam on. At the end of the class, she was still in the same spot, shivering. I helped her out of the pool and wrapped her in a towel. I got my certificate, but somehow I didn't feel good about it.

Years later, I asked her why she didn't finish. She said she just knew she couldn't do it. It was like she was setting herself up to fail because she couldn't see herself win. It was always like that with her.

"You told Benny?"

She leaned her head on my shoulder and I put my arm around her. She felt small and fragile, like a sparrow. "You're the only person I told so far."

"You don't have to go through with it, ¿sabes? It's still early enough…" I started.

She cut me off. "I ain't going for no abortion, Magdaleno."

"I'll get you the feria. You don't gotta pay me back."

She raised her head. "I want to have something that's mine, something I can live for, something that makes me someone. If I'm a mother, then I'm important to someone, don't you see? I'll matter. I'll have a place in the world. And a baby, it's always yours, connected to you no matter what."

Her words hit me right in the middle of my chest. I guess we were all searching for that place in the world. To belong. To matter.

"Sis, when Moms and Pops …"

"I know."

I wanted to be miles away when mi papá found out. "You gotta get a test first. Maybe you're worrying for nothing."

She lowered her head onto my shoulder again. "I'm too scared," she whispered.

"I know, but you got to. It'll work out, sis. Babies are part of life. This happens all the time."

I put my arm around her, trying to ignore my hollowing stomach.

EIGHT

My life was beginning to feel like a fuckin Rubik's cube. Every time I got the squares of one color lined up, the other colors got twisted out of place. There seemed to be no way to get everything straight. There wasn't much I could do about Lissy. I would help her any way I could, but she had to do what she had to do. Just like I had to do what I had to do.

Talking to my sister made me realize I had to see my situation in a practical way, too. Getting a good job was next to impossible. With the Cycos, I could earn at least. I could save up money for Paloma and me. We couldn't go anywhere til parole discharged me anyway, unless I wanted a warrant out on me, and earning with Cycos would buy me some time. I needed to find a way to go around Rico and get to Chivas so I could leave the clica on good terms and live without a bull's eye on my back. Once I got out, Paloma and me could be together. Plus, I had to admit, deep down, I wanted payback on Rico.

I thought about what Lissy said about having the baby. Being in the clica ran deeper than money and homeboys. Outside the barrio, I was nothing but a small brown man, a dumbass wearing arrows and a clown suit. In the barrio, I was somebody. I was respected. I had a place and that felt good. The life and my homies were all I knew. If I left, I'd have to start all over, and that truth be told, thought was kinda nerve-wracking. That was what made it real hard to leave the life, even though I wanted to. This was turning out to be a lot more complicated than I thought.

Still, I didn't want to go back to prison or die or, worst of all, end up in a wheelchair, like one homeboy I knew.

He got capped in the back by a cop and was paralyzed from the waist down. He sued the police department and ended up with a big-ass settlement, like a million dollars. In a couple years, he'd blown all the plata on dope, liquor and girls he couldn't fuck but swarmed around him like bees to honey.

Anyway, for me, it was like I was on an elevator stuck going down. I was pushing the buttons, but the doors wouldn't open. The only way to escape was the trapdoor in the ceiling of the elevator. The trapdoor just led into the elevator shaft but from there, I could haul myself up to a door in the building and force it open.

The trapdoor was the clica. I had to use it as a middle step to re-enter the building, my new life. Once I got through the door, I could close it behind me. Getting back in the life again was the only way I could get ahead. But how the fuck was I going to tell Paloma?

We were laying in her bed a couple days later. It was late afternoon. Her mom had gone to work and Blueboy was out. I ran my fingers up Paloma's thigh into the thicket of wiry curls and slid them into the chasm. When her fingernails bit my biceps and then melted, I was happy because I made her happy.

She cradled me, my head in the crook of her neck leg thrown over hers, hand cupping the comforting swell of her teta. She rubbed her palm over the hairbrush bristles on my head and I listened to the thump of her heart.

The air in the room was thick and warm and smelled of us.

"I been thinking, nena. I know you're not gonna like this, but it's the only way." Her body stiffened. "I gotta get back in with the Cycos, just for a little while. I need pisto and I want to earn big so we can get away from here, make a life on our own."

Her breath fanned my forehead as she exhaled. "So, you were bullshitting me with all that talk about getting out. I fuckin knew it."

I shifted our bodies, so I was looking into her eyes, hers were pearled with hurt. I brushed her cheek with my thumb.

"I wasn't bullshitting you. I am serious. I don't got a lot of options right now, and I got Rico on my back. I gotta get to Chivas, play this real careful."

"What about Blueboy? You haven't told him about us, and you

said you were gonna do that, too."

"I got too much on me right now. I gotta take care of one thing at a time. Right now, I gotta get me some feria. It's for us, nena. After Chivas gives me the okay to go inactive, it's not gonna matter what anybody says about us."

"How long you think this is gonna take?"

"We can't go nowhere til I discharge from parole anyway."

"How long is that gonna be?"

"Not long, three months."

"A lotta things can happen in three months." She paused. I waited, sensing she wasn't done talking. "I don't like it, but I can't stop you. I just don't want you to get killed or busted again."

My heart swelled. "Don't worry. I'm staying on the downlow all the way." I was relieved. She took it a lot better than I expected. She stayed lost in thought for a while, then got up and started getting dressed. I stood and hooked her bra strap then she swiveled to face me.

"It's Rico, right? You want comeback and the only way to do it is getting back in with the Cycos."

"I can't lie to you, nena. He's way overdue for comeback, but I also got other plans, and they're the most important. It ain't all about him."

"Just be careful, baby."

I knew Blueboy wouldn't need to be convinced about me going back to the barrio.

After leaving Paloma, I found him at the abandoned house and sat on the step next to him.

"The dead dog's gone, homes," he said. His words were blurring. He was flying.

"I made a decision, homes. I'm gonna get back in."

Blueboy nodded slowly.

"I thought you might. Seems like you were heading that way, not that you really left anyhow."

"Just temporary, so's I can make some feria to go someplace else."

"I'm glad you're back in. Maybe we'll get some sense round here.

You see how Rico's acting."

"I talked to Lissy."

"What she got to say for herself?"

"The fool's in county, but he put a belly on her." Blueboy slid his eyes sideways at me. "She's got some dream of making a family and living in a house with a white picket fence."

"What's a picket fence?"

"Them cutsey wood fences round a garden with flowers like on TV," I said.

"Like that's ever gonna happen."

"Not with no methhead. I'm hoping he gets sent down and she forgets about him."

"You better pray on that one. Hard to forget when you got a baby crying all night. But at least he's outta the way in lockup."

"She ain't told los viejos yet either."

"You're taking this real tranquilo, homes. You ain't mad about this? I mean, damn, if it was my sister, I'd be all over the fool in two seconds."

My throat went dry. I took a Snickers from my pocket, broke it in two and gave half to Blueboy.

"They taught us in anger management that you can't control other people's actions. You can only control your own reaction. If you react wrong, it can make the situation worse. So, I'm tryna take it calm. It's her life anyways."

"Damn, Mags. You're a real wise man now."

How was I ever gonna tell him about me and Paloma?

"Guess el bote was good for something. Let's roll, fool." I was sweating hard.

"Showtime."

We entered the garage by the hole in the wall, but the front garage door was open. A sun-colored pickup truck, gleaming like it came straight from a dealer showroom, was parked in front.

"Rico's," Blueboy whispered, although I'd figured as much.

The engine ticked as it cooled. Where'd he get the feria for this? I walked around it and tried a door. Locked.

"He don't like anyone touching it," Blueboy said.

"No, he don't." Rico came around the side of the building, footsteps crunching on shards of glass. "You fools are late."

"Just admiring the ride, homie," I said. "Real tight."

The rest of the homeboys came up behind him.

"Mouse!" Rico pointed at a rear wheel. "The rims are still dirty on the inside. Do them again tomorrow."

"You got it, Rico."

Rico had really taken Chivas's lessons to heart.

"Mags and Flaco ride shotgun with me. The rest ride in the back. Stay down in case the five-o's around. Cojo, lock up the garage. It got enough air. Place smelled worse than a puta's chocha. Vamonos, fools."

Cojo pulled down the door and closed it with a padlock. We jumped in and pulled out into the night. The air pricked with jags of energy. My stomach fluttered with the edge of anticipation, that sharp blade of action— la carga, the charge that was the essence of gangbanging. No high or jaina could take the place of this. The thrill of a mission. The adrenaline rush of the unknown. We were going to take life and shake it, so it rained down on us. We were going to crash ourselves against our limits and push ourselves through them. We were going to make something happen.

My good mood made me feel generous toward Rico. "The ride's stylin, homes, real firme." He nodded. "How's your uncle doing?"

"Mi tío Alfredo? He's good."

"Still got them gallos?"

"Best roosters in Southern California. I'm working the next fight, out in Moreno Valley."

He swung onto the 110 and hit a sea of red lights. "Fuck, look at this shit."

"Dodgers' game must be over," Flaco said. "Maybe we could cut through Echo Park, it's shorter."

"Too risky with the truck, fuckin 5150s'd be right on us," Rico said. I wondered if he was worried about the homies in the back, or about bulletholes in his shiny new truck. Knowing Rico, prolly the latter.

Rico was raised by his tío because his mother was loca, the real deal, loony-bin crazy. His dad took off because he couldn't stand her shit. After his pops left, she got worse, locking the little kid out of the house at night, or in a closet by day.

One day she took a knife to him, nicking him, calling him "hell child" and threatening to slice him into chicken tenders. Her brother, Alfredo, happened to come by. He took Rico, got legal custody of him and everything, and she went into the crazyhouse.

Rico was seven years old. He never saw his mother again and never talked about her or his hijo de puta dad. But he sure worshiped his uncle. I woulda worshiped him, too.

Rico pushed the truck through the traffic, nosing into the narrow gaps between cars, forcing drivers to let him in. Horns honked. Rico flipped them the finger. Then the jam cleared in that magic way traffic backups do, and we were pedal to the metal.

The homies in the back hunkered down low, sinking into their hoodies to hide from the wind as well as the cops. We passed the baseball stadium then turned into Elysian Park.

Rico whipped up the hill's curves, past the LAPD Academy. The truck's headlights slashed the forest hugging the unlit road. At one point, the trees cleared, and a postcard view of LA spread out before us.

"Damn! Check it out," Flaco said. "Slow down, Rico."

"This ain't no Hollywood tour bus."

Rico punched the gas and the truck jack-rabbited up the slope.

At the crest of the hill, the road opened into a flat parking lot surrounded by trees, their branches looking like claws in the dim light. Several cars were parked around the perimeter. Rico cut the engine. We got out and met at the front of the truck. The air was soundless.

"How we gonna do this, Rico?" Tweety asked in a normal voice.

"Shut the fuck up, fool!" Rico hissed. "I'll tell you how. The maricones do their chupi-chupi thing down in the bushes. There's a path leading down there. You got that flashlight, Jackie Chan?" He handed it to Rico. "We're gonna get em as they go in and out."

We moved off. "Look at the rides," Mouse said. "Mercedes, Lexus. Is that a fuckin Maserati?"

"Calláte, vos. You can play Hot Wheels later," Rico said.

We posted up near the path entrance. A few minutes later, the sound of heavy footsteps and huffing breath came up the path, then the too high-pitched voice of a fake female.

"You can come back for more anytime, sugar. I got lots you ain't even seen yet."

Rico shone the flashlight into the face of a skinny black girl who wasn't a girl. She jumped, clapping her hand on her chest like a cheesy novela actress.

"Oh my! Is this a welcoming committee?"

We swarmed around her and the trick, a chubby white fool with hair the color of a sugar cookie.

"What is this?" he said.

"Get the fuck outta here," I said. "This ain't with you."

"No! You stay right there, doughboy," Rico said. The john froze.

"Please, I ..."

"Shut the fuck up or I'll use your dick to shut it for you." Rico gestured to Cojo, who moved next to him.

What the fuck was Rico doing? The action was shaking down the pros, not the johns. You didn't jack the clients because then they wouldn't come back, and there'd be nothing to tax.

Rico turned his attention to the puta.

"Bitch, you play, you pay."

"Damn, this shit again." She jammed a hand on a cocked hip and flipped her long hair back. Her face could pass as a woman's, but her arms and legs were knotted with muscle and there was no waist to curl your hand around. Her tits looked like she'd stuffed a bra with tennis balls.

"Nothing in life comes free, sugar." Rico sneered the last word.

"Why you comin back up here? We pay you down on the boulevard."

So that was the arrangement with the 5150s. They hadn't left the turf open. I knew there had to be a catch.

Rico whacked her upside the head with the flashlight. "No questions."

She stumbled off her stiletto heels and tumbled to her knees, her wig askew. Rico swept it off, revealing an eight ball covered with a layer of steel-wool hair.

"You don't gotta get nasty. How much we talkin about?" she said.

"Fifty a week."

"Fifty!"

Rico stepped toward her, holding the flashlight like he was going to crash it on her head again.

She raised her arm in defense. "Okay, okay." She dug into her cleavage and plucked out a wad of cash with fingers that ended in glittered silver nails. Rico snatched the money.

"Hey, you said fifty," she protested.

Rico counted off several bills and threw the rest back at her.

"You're lucky I'm in a good mood tonight," he said. She scrambled to pick up bills. Rico scooped up her wig.

The gabacho was getting antsy. "Can I go? Please. I have a wife and three kids." He offered bills out of his wallet. "Take it, all of it. See, that's all there is. Just let me go." Cojo looked at Rico, who nodded. Cojo grabbed the cash.

"Get your fuckin fat ass outta here before I puke on it, maricon motherfucker," Rico said.

He jiggled off.

The tranny wobbled to her feet, dusting off her pink miniskirt. She stuck her hand out. "My wig."

"Nice hair." Rico twirled it on a forefinger, lips curled, eyes like nail heads.

"Just give it to me," she said.

Rico grabbed a strand of the hair and yanked it.

"You got your money. Give me my wig."

"Give me my wig," he repeated, imitating her high voice.

The scene was making me fuckin sick to my stomach. "Give it to her," I barked. "She don't have the wig, she can't work, we don't get a tax."

It took Rico off balance for an instant. She pounced and seized the wig.

"Don't be scaring off my tricks again." She was feisty, I had to give her that. "By the way, I'm open to barter arrangements. Once I go down on you, baby, you'll never want it from no other bitch." Her laughter trilled into the darkness as she hobbled off.

In one stride, Rico had her by the neck. Eyes bugging, she gurgled, grasping his arm with both hands.

"You show more respect next time."

Rico squeezed her throat, then threw her. She landed in a heap and lay there, sucking air. I exchanged a look with Cojo. This wasn't down.

The night wore on, tripping out the putos, jacking the tricks, threatening to take one fool's Mercedes.

Rico had always gone overboard on missions to impress Chivas, but now that he was the boss, it was like he was flying so high, he couldn't see the ground. When he gave the word, we trooped back to the truck.

"Piece of fuckin cake," Rico said.

Nobody answered. A successful mission made you feel supreme, a failed one brought you real low. This one was successful but everybody, except Rico, seemed low.

At the garage, he made a big deal out of congratulating the homies. "We made good pisto tonight," he crowed as he sat and started counting the billetes.

Everybody exchanged uneasy glances, shuffled in their chairs, stuck hands in their armpits. The sour silence made Rico look up.

"What? Nobody got nothing to say?"

"This shit ain't down, Rico," I said.

"Whatta you talking about?" His eyes slitted into dark dashes.

"The 5150s still got that turf. You heard that tranny. The putos pay the 51s on the boulevard so they don't come up the hill and disturb their business. And the way you smacked her and the others around, they're gonna complain."

"Who's she gonna complain to? She thought we were the 51s," Rico said.

"She can go to the shotcaller. Then they're gonna be looking for whoever it was. Another thing, we can't be jacking the tricks or they ain't gonna go there no more. You shoulda let them go."

"I guess the pen made Mags some kinda maricón lover."

Rico laughed and looked around at the homies for support. I bolted from my chair and lunged at him. '

But Tweety was faster than me. He grabbed my arms and pulled me back. The others piled on and pushed me back in my chair.

"Everybody chill, respeto," Flaco said. "Mags is right, Rico. We step to the tricks, they ain't going to come back."

Rico slapped the wad of bills against his hand. "Listen up. Them motherfuckers were giving us the money. I ain't walking away from free feria."

"The business was with the putos," I said.

"I don't even like being around that shit, Rico," Tweety said. "We saw some kid taking it up the ass in a bush." Cojo and Jackie Chan nodded.

Rico rubbed his chin. "Tell you what. We chill on it til the next meeting, then we take a vote."

Everybody agreed. Rico distributed the night's earnings. He was generous with the cuts, trying to win favor. But he was no fool. Once he got his way, the cuts would be lowered.

The homeboys filtered into the night. I watched Rico driving away with Mouse.

"You ready for Gato's now, homes?" Blueboy said.

"Straight up."

The beat of cumbia music pounded the air as we approached El Gato Rey from the alley. When Blueboy swung back the metal door, it was a full-frontal assault of rhythm. I passed the dark niche used by the strippers and other girls to turn a quick trick.

It was occupied—a guy in a straw cowboy hat was humping a girl, his shirttail covering his ass with his jeans puddled around his ankles. The girl's eyes widened over his shoulder as she recognized me. She twinkled her fingers as I passed. I smiled at her and leaned into Blueboy's ear.

"What's her name again?"

"Lola."

"I did her a couple times."

"Me, too," Blueboy said. "I was figuring on trying again tonight."

"Used goods already."

A dancer was wrapping her legs around a pole on a stage, playing with her tassel-tipped tits and pouting her lips. Neon lights flashed orange, purple and green. Fools with cowboy hats and belt buckles the size of plates clumped in their boots on the dance floor with some of the regular girls. By the end of the night, they'd have empty arms and empty wallets. We found a corner table and ordered beers from a waitress with a downturn to her mouth. A minute later, a middle-aged man with an eye patch and a belly bursting his shirt buttons scurried over.

"Magdaleno!"

"Gato! Quihubo, hombre?" I greeted him with the Colombian expression as I stood and hugged him, slapping him three times on the back.

Gato was a refugee from another civil war. Back in Colombia, he'd been a paramilitary soldier who fought the guerrillas. He joined the paras to protect his family's banana plantation because the Army couldn't.

After his name got on a guerrilla hit list and his eye got blown out, he took a couple kilos of coca north and with the profits, opened El Gato Rey, the King Cat. It had no sign out front, just a purple neon outline of a cat wearing a crown and an eyepatch staring out a small window.

"I got business to discuss with you, Magdaleno, but I'll let you get settled in first. Drinks on the house." He snapped his fingers at the waitress and made a circling motion at our table with his forefinger. He patted me on the back and left. "Enjoy yourselves."

"What I tell you, Mags?" Blueboy said. "You been missed."

The girl delivered the beer. She smiled at us big, now that she knew we were compas with the owner.

I took a slug of beer. "So, where'd Rico get the pisto for that truck?"

"He says from betting on his tío's gallos."

"Let me guess. Since Chivas been locked up, Rico's been doing real good with his bets."

"Now that you mention it, yeah."

"You ain't figuring he's skimming clica earnings?"

Blueboy shrugged. "Rico does work for his tío. He could've made enough to make a downpayment."

"Anyone talk to Chivas since he got locked up?"

Blueboy shook his head. "Rico gets messages through Chivas's lady, but he always goes alone. We don't even know where she's at. He keeps that a big secret."

"I know. She's over in East Los. Chivas took me to the house a couple times."

"He trusted you, homes."

"Yeah, but does he still trust me, and if he does, does he trust me more than Rico?"

"You gonna go to Chivas?"

"Maybe."

Blueboy pointed his bottle at the dancer on stage. "She's been looking over here real hard."

I turned my head. She twitched her hips and stroked herself real slow in a show for us.

The song ended and her body immediately sagged. She tottered off the stage in her six-inch heels.

"You better get over there quick, so she sees them blue eyes," I said.

Blueboy drained his beer and slid out of his chair. A few minutes later, Gato joined me. "Like any of the girls?" he asked. "Colombianas are the prettiest."

I smiled. "Not tonight, Gato, but I appreciate it."

"Anytime, compadre. What you up to these days?"

"Little a this, little a that."

"I got a new business going."

"You building an empire or what?"

He laughed big, showing a row of crooked teeth. "I thought you might want in on it."

That's why he was offering me free booze and girls. Gato was always playing an angle. "Legit or illegit?"

"Big money."

"Illegit." He see-sawed his hand in the air. "I can't pull street shit no more, Gato."

He leaned back and threw his hands in the air, as if to say, "Come on, what me do street shit?" He was a real character.

"I bought an old salvage yard down in Watts. I'm going into parts." He pulled on the sides of his greying Pancho Villa mustache.

"A chop shop." That was good money.

He held up his thumb and forefinger about half an inch apart. "Just a little, to round out the income. I want you to come work for me. Legit. I'm gonna buy a lot of wrecks that need to be chopped. Some that I can fix up and resell, too. And you can earn overtime on the other shit. How bout it?"

I twirled the beer bottle on the table. "What happened with shipping rides to Colombia?"

"My guy got too greedy. He told me the customs officer wanted a bigger take. I said fine, pay it. There's plenty of billete to go round. Then I find out the customs guy is making the same and my guy was skimming the extra. Eh, it's a lesson. You can't do business from a distance. You gotta be where you can see it. With parts, I can make just as much with a lot less risk."

"Round out the income."

"Precisamente," Gato said.

Like I was going to say no. I nodded. With a wide smile, he snapped his fingers in the air. "El especial," he called.

I leaned back in my chair, although I really wanted to jump up and down. Finally, I'd caught a break. I shoulda come here my first night back home, like Blueboy said.

The waitress delivered a bottle of clear booze and two shot glasses, bending slightly as she placed them on the table. Gato's hand crept up the rear of her miniskirt. "Every job has its perks," he said. She flashed him a sly smile and left.

He poured shots. "Anís. Colombia's finest. This will set you on fire."

We clinked glasses and tossed back the liqueur. It tasted like licorice. Dynamite crackled through my veins. "Shit's good, man."

"Told you."

"Gato, I always wanted to ask you something."

"Ask." He was pouring more shots.

"Why didn't you keep going with the coca? You coulda made big money."

"I could've. But I was ahead by a couple hundred grand and that was good enough for me. Greed is one of three things that lead to a downfall. I've seen it happen time and again. If I'd kept going, eventually I would've popped up on the DEA's radar and I'd be getting out of federal prison right about now, with absolutely nothing."

"What are the other two things?"

"Women and a big mouth. My advice to you, get in, get out, tell only those who need to know and always think with this." He tapped the side of his head. "Not that." He pointed to his lap.

"I bragged to the prettiest girl in town about how I was such a hotshit para that la guerrilla had put a bounty on my head. I was trying to impress her, so she'd let me fuck her. Next thing I knew, I was ambushed. I got away but left an eye behind. I fled to Santa Marta, got in the coca business, made enough money but not too much, then got out. And here I am, still running scams."

He tossed back another shot of anís and stood.

"I have to check on the cash register. I think the bartender's been stealing. You want anything, just let la muchacha know." I nodded. "It was fate you walking in here tonight. Increíble."

He patted me on the back and headed for the bar.

I liked the way Gato thought. He was smart, weighed the risk, always thought ahead.

Maybe I could work for him just long enough to make a grip of cash to start a business somewhere, something I could run with Blueboy.

If Gato could do it, why couldn't I?

Blueboy loped back to the table. "I'm bouncing." He had a

triumphant gleam in his eye.

"Don't tell me. She fell for them baby blues," I said.

"Hey, if you got it ..."

I smiled and swiped the air as if to say get out of here. He vanished into the crowd. Since he was going to be occupied, I knew where I was headed. I walked woozily to the back door.

The cool air sobered me up by the time I arrived at Paloma's. The light was on in the living room. I knocked. Doña Flor opened the door. Shit.

"Magdaleno, what brings you by so late? Come in."

I stepped inside and she kissed me on the cheek. She must have been pretty once, with big eyes and round cheekbones, but now she had dark splotches on her tea-colored skin and lines that tugged at her mouth. She was wearing a coffee-stained bathrobe with no bra. Her tetas hung like eggplants.

"Sorry to disturb you. I had something to tell Blueboy."

"Don't worry. Working the night shift means I'm always up late."

"Who is it, mamá?"

Paloma appeared in the living room. Her face lit up when she saw me. I felt mine do the same.

"Magdaleno." Flor beamed at me. "He's looking more grown up. Time goes so fast. I hope you're on a good path now."

Behind her mother's back, Paloma licked her lips slowly at me. My whole body ached.

"I just got a job at a salvage yard," I said. Paloma raised her eyebrows at the news.

Doña Flor smiled. "Qué bien. Maybe you can encourage Rubén to do the same. He's always looked up to you." It sounded weird to hear Blueboy called by his real name. I nodded a little sheepishly, aware of how I was going behind his back. "You want to wait for him, have something to eat? I have no idea when he'll be home. Sometimes he's out all night. You know how he is."

Paloma was pointing her finger at her room behind her mother's back and mouthing something. I was trying to read her lips and pay attention to Doña Flor at the same time. "No, thanks, Doña. I better be getting home."

"Come over for dinner one Sunday, okay?"

"I'll do that," I said, edging toward the door.

I walked slowly up the drive, then doubled back and sneaked

round the side of the house and tapped on Paloma's window. The blinds rustled and the window slid up. I crawled through, catching my foot on the sill so I almost fell on my face. I hopped for a second, and Paloma gave a snort of laughter, pressing her hands over her mouth to muffle the noise. After getting both feet situated, I pulled her hands away and covered her lips with mine.

Still kissing, we lowered ourselves onto the bed, which groaned with our weight. We had to move slowly to avoid making noise. The slow motion intensified every caress as we slid our clothes off. Her sweat-filmed skin was warm butter. She pushed down my pants and stroked me. When the moment came, I buried my face in her neck as the shock waves rippled through me. When it was her turn, she gnawed on my collarbone with her teeth. The pain was sweet.

Paloma traced my face with her fingers. "What was that about the salvage yard?" she whispered.

"I'm gonna be working with Gato. A real job with real money, nena. Things are gonna work out now, I can feel it." We fell asleep, our limbs knotted like string around a package.

I woke up with dawn filtering through the blinds. I got dressed silently, kissed Paloma's forehead and climbed out the window.

When I got home, I found Pops sitting in his armchair in his boxers and undershirt, hair mussed, red eyes staring into space, an empty whisky bottle and beer cans round his feet. Whisky meant Moms didn't get his paycheck fast enough, and there'd be rice and beans for the week. I switched off the yakking infomercials on the TV.

"Papá?" Had he been up all night? Or had a nightmare and got up? He looked at me blank as a sheet of paper. Then he stood and stumbled through the cans to his bedroom.

NINE

The bus rolled deep into South LA, past liquor stores on practically every corner, 99 cent taquerías and walls alive with fat-lettered graffiti saying things like "LA Bombin," "Toothy" and "Peace-n," starbursts bouncing off the edges.

Nation of Islam foot soldiers in their suits and bowties, their heads striped with straight-edge side parts, sold bean pies and their newspaper, The Call. Grown men rode bicycles, shopping bags swinging from the handlebars.

A guy weighed black-spotted bananas and potatoes growing ears on an aluminum scale hanging in the back of his battered truck, his mobile store. Women, purses in hand, clustered around to buy that morning's cut-rate seconds from the wholesale market. A blob of a black female security guard sat behind the high steel fence surrounding a middle school. These were the hoods where nobody asked questions. Nobody saw nothing, heard nothing, knew nothing. Perfecto for a chop shop.

I reached my stop in an industrial section of Alameda Avenue, full of grimy Mexican businesses squeezed side by side—tire places, a store selling used fridges and washing machines, probably third or fourth-hand judging by the ones on the sidewalk—and turned into the street on the address Gato gave me. The salvage yard had no sign on it, just an eight-foot-high fence of rusty corrugated iron with two strands of barbed wire on top of it. The street number was scrawled in white paint on a corner of the open double gate.

As I walked in, I was startled by two Dobermans barking. They were tied with long chains so they could trot along the gate. The metal links scraped on the ground as they moved.

Gato came out of a shed marked "Office." "Don't worry. They'll get used to you." He walked over to me, snapping his fingers at the dogs.

"Miren, Duque, Duquesa." Duke and Duchess. Cute. He made a show out of patting me on the back. "Amigo." They sat on their haunches, tongues curling out of their mouths. "Better and cheaper than any security system." Gato swung his arm in a semi-circle. "So, this is it. What do you think?"

Doors, grills, trunk lids, body panels, mufflers, rims, all kinds of engine parts, were piled in towering rows, tiny pathways in between. A bunch of car carcasses rusted in a corner.

"Looks like a crazyass junkyard to me."

He laughed. "Come and see where you're going to work."

He led me to a cinderblock building off to the side and slid up the door to reveal a double-bay garage with a long tool bench along the back and side walls and some car seats forming an L-shaped sitting area in the right front corner. A yellowed calendar with a bare-butt babe straddling a motorcycle hung on the wall. It was ten years old.

"Tools?" I asked.

He pointed to a chest-high red toolbox. "Everything you need. Check it out."

I pulled open one drawer after another. Ratchets, sockets, hex keys, calipers, pry bars, gear pullers, screwdrivers, air drill, torque wrench, oil filter wrench. A welding kit with an acetylene torch and mask stood next to it.

I looked at Gato. "Where's the first ride, man?"

When I got home, I headed straight into the kitchen where Moms was patting out pupusas, Salvadoran thick corn tortillas stuffed with fillings, and counted off seven of the ten twenty-dollar bills Gato had given me as an advance on my first paycheck. In my front pocket jingled the keys to an 89 Nissan Sentra—132,000 miles on it but still running. Gato said I could use it while I fixed it up then he'd roll back the mileage and sell it.

"Mamá, I want you to buy a new armchair," I said.

Seeing the fan of billetes I was holding, she looked at me hard.

"I got a job at a salvage yard in Watts." I thrust the bills at her.

She hesitated, then plucked them from my hands with doughy fingers and tucked them in her apron pocket.

"Maybe you should come with me to church tonight."

That was more than I bargained for. I was planning to go see Paloma at the restaurant. "Ay, mamá."

"¿Porqué no? Do you some good." She patted out a pupusa between her palms.

I knew she was thinking that I was involved in some illegal shit and going to church would make me mend my ways. What the hell. I wanted to make her happy. I didn't want to disappoint her anymore. Paloma would understand. "Sure, mamá." She smiled.

When we were growing up, Moms never skipped Sunday Mass, and sometimes she went during the week, too. Pops never went. "There is no God," he would say as he sucked down a beer. "God packed up and went home a long time ago. Churches are nothing but empty houses."

Moms would wave her hand at him. "Don't take any notice of him. He believes."

Maybe he did because he never sided with us when we appealed to him to get out of going to Sunday school and never objected to Frank becoming an altar boy. But he refused to set foot inside a church, even to attend our First Communions. But while I was locked up, to the shock of everyone, Moms switched to one of these holy-roller churches a couple blocks back from MacArthur Park.

That was where we were going after dinner. Zully snickered when Moms handed me her black leather-bound Bible to carry, maybe so some of its holiness would rub off on me. But any virtue I had was like the gilt letters reading Santa Biblia on the cover, chipped and faded.

As we walked along the sidewalk, I couldn't remember the last time I had gone anywhere with my mom. I'd forgotten how short her stride was. I had to slow my pace to match hers.

"Why do you like this church, mamá?"

"This church feels more joyful, more alive, freer. Everybody helps each other. Everybody accepts each other for who they are. Pastor Julio used to be a cholo running in the streets. He was in prison for a long time. That's where he repented and found God."

So that's why she wanted me to go. "You gonna get papá to go?"

"You never know. I keep hoping."

"How come you never lose hope with him, mamá? I mean, why do you even stay with him? Why didn't you ever take us kids and leave?"

"Ay m'hijo. Tu papá y yo, we've been through so much. The years are like cement."

I thought she'd say something about never being able to support us on her own. That's why I had figured she stayed.

An ambulance whisked by. She said something else, but the siren stole the words. I sensed they were important for me. "What was that, mamá?"

"No importa."

"It does matter. I want to know."

"I never give up hope that your papá can be what he used to be, even a little bit."

The words churned in my head. "Like before he started drinking, in El Salvador?"

She hesitated. I could feel her weighing whether she should untie the knot of the past. Then she pulled it loose. "Tu papá was a radio operator in the war. It was one of the most dangerous jobs in la guerrilla, and also one of the most important. He volunteered for it. He had to march all day through the mountains with a portable radio set in a backpack. At night they would make camp and set up the radio. It was called Radio Libertad. It was the guerrillas' way of countering the government's misinformation campaign and getting their message out to the people and the media. They could only be on the air for a couple hours at a time because the army listened in and tracked the signal. As soon as they got the location, they would send a squad to destroy the radio, so the radio operators had to keep moving, watching their backs all the time."

"Papá did this? How come you never told us?" They'd been so secretive about Pops' past that sometimes I'd even wondered if the guerrilla story was really true, if they had made it up as an excuse for his drinking and his moods, and that's why they never talked about it.

"What's the use? It was another lifetime. It's so distant now sometimes it feels like it never happened, like it was just a dream, or a nightmare. But it did happen. That was the man I fell in love with when I was just a little older than you. Here we are."

I wanted to ask her more, but she entered a storefront. The

window bore the name La Iglesia de la Redención de Galilea, the Galilee Redemption Church, in stenciled red letters along with a cross made up of red-light bulbs. The church was wedged between a store jammed with pine wood furniture and a place with sun-bleached Bruce Lee posters taped on the window. Inside, a couple people placed plastic chairs in rows facing a podium. A plain wooden cross hung behind it on the wall.

"Where's Christ on the crucifix, the saints?" I whispered.

"That's how it is here, plain and simple."

"Esperanza." A beefy guy, maybe forty or so, strode over. He wore rectangle-shaped glasses, grey-streaked hair brushed back from his forehead and a goatee to match. Two tattooed teardrops dripped from the corner of his left eye.

"Pastor Julio, I brought my son Magdaleno."

"Glad you could make it."

His eyes sized me up, one banger to another. I knew I couldn't hide nothing from this fool. I was open as a sunny day to him.

He gestured at the chairs. "We're about to start so grab a seat."

I figured I could slip out in the crowd once the service got going, but mamá's smile pinned me in my seat like a clamp. There was no crowd, anyway. I kept twisting around in my chair to check, but only about six people showed up. They prayed standing, hands reaching into the air, eyes closed, bodies swaying. They sang a song and clapped as a chubby girl, her hair in a bun, played a guitar and made eyes at Julio. Then he moved to the podium, speaking in a voice that was quiet yet commanded attention.

"We are all sinners in one form or another, but it is never too late to ask for redemption. It is never too late to change our ways. Sometimes we think we want change, but we are not truly ready. Only when we are truly ready to repent, truly ready to humble ourselves before the eyes of the Lord Jesus Christ, will He grant us His mercy and salvation. When that happens, heaven opens and shines its grace upon us.

"We feel that shift in ourselves, an inner peace of knowing things will get better. All we have to do is trust in the Lord's infinite wisdom and hand our burdens to Him. It's not so easy. As many of us know, it takes a while to get to that point. We are prideful, think we can do it ourselves, we think we can manage."

He paused. I looked at Moms. She was absorbed.

"I used to rob, stab and shoot," Julio continued. "I wounded and yes, I killed. I was a drug dealer selling death to young and old. I spent more years of life behind bars than in the streets. I was hard, and proud of myself for being hard. If I thought someone looked at me funny, said something disrespectful, I was right on them ..."

His words felt like brands on my skin. I was sweating. I had to get out of there. I jetted, feeling people's eyes on me as I rushed out. I gulped the air outside and glanced back through the window. Julio was looking right at me. He nodded. I nodded back then ran. I needed a Snickers, bad.

TEN

Tweety and Jackie Chan were carrying into the garage a fraying couch upholstered in a rose pattern that had faded from red into a shit brown. They set it against a wall and Jackie dusted off his hands.

"Hey, ain't bad," he said.

Tweety flopped on it. "Now I can crash here after parties."

"That couch is gonna be used for more action than you snoring," Jackie Chan said.

"Maybe we can get one of them couches you pull out into a bed," Cojo said. "Then we're talking action."

"You fools are gonna infect it with fuckin HIV or some shit," Jackie Chan said.

"Only if they get lucky and that's a long shot," Blueboy said.

"Yeah, anyone who sits on it is gonna jump up and be itching their ass like a motherfucker. I feel it already!" Tweety sprang up, wildly scratching himself. Everyone laughed except Flaco, who was looking down and distant off to the side.

I sat next to him. "Sup, homes?"

"Shit with mi viejo. La migra busted him like eight months ago. He got convicted on a DUI and they came looking for him."

"He in detention?"

"Yeah. He ain't doing too good, sick all the time. His hearing's coming up. He says he just wants it over with, even if he gets sent back. He's tired of waiting, not knowing what's gonna happen."

"He got a chance?"

He shook his head. "They're kicking everybody out now. Mi viejo says if they deport him, he's just gonna turn around and come right back. He told me to start getting the pisto ready for the coyote. Five grand. Pisses me off, homes. Mis viejos came here for Andrés, so he could go to school, have a chance in life. Now this. Ain't fair."

I felt bad for Flaco.

Rico stuck two fingers in his mouth and blew a sharp whistle. "If you fools done with your decorating, maybe we can get to our meeting." The laughter dropped. "We got business to discuss."

Everybody found a seat and focused on Rico. "Cojo, give us the 411 bout this cabrón who ain't paying his taxes." El Rey Rico Maximus. Telling people when to talk, when to shut up, when to piss, when to shit, when to fuck.

"He moved his international driver's license shit outta the park so he thinks he don't gotta pay us no more. He's selling outta the bathroom at the Pollo del Campo."

"Is it the guy with a mustache bigger than his face? Tells everybody they can drive legit with some international shit?" Blueboy asked.

"Yeah, that's him," Cojo said.

Flaco leaned forward. "We can't let him get away with this or they're all gonna start selling out of Pollo del Campo."

"Me and Tweety can give him a message," Jackie Chan said. "One with a lead pipe."

"Messages are my thing," Tweety said.

"A lead slug is more like it." Rico was smoothing the sides of chin. He suddenly slammed his hand down on a table, making us jump. "How dare he laugh at us? Ignore us? Does he know who he's dealing with?" His voice rose with every question, then he leapt to his feet. "We are the Cyco Lokos, fools! Nobody disrespects us!" He shrieked the last sentence, then licked his lips and sat, chest heaving. His outburst took me aback, but only because I hadn't witnessed one in a long time. Rico was always excitable. You never knew what would trip his trigger. It always felt uncomfortable after he pulled one of those weird tantrums. Nobody knew what to do. Except ignore it.

Jackie Chan broke the silence.

"You saying smoke him, Rico?"

"Just cap his ass so he don't even think of dissing us again. I guarantee you cuz of him, other fools are thinking about pulling the same shit."

It was stupid, getting so wound up over this pendejo. I spoke up. "That may be, Rico. But if we light him up, he's gonna go to the ER and the hospital's gonna report the gunshot wounds to the five-o. That's gonna bring heat. It ain't worth it. A two-by-four up his ass and a lead pipe to his knees, he and everybody else gets the message, and la ley thinks it's just a fight in the alley. They don't give a fuck about that."

Rico banged his fist on the table. "We gotta be feared on the street so when we come knocking, people pay up nice and easy."

"Mags is right, Rico," Blueboy said. "We should keep cool."

"Anybody else?" Rico said, looking around.

The rest of the homies stayed silent. I thought they'd be on my side, but they weren't backing my play.

"Flaco, Cojo, this one's on you," Rico said. They nodded. "Aight. The business in Elysian Park." He smiled oddly. My nerves pricked into alert.

"We gotta pass on this," I said. "It's gonna bring payback from the 5150s. That tranny said they're already paying a tax to them down on the boulevard."

I glanced at the others for support, but everybody looked at the ceiling, tied a shoelace, coughed, scratched an elbow. Rico had gotten to them with something. Blueboy, realizing the same thing, slid his eyes at me.

"We got a lot on us with this shit with Chivas. We don't need more," Blueboy said. "He told us to stay lo pro, remember?"

"The street's gonna think we're weak without Chivas. We gotta show we're stronger than ever," Rico said. "Anybody else?" He made a show of looking around the circle. Silence. "Only two members opposed. We keep on doing what we been doing."

Rico's face played a trumpet of gloat. I wanted to put my hands around his chicken neck and twist it. And bang all the homeboys' heads together.

"Tweety, Mags, you take over tax collection. Take Mouse with you. Flaco and Cojo, after you hit that fool, you switch to Elysian Park. Blueboy and Jackie Chan, step to the street slingers. Make sure they ain't holding out on us. Chivas needs more plata for his lawyer."

I was burning with fury. This was the last time Rico was going to get one over on me. I stood. "That it?"

"One more announcement," Rico said. "My kid's bautizo is gonna be at mi tío's this weekend. Everybody's invited. There's gonna be plenty of carne asada y cerveza."

The homies smiled, but the atmosphere was unsettled as a choppy sea.

As soon as I got in the alley, I picked up a big blue trash container and hurled it, yelling. The shit bounced when it hit the ground. The lid cracked and garbage flew out. I grabbed a wooden fruit crate, tore it apart and pitched the wood pieces down the alley.

"Chill out, homes," Blueboy said.

He was right. I pulled my hood up, stuffed my hands in my sweatshirt pockets, and power-walked. I gradually got my temper under control and slowed down.

"The fuck happened in there?" Blueboy said.

"Politicking. Rico bought em off. I shoulda known he'd pull something. ¡Hijos de putas, todos!"

"Rico's playing hardball."

"Chivas always said play things cool, play smart. Take action only when necessary and only the necessary action. Rico's doing just the opposite. He's gonna get us into a war."

"What you gonna do?"

"I'm gonna pay a visit to Esme, Chivas's lady, that's what. I'm gonna get a message to Chivas about what's going down. Rico played me like a fuckin fool. That's the last time. I ain't letting Rico get away with doing this to me no more. The game is on!" My words streaked the air.

We walked a few strides then Blueboy spoke. "My moms told me you stopped by the other night after we left Gato's. I thought you knew I was going with that dancer."

Fuck. I was a number one dumbass. My brain raced. "I wanted to tell you about the job with Gato. I was really out of it, homes. Gato was givin me shots of that shit from Colombia, anís. I really didn't know what the fuck I was doin. How was that girl?"

"You really wanna know, don't you?"

"You holding out on me?"

"Ever hear of girls with a pussy like a crab, squeezes you in and out?" He made a fist in the air and tightened it.

"Damn, she got one of them?"

"Where you think I'm going now? I ain't kicking it with your beat ass."

I laughed. "Go for it."

Blueboy peeled off. I sped up to get to El Capitán. Paloma was finishing her shift, and if we moved fast, maybe we could get a quickie in before her mom came home. At first, it was kind of fun, romantic even, sneaking around like this, but it was getting tired. Paloma was bugging me to tell Blueboy about us. I kept telling her it wasn't the right time. Then again, I didn't know when would be the right time.

ELEVEN

I had a parole appointment with Angel the next morning. He was happy to hear about my job. I pissed clean. All good. "Keep it up, Mags," he said.

Afterward, I stopped at a toy store downtown to buy a couple things for Chivas's kids and headed to East LA, where he had his family stashed in a tidy bungalow with a porch and yard. Although it wasn't so tidy anymore, I noted as I pushed open the gate.

The grass was shin high and clumped with weeds. A rusty scooter lay on its side. The railing on the steps was busted. A baby wailed inside. Things had definitely zigged and zagged with Chivas locked up.

I climbed the steps to the porch and rapped at the door.

While I was waiting, I pushed one of the weathered rocking chairs sitting there into motion. That was what everybody did in East Los, rocked on their porches and watched their neighbors' lives and, of course, gossiped about them.

I heard shuffling then the door opened. Scooped out cheeks, hollowed eyes, lank hair. What was she on?

"Hola Esme, whassup?"

Esmeralda squinted at me. I heard a noise and looked down. A toddler wearing only diapers clung to her pants, a snail trail of clear snot running from a nostril. Feet pattered and a pair of brown eyes belonging to his older brother peered round her legs. At least she'd gotten this one dressed, in a T-shirt and shorts.

Her face cleared in recognition. "Magdaleno! When did you get out? Rico with you?" She poked her head out, her mouth twisting when she saw I was alone.

"Just me. Here, I brought something for los cipotes."

I gave her the bag I was holding, and she invited me in. The interior was dim with the shades all pulled down. A foul smell hung in the air.

Esme fished in the bag and took out the toy fire truck I'd bought. "That's for the older one," I said.

She handed it to him. The toddler immediately tried to grab it and started to cry when his brother snatched it away. "There's something for him, too." Esme took out the little monkey. "You wind it up and he plays the cymbals."

"Mira," she said to the kid, winding the key in the monkey's back. He took the toy, quietening down as it clapped its hands. "Now go play." What they really needed to do was take a bath. She looked at me expectantly. "Rico give you anything for me?"

"No, it ain't like that. I just stopped by to say hi, see how you doing."

Her face fell a little. "Oh yeah, sure. Sit down. So how you been?"

I sat in an armchair. I realized the bad smell was dirty diapers. "Doing aight. You?"

"Okay. Ain't easy without Chivas, you know."

She reached for a pack of smokes on a side table, exposing the inside of a pale, skinny arm and confirming my first impression. Needle tracks. Chiva, most likely.

Then it clicked. That was what all the shit about asking for Rico was. He was her supplier. The clica's earnings weren't paying for just his lawyer. They were also going right into that freeway of veins. Holy fuckin shit.

Her hand shook slightly as she lit up. She steadied as she drew on the cigarette and blew out a plume of smoke. It was a real shame. Esmeralda was a beautiful girl. Light skinned, refined features, a thick jet of inky hair, everything in the right proportions. Chivas was crazy about her. Did he know she was strung out? One of his rules was no dope in the clica, and he was real strict about it. Said dopers were weak links, unreliable and untrustworthy because their loyalty was always to feeding their habit. There was no way I could give her a message about Rico to pass to Chivas. She'd tell Rico right away, and of course, she'd be telling him I stopped by. "How's he doing?"

"Hanging in."

"Next time you see him, tell him I'm back, get in touch if he needs anything."

"Sure." She nodded. "He'll appreciate that."

A moment ticked by. In the past, she'd offer me coffee and pan dulce, show off the roly-poly baby. Now she seemed to be waiting for me to leave. I tried one more time. "The kids are getting real big," I said.

"Yeah, they're growing fast." One of them screamed from the kitchen. "I better go see to them."

"I gotta get going. Just wanted to see how you were doing."

She walked me to the door. "You gotta twenty you can spot me? I'm a little short this week. The kids need milk and cereal and shit."

I pulled out a twenty and drilled her eyes. "You feed them babies." She snatched the bill.

I flopped down the porch steps. Maybe she'd spend some of that on food for the kids. I hoped so.

I drove off with my mind spinning. Rico had Esme wrapped up pretty as a Christmas present tied with a bow. I had to find a way to get to Chivas, but it wasn't going to be easy. Gang members weren't allowed to visit homies in county, and I was on the DA's gang affiliate list. I could write him a coded letter, but there was no guarantee he'd get it or answer. No, personal contact was the best. I'd have to think of another way.

TWELVE

I needed to find out what the fuck went down with everybody at the clica meeting, and if there was one homie who would spill, it was Tweety.

Tweety's crib was a bashed up RV behind Maldonado's gym, where he trained. He'd lived in it with his dad after his moms split to Salvador, taking his two younger brothers. He and his pops drove the RV around LA, parking on a street til the neighbors called the cops to move them on and they'd drive to a new place, where the same thing would happen.

Tweety's viejo owed a grip of taxes but by not having an address, he said the government couldn't find him and he was beating the system. Then he had a heart attack and died. Tweety stayed in the RV. Then the RV died and Tweety didn't have the money to fix it, so Maldonado let him park it in a back corner of his lot.

The gym was on a street full of factories in an area of seafood plants near Skid Row. I got used to the smell after a minute, but that first nose full always made my stomach flip.

The front of the gym was painted with a mural of Aztec warriors playing handball against a backdrop of red, white and green, the colors of the Mexican flag. It was a damn sight better than the chicken-scratch gang tags that used to cover the wall.

I checked round the back. The RV was still there, paint peeling, tires flat, hitch and hubs rusted out. The door was closed, which meant Tweety was in the gym. When he was there, he always left the door open to get some air. He'd decorated the inside with skin magazine centerfolds. Sometimes a bunch of kids would be crowded around the door getting an eyeful.

I pushed open the gym door, wrinkling my nose at the moldy sweat stink.

I looked around for Tweety and spotted him jackhammering the bag, bouncing like he had springs in his feet. With every punch, the bag whooshed like the breath was knocked out of it. I watched him til he finished. He was so sweated down he looked like he just stepped out of the shower.

I walked over. "You damn sure gonna win a belt one day, Tweety."

He smiled. "Maldonado's gonna start me on the pro circuit soon, get me on some undercard fights to build my record."

"Bout time. You ready for tax collection?"

"Yeah." He sat on the bench and stuck out his hands. I unlaced his gloves and tugged them off, then unwound his hand wraps.

"So, about that meeting the other night."

He hung his head like a little kid. "I feel real bad, homes."

"Not so bad because you didn't back me up. What did he give you?"

Tweety shrugged. "Nada."

"Nada, my ass. Tell me. He either promised you something or threatened you with something."

"Things been real bad lately, Mags. We're all hurting for pisto. La migra busted Flaco's viejo. The judge tossed out Jackie Chan's mom's lawsuit 'gainst the city cuz that was her third one for tripping on the sidewalk. Cojo's lady caught him cheating on her so he's cribbing with me and giving her money for the kid. I owe Maldonado money. We gotta give bigger cuts to the clica for Chivas and shit."

"Yeah." I tossed the wrap from one hand onto the bench and started on the other.

"Well, you know Rico's tío got that business mowing lawns and shit."

"Rico got you jobs with his uncle?"

"That's about it."

Tweety made a fist with his right hand and plunged it into a bucket of rice, twisting it like a washing machine.

"But it ain't nothing against you, Mags. I mean, you were right.

We all thought that.”

“So, you hung me out for cutting grass? You all a bunch of sorry-ass punks, you know that? Why you didn't give me the lowdown beforehand?”

“Rico told us not to tell you or Blueboy.”

I took a deep breath and calmed down. The one who had the money had the power. That's the way it always was. “You think Alfredo's got so many lawns to cut he's gonna hire all a you? Rico's really gonna give away his chamba?”

“Rico said he's gonna have a lotta work soon.”

“I could tell you Santa Claus is gonna be riding into town on a surfboard, you believe that, too?” I shook my head, disgusted. “Well, you do what you gotta do, that's all I gotta say.”

“My bad, Mags.”

“Yeah, well, let's roll. We got work to do. These fools in the park might need some physical education.”

He brightened. “That's my thing.”

“You the A-plus physical educator, homes.” He shook off the rice grains sticking to his hands.

“Tell me something, Tweety. Why you like boxing so much, getting beat down all the time?”

He looked down as he flexed his fists. “Cause fighting's the only time when I really feel something, you know, the pain. When I hurt, I know I'm really alive.” He paused. “You feel me?”

He play-punched my thigh and bagged up at his stupid joke, leaning back and lifting his feet off the ground, back to his regular old Tweety self.

He headed to the locker room to shower and change. I couldn't stay mad at Tweety or Cojo, but Flaco and Jackie, I thought they were smarter than buying Rico's shit. At the same time, I knew the feeling of desperation when your pockets were empty.

Would I have done the same thing? I liked to think I wouldn't have, but I didn't know.

Maybe I would've.

Loyalty and respect were the DNA of life in the hood. I always thought loyalty was gained through respect. That was the code drummed into you. But now I saw loyalty had nothing to do with respect. It had to do with getting something you wanted. You could be loyal to someone you didn't respect at all, like Rico, as long as they offered you something.

Night was falling when Tweety and me hit the street. We picked up Mouse at the garaje on the way to MacArthur Park. The kid was fiddling with something in his hand that he slipped in his pocket when he saw us.

I frowned. "What you got in your hand?"

"Nothing," he said.

I grabbed him by the collar with one hand and stuck the other in his pocket. I felt something hard and pulled it out.

A Hot Wheels car. It was a souped up jalopy, the purple paint on the body half gone, only flecks of gold left on the engine. I looked at him. He rubbed his nose, folded his arms with his hands in his pits, shuffled his feet.

"This for good luck or something?"

"Something like that."

"Looks like you had it a long time."

"Yeah, forever."

He was just a kid. I handed it back to him. "I had a grip of em too, once upon a time."

We walked over to the park and headed for a guy wearing a denim jacket, propping a bent leg on a bench. We stopped as a pair of men went up to him, Oaxacan Indians by the look of them. He took out something from inside his jacket and showed it to them. Fake social security cards, drivers' licenses, birth certificates. The guy sold everything. We waited while they haggled, then the two men handed over money and took their cards. We moved in and surrounded the seller with our arms crossed, legs apart, and stared him down.

"¿Que onda?" I said. His face fell flatter than a tortilla as he surveyed the three of us. "Rent day."

"Where are the regular guys?"

"On vacation," I said.

He pulled at his mustache. "Hombre, it's been a rough week."

"Don't look that rough to me. You just made a sale."

"First in days."

"Good weeks, bad weeks, the rent stays the same. You know the rules."

"You gotta cut us a break. La policía was putting on the heat in the park and for a week we couldn't come out here."

"Rent is rent."

I beckoned to Tweety. He seized both sides of the guy's jacket, pulling them so tight he gasped, his eyes wide.

"Está bien, está bien."

I nodded to Tweety.

He released him, and the guy pulled out a roll of bills from his jacket. He counted off twenty.

"That's the way I like it," I said. "Con respeto."

The other vendors handed over their rent money without hesitation after seeing the first guy get roughed up. I hated this petty shit, threatening people to hand over a few billetes. They were just trying to make a living like the rest of us.

Frank was laying on the couch watching TV when I got home after stopping briefly at the restaurant. Paloma was busy and the jefe was giving her a hard time, so I left.

"Where you been?" Frank had his stern "father" look on his face.

I'd thought he was past treating me like a snot-nosed kid, that finally he was viewing me as an equal, but old habits were hard to break.

"Work."

"You been kicking it with the homeboys?"

My wall of defense shot up, just like it used to. "You fight with Glenda?"

"I got eyes around. You been out with the homies."

"Maybe them eyes ain't seeing too good."

"Don't lie to me, Magdaleno. I'm doing you a favor. You're gonna get violated."

"Don't be throwing your shit on me!" I yelled.

The bedroom door opened, and Moms stood in the doorway, clutching her shawl over her nightgown.

"Mamá, he's going back to the mara, just like I told you," Frank said.

"Paco, why don't you go fuck yourself instead of Glenda!"

His eyes hurled blades at me. I glared right back at him, daring him with my eyes to hit me so I could slam him back. I couldn't throw the first punch in front of Moms. He froze.

He couldn't throw the first one either. I marched into the bathroom and slammed the door.

It was the only place to get a little privacy in this family, and then it only lasted five minutes before someone wanted in.

I took a deep breath. Frank was right. If I kept on working the street, it was just a matter of time til I got violated. Morales had already made it clear that he was standing nearby, ready with the wrist bracelets. And getting me violated and put back inside was probably just what Rico wanted.

I slumped against the sink. I was getting caught up in the web I promised myself I wasn't going to get caught up in again. I ran cold water into my cupped palms and splashed my face. I looked in the mirror as the water dripped off, the drops plinking as they hit the porcelain. I couldn't get out of the clica so I had to put in the work. I had to keep off the street, but I couldn't look like a punk. I was stuck.

A soft tap sounded at the door. "Mags, it's me."

Lissy. Maybe she had to throw up. I unlocked the door and she entered, quickly closing the door behind her. "You gonna be sick?"

She shook her head and sat on the edge of the bathtub. Relieved I didn't have to witness that, I leaned against the wall. Her face had gotten rounder and chubbier.

"Where you been at lately?" I asked.

She turned on the tub faucet in case of eavesdroppers outside the door. "Staying with a friend." She took a deep breath. "I took one of them tests."

"And ..."

"Positive."

"So, you going through with it?"

"Benny wants a kid."

"Sis, you're gonna be the one raising that baby."

"I want it, too. Benny's mom is gonna help with babysitting and stuff. She's happy about it. She wants a grandbaby." Defiance rang in her voice, a sign I had to back off.

"You gonna tell mamá?"

"I have to."

"It'll be worse the longer you wait." I smiled. "You're gonna look real cute, sis, like a big ole basketball."

94

She slapped me playfully. "I want you to be the padrino, Mags."

I didn't think there was much chance of that with Benny being a 5150. "We'll see."

A fist pounded the door. "I gotta go." Zully.

We stood and I hugged her. "Felicidades, mamacita." I tried to sound happy.

THIRTEEN

I threw myself into working for Gato, stripping down wrecks he bought at auctions, a lot of Hondas and Toyotas since they were the parts most in demand. I got my chop system down fast—unbolting doors and seats, cutting out the windshield, shearing off the roof with the torch. In a couple hours, the car was a pile of parts.

If there were no cars to chop, I cleaned up the yard, put the parts in order, catalogued them, worked on the Nissan. I wasn't satisfied with the day's work til my muscles ached. It felt real good to be working. It got my mind off Lissy and Rico. It even felt good not to think about Paloma for a while, like my mind was my own again, free.

But I couldn't deny having money in my pocket was the best thing. It was like someone stuck a needle in my vein and shot me up with juice. Money gives you power, freedom. It makes you somebody. There was this mayate in prison who was into black power and Islam and all that. He would say that the Christian Bible and all that shit about "blessed be the meek for they shall inherit the earth" was just another tool of oppression by the white man to keep the chains on black and brown people, to keep us down. Inside, I never paid him no mind. I kept myself to myself mostly, but now I saw there was some truth in what he said. No one ever got anywhere being meek and mild, especially the white man.

On my first payday I bought a dozen white roses for Paloma and took her out away from the barrio, far from ears and eyes. We drove up snaking roads into the Hollywood Hills near the

Hollywood sign, past houses hanging over the cliffsides propped up by just a couple poles. Halfway to the top of the ridge, the Nissan started jiving and shaking. I pressed the pedal to the floor. The car went even slower.

"You sure this bucket is gonna make it?" Paloma said.

"We'll make it," I said. "I'm thinking of buying this off Gato and cherrying it out better than Frank's. It's gonna be our getaway car, nena." I pointed out the window to distract her attention. "Hey, check it out. You can see the ocean from here."

The city spread below us like a blanket with a stripe of blue at its far edge.

"It'd be the bomb to live up here." Paloma's hand clutched my thigh in a dangerously high place. "I mean, smell the air!"

I knew what she meant—it was clean, pure. "One day we're gonna live in a place like this."

"Keep wishing," she said.

"You don't think I can do it?"

"You gotta be real, baby."

"I'm gonna make a grip of money then we're getting outta here. We'll go somewhere and start a business, like Gato. I'm serious, nena."

The road got steeper. The car spluttered like an old man in the morning as the temperature gauge headed into the red. There was no place to pull over. The road was barely wide enough for two cars. I had to honk the horn before going round bends.

Paloma was frowning. "We're not gonna make it."

I didn't answer. She was right. Suddenly smoke poured out of the engine. I pulled over, and the car tilted into a ditch.

Paloma yelped. "¡Dios mio¡ The car's on fire!" She scrambled out and stood back while I popped the hood. Steam billowed out. "Mags!"

"It just overheated. We gotta wait for it to cool." ¡Puchica! I shoulda waited til I got more work done on the engine, but no, I wanted to show off, be the big chingón in front of my girl. Instead, I ended up smaller than ever.

"Now what we gonna do? We're in the middle of nowhere," she said.

"We gotta get some water."

"Where we gonna get that?"

"We walk down the hill."

"Walk! I got heels on."

I stared at the car, seeing it for what it really was, how Paloma saw it—rusted out wheel wells, half the side molding busted, missing hubcaps, patches of primer, windows with broken motors so you had to pull them up and push them down with your hands. A piece of junk, that's why Gato let me have it. And me, overjoyed, acting like it was really something. Everybody had to be laughing at me.

Rico's shiny yellow truck flashed through my mind. Him sitting in it high and mighty, ordering Mouse to wax and rewax it. ¡Caaaaabrón! I slammed my foot into the Nissan's front tire. I kicked it again and again and again. Yellow, yellow, yellow. I fuckin hated that color.

"Mags! Cut it out. Let's go find water." Paloma tugged my arm. I stopped and let my chest settle.

"You stay here, I'll go."

"I ain't staying by myself."

"A'ight. Nobody's gonna jack this piece of shit anyway."

We walked down slowly, Paloma stumbling and clinging to my arm. A gabacho was unloading groceries from an SUV in a driveway. I went up and explained what happened, real polite in my best white voice, and asked if he could give us a jug of water. He looked at us for a moment, prolly debating if we were going to stick him, then said sure. He went into the house and returned with a bucket of water.

"Keep the bucket," he said. He didn't want to give us an excuse to return.

It got us home. I parked down the block from Paloma's house under a tree. "I'm sorry we didn't make it to the top, nena."

She smoothed the nape of my neck. "One day, baby, one day we'll make it to the top."

We kissed. "By the way, you owe me a new pair of shoes." She held up a heel that had come off.

"Damn, when did that happen?"

"When we were walking down the hill."

"And you didn't say nothing?"

"I figured you had enough fixing to do."

The day's disaster melted away. I had nothing to offer except a tattoo over my heart and a tin can on wheels, but Paloma was still with me. That was all that mattered. I grabbed her hand and kissed her palm. "You're the best, nena. I love you with all my heart, te lo juro."

At lunchtime, Gato would call me down to his office to share the food he brought from home, courtesy of his Colombian wife Migdalia. Cornmeal patties called arepas. Sancochos, thick soups with chunks of corn, yucca and chicken. And the best, a plate of rice, beans, meat, fried egg, chicharrón, sausage, plantains and avocado, which he called la bandeja paisa. He told me stories about Colombia as we ate.

"Your wife sure can cook," I said one day as we leaned back in our chairs after polishing off a beef stew.

He patted his paunch. "I was a lot thinner before I got married. She loves to cook, and I'm not gonna tell her not to even though I'm getting fat. My next business is going to be a restaurant with Colombian food, but it takes money to set that up right. I want it to be a nice place, not like these Mexican taco dives."

Gato so far hadn't mentioned anything about the chop shop operation that was supposed to "round out the income," and I was wondering when it was going to get rolling. My income could definitely use some rounding out. The time seemed right to bring it up.

"What happened with the chop shop you talked about?"

He looked pained. "I'm having supply problems."

"You mean getting the rides?"

"It's my wife's brother-in-law's family. We agreed on a price per car, but now they want more. I told them my price stands, take it or leave it. They think they got me over a barrel because of the family connection, but business is business."

"You gotta stand tough."

"That's what I tell my wife. She wants me to give them more plata, but if I give in now, they'll just want more money down the road."

The ghost of a plan glimmered in my head.

FOURTEEN

Rico's tío Alfredo lived in Pacoima, out in the San Fernando Valley, in a low slung, sheetrock house with a yard that tried real hard to grow grass but stayed a patch of grey dust no matter what. Pacoima was full of South LA transplants like him, immigrants moving up the food chain who thought they were leaving the ghetto behind when they arrived in suburbs, but they just brought the ghetto with them.

You could send money orders to Tegucigalpa, catch a bus to Tijuana, buy Gallo beer from Guatemala, get scammed by viejas standing outside the Food 4 Less selling "winning" lottery tickets, by notarios promising green cards for $500 upfront, or run your own scam—gambling and betting, slip-and-fall lawsuits, claims for welfare checks for fake kids in a day care center. The only difference between South LA and Pacoima were the Valley summers that made you feel like you were breathing through a blanket.

As I parked the car down the block, I could taste the meat cooking on the grill from the aroma. Zully reached for the present for Rico's kid, tied with a blue bow, in the back seat.

I had to bring her. When I came home from work, Moms was sitting at the kitchen table, her face solemn as a priest's.

Lissy sat across from her, looking like she was either going to burst into tears or throw a punch or both. I knew what must've gone down—Lissy told Moms about the baby.

I was hungry but decided it was best to stay outta the kitchen for the time being. Zully came out of her room as I headed to the bathroom. "Where are you going, Magdaleno? Can I go with you?"

"I'm going to take a leak. You wanna watch?"

"You know what I mean. I wanna get outta here, go somewhere. I guess you know what Lissy is telling mamá."

Her doll face turned up at me, full of expectation. I remembered what she said about wanting me as her brother. I could take her to the party, no biggie. "I'm going to the bautizo for Rico's kid. You can come if you want."

A lightbulb clicked on in her eyes. "Really?"

"I'm leaving in five minutes so be ready. I ain't waiting."

"I'll be ready."

She was true to her word, wearing Barbie pink pants and sitting in the living room when I emerged in clean clothes from the bathroom. I yelled to mamá that Zully was going with me and we bounced.

"So, what do you think about Lissy?" I asked her after we got in the car.

"I'm gonna be a tía and you a tío."

"What did Moms say?"

"She wasn't too happy, but I think she'll like being an abuela."

"Yeah, you're prolly right."

If there was one thing I loved about mi mamá, she always took things real calm. I couldn't think of a time when she lost her temper. Maybe it was all these years of dealing with el viejo or maybe that was just her.

I wondered who I woulda been if I inherited her calm gene instead of the angry gene from Pops.

"We're gonna get through this," Zully said, all matter-of-fact. "A lot of stuff happens in our family, but we always work it out."

I glanced at her staring at the road, so confident about the future, so full of faith. I suddenly admired my bratty little sister. She put the peg in the hole. "Yeah, you right on that one. It always works out somehow."

Alfredo and his wife Guillermina had decorated the backyard with colored Mexican cut-out flags. A blue, yellow and pink donkey piñata hung from the roof overhang, ready for the kids. Speakers set up on the patio outside the sliding glass doors boomed Los Tigres del Norte.

I walked over to greet Alfredo as he stood over his homemade barbecue—an oil drum cut lengthways so the upper half formed the lid, and the bottom half held the charcoal. His hands were full, a beer in one, grilling fork in the other.

"Glad you could make it, Magdaleno," he said.

Next to him, Guillermina was filling up two paper plates with blackened chorizos, hamburgers and steaks. She was as obese as ever, her eyes watermelon seeds sown in the pudgy folds of her face. She kissed me on the cheek, and I introduced Zully to both of them.

I looked round. The homies were sitting together. Flaco was with his girl, Yajaira. A bunch of people I didn't know—Alfredo and Guillermina's family and friends, I guessed—hung around the yard, sipping beer, as rugrats chased each other.

"Ey, Mags!" I turned to see Blueboy and got a start. Paloma stood next to him, smiling coyly at me with shiny scarlet lips. "I was wondering when you were getting here, Mags," he said.

"I had to put in a few hours with Gato. How you doing, Paloma?" I said like I hadn't seen her in weeks.

I kissed her on the cheek, smelling her soaped skin and resisting the urge to brush my hand over the curve of her melones outlined in a form-fitting shirt.

"I guess we both got stuck with little sisters," I said to Blueboy. "I brought Zully." She waved.

"Paloma bugged me to come."

Paloma gave me a saucy smile. "I didn't see why I couldn't."

"It's cool," I said.

Rico bustled over. A drooling baby dressed in a sailor suit sat like a little prince in the crook of his arm. His other hand held a beer. He was all smiles.

"Mags, you made it, homes." His eyes fixed on Zully. "This who I think it is?"

"Yeah, you remember my lil sis, Zully."

"Not looking like this, I don't."

He stared at her. She looked at the ground out of shyness, tugging a strand of hair. I didn't like how he was eyeballing her—it was disrespect to me, and my sister—but I didn't want to cause a scene at his party. Instead, I wagged the baby's chubby fingers to draw Rico's attention away from Zully. "So, this is the hombrecito, huh? What's his name?"

"Kevin. He was real good in church this morning. Didn't cry or nothing when the padre put the holy water on him." Rico kissed the kid's puffy cheek.

"We brought this for you." Zully offered the gift.

Rico's eyes brightened. He passed the baby to Paloma and set his beer down so he could open the present. He pulled out the honey-colored teddy bear I bought.

"Real nice, Mags."

"I don't know nothing about baby shit, but I figure all kids like a peluche."

"Get yourselves some food. Beer's over there on ice. I gotta show Maribel."

He took back the kid and gave him the bear, which he instantly dropped. Zully picked it up and dusted it off, handing it back to Rico. I caught him hooking her with a smile.

Paloma took Zully and they joined Maribel and some other girls. I waved at Maribel. She'd dyed her hair red and piled it on top of her head like a bouquet of curls. I could see she still had a little of the baby fat on her. She smiled and waved back.

I grabbed a beer and steered Blueboy to the side so we could talk.

"I got a business for you." I told him about Gato's chop shop plan. "If I can get Gato to ditch his wife's family, you wanna go in with me on it?"

"You gotta ask?" He held up his hand and we fist pumped. "You gonna say something to the homies?"

"The traitors, you mean?"

We ambled over to Flaco, Jackie Chan, Tweety and Cojo. They fell quiet when I rolled up.

"Mags, it was nothing personal against you, homes," Flaco said in a low voice.

"You coulda at least fuckin warned me what was going down, so I didn't look like a fuckin pendejo," I said.

Jackie Chan nodded. "We shoulda told you."

"You sold yourselves, let yourselves be used."

They all looked at their shoes. "Things just been real bad since Chivas got locked up," Cojo said.

"Yeah, well, they're bad for all of us." I walked away to make them feel my disappointment.

It was the tipping point of late afternoon when the day saves its best for last—a light like liquid gold before twilight takes over. I was bathing myself in the rays, eyes closed against the sun, kinda just taking in the moment. When I opened them, I spotted the silhouette of someone walking up the driveway. Could that be ... I shielded my eyes with my hand against the light. Damn, it was. Esme stood there, holding her two kids, as she twisted her head around, looking for Rico, no doubt. She had fuckin nerve, or desperation for a fix, which was more likely the case, judging by the film of sweat glinting on her pasty face.

I stepped over. "How you doing, Esme?"

"Good." She smiled past me. I turned. Rico was rolling up.

He seized her elbow. She winced. "I told you to wait til I called. Now's not a good time," he hissed.

"Let go of me. I was bored. Felt like getting out." They seemed real familiar with each other. Maybe he was more than her chiva supplier.

Rico suddenly seemed to realize I was standing there and dropped her arm.

"I was just saying hi to Mags," Esme said. "Chivas used to bring him over all the time." She turned to me. "I'm going to see him tomorrow. I'll tell him you stopped by."

Rico's eyes shot bullets at me. I met his staredown straight on from under the hoods of my eyes.

But I didn't want to get in the middle of the battle brewing between him and Esme. "I better see where my sister's at. Catch up with you later."

I got a fresh beer and took a long swallow as I observed Rico and Esme. They were standing too close together and it didn't look like a friendly conversation.

I turned to look at Maribel. She and the other girls were watching, too, scowls on their faces.

"Rico!" Maribel called.

"Gimme a minute," he shot back. She frowned, muttered something and one of her friends grabbed her arm.

Tweety came over. "Alfredo's gonna show us his birds."

"There's gonna be a better bird fight out here," I said, but I went with Tweety.

We walked over to a long shed in the rear of the yard where

Alfredo was unlocking a padlock as the other homies waited. He pulled the door open, blasting us with the tangy perfume of chicken shit. Roosters in cages lined a wall.

"I got eleven right now, all good fighters, no weak ones." Alfredo grabbed a sack of corn and poured it into the feeding troughs along the cages. "I'm fattening them up now. Couple days before the fight, I cut their food in half. Then they're real lean and mean as all hell. Here you are, boy, how's my beauty."

He stuck his forefinger in and stroked a bird as it pecked the corn with jerks of its head.

Its feathers were like a sunset, red, yellow and orange mixed with browns and greens. A beauty all right.

Alfredo petted and talked to them as he filed along the row, filling their water containers.

"This one's a feisty one. He never gives up, do you boy? This one is my heavyweight champion. Goes straight for his opponent's eye, pecks it right out. I call him Gladiator. This one got cut up bad in the last fight so he's still recuperating. Feeling better, boy? I'll let you run around tomorrow.

"I usually let them run in their corral, but there's too many people around right now. They'll get too excited. They have to stay calm between fights."

"When's the next fight?" Flaco asked.

"I got one up in Lancaster in a couple weeks, then down in San Diego."

"You go all over with them birds," Cojo said.

"All over California. Nevada and Arizona, too."

I picked up a gaff, the curved steel spur that attaches to the roosters' legs to wound their opponents and ran the pad of my thumb along it. It was sharp and ended in a nasty point.

"I wouldn't want to run into that in a dark alley," Jackie said.

"Me neither." I put it back in the box.

Alfredo finished his chores and we strolled back to the party. Evening had dropped and strings of white lights sparked to life around the yard, giving the place a real nice glow, romantic like. I looked around for Zully but couldn't see her.

"When's that cake coming, mamita?" Alfredo called.

"I'll get it." Guillermina waddled into the house. I tapped one of her fleshy arms.

"Doña Guillermina, you seen my little sister around?"

"She might be in the bathroom." Her tent dress billowed around her like a parachute.

I felt fingertips tickle my palm. I turned. Paloma was twirling a lock of hair and giving me a sex-kitten smile with her head cocked to one side. "Let's find some place to hide out for a while. No one will notice."

I realized she was tipsy. "How much you had to drink?"

"Not enough."

She gave me a smoldering look and ran a finger up the inside of my forearm. My curiosity was aroused, as well as something else. I looked around. The party had reached that stage when enough beer had been drunk so everyone was loose, but not enough to get rowdy and ugly. A couple was making out on the shadowed edge of the patio —Cojo and one of Maribel's friends. Another girl was sitting in Blueboy's lap. Flaco and Yajaira were entwined on a loveseat. Jackie and Tweety were trying to make two girls who did nothing but giggle. Mouse was refilling the ice chest with beer. I couldn't see Rico or Esme.

"Behind the rooster shed," I said.

She left as Guillermina came out of the house holding a sheet cake frosted in blue and white. Zully followed, carrying a stack of paper plates and napkins, and behind her, Rico, holding a knife. The music pumped louder and some of the girls jumped up to dance to reggaeton. The guys gathered to watch.

I slipped into the dark and found Paloma leaning against the wall of the shed. She flung her arms around my neck and drew my head to hers. She pulled up my shirt and her fingers slid around my waist and walked up the valley of my spine. My hands cupped the roundness of her nalgas.

We rubbed and humped and ground until finally we unzipped. I hoisted her on to me, pressing her up against the wall, and she wrapped her legs around my hips.

"¡Mira!" A high-pitched voice piped as we were pumping. Damn! We turned our heads.

In a shaft of light beyond the shed, a little kid pointed at us. We froze. Arms scooped him up.

"You come back here. Don't be running off like that again." Rico. My heart hammered all over my chest as I held my breath.

"Come eat your cake." They left.

"Did he see us?" Paloma whispered.

"He prolly saw a couple going at it, but I don't think he recognized us. It's totally dark." I lowered Paloma and we zipped up. "You go out first."

She kissed me, long and wet. I loved it when she was a tease. "You have fun?" she said.

"I'm going to have to get you drunk more often, nena."

She slipped around the corner of the shed. I waited a few minutes, which ticked by like hours, then rejoined the party.

Rico was talking to Paloma. I headed for the table where vanilla cake was set out on plates and took one.

"Where you been hiding at, Mags?"

Rico came up behind me. I wanted to smash my cake in his face. Instead, I stuck a forkful in my mouth.

I raised the plate at him.

"Good cake," I mumbled. I was trying to stay cool but watching his face to see if he'd recognized us.

"We're getting set to do the piñata now," he said. He seemed normal.

Blueboy rolled over.

"I was looking all over for you, homes," he said. Since when was I so popular? "You up for arm-wrestling Cojo?"

"Tell you what," Rico interjected. "How bout I take on Mags? And the winner goes against Cojo."

"What about the piñata?" Blueboy said.

"That can wait."

I set down the plate. "Bring it on, Rico."

We sat at a picnic table. The homies left off watching the girls dance and crowded around. Then the girls came over to see what the big draw was. Rico and I put our arms up, elbows on the table, clasping hands, staring each other down. I steeled my arm.

"¡Dale!" Cojo said.

I tightened my grasp and pushed with all my might against Rico's wall of resistance. I pushed harder. He pushed harder. My eyes focused on my hand. It seemed disconnected from my body, engaged in a death struggle on its own. If I lost concentration for even a fraction of a second that would be all Rico needed. I gritted my teeth as my neck muscles contracted into cords, my arm turned into wood.

Our fused fist quivered. It was harder to keep it upright. I glanced at Rico. His face was taut, shining with a breakout of sweat. He faltered just the tiniest bit. He was getting tired, like I was. But I summoned every bit of strength I had and pushed. His arm gave way a couple inches.

The crowd gasped. I had the edge I needed to crash his hand to the table. Rico's arm slipped another inch. He was tiring. I applied more pressure. Trembling, his arm lowered slowly.

It was only about two inches from the table. Then he recovered with a burst of energy that took me by surprise. He gained on me, pressing me back. I couldn't fight his momentum. I was getting tired. Our arms were upright again. My arm wavered.

It was falling back. I closed my eyes, and images flashed through my head.

Rico running. Morales holding the cuete in front of my face. The judge scolding me. The tiny exercise yard for SHU inmates. I couldn't let Rico win again. I pushed and pushed and pushed against that gloating face, that fleeing back, that raspy voice. He grunted as he tried to hold me off. I grunted as I powered against his fist, down, down, down. I almost had him on the table then he stopped me. For a second, our gripped hands wavered. Sweat dripped off my forehead into the table. I drew on the last bit of muscle power I had and slammed his hand to the table.

My head drooped and white spots flashed in my eyes. My back was slapped, congratulations said. A beer was shoved in front of me.

"Mags, you okay?" Paloma. My vision cleared. "You white as a gabacho."

Rico had left the table. I was exhausted. My body felt as limp as an old man's dick. I had to get outta there.

"Where's Zully at? We gotta jet," I said.

FIFTEEN

Once I got some distance on the road, I felt steadier and my triumph over Rico hit me. He was not invincible. He could be beat. *I* could beat him. I banged the steering wheel with my fist.

"What are you doing, Magdaleno?" Zully asked.

I jumped. I'd forgotten she was in the car. "Just thinking."

"Bout the arm wrestle?"

"Yeah."

"Rico was real nice to me when we were in the kitchen getting the cake."

"Oh yeah? He was rapping you?"

"Just asking me about school and stuff."

I glanced at her. She was twirling her hair, looking out the window. "Rico's cheating on Maribel with that girl, the one with the two kids."

My ears pricked. "Maribel say that?"

"Maribel called her a puta and wanted to kick her ass, but her friends told her to chill out and not ruin the party. Then Rico took the girl into the house and I guess she left out the front door cuz we didn't see her again. Maribel had a fight with Rico about it. He said she was a homeboy's lady and just came by to pick something up, but Maribel wasn't buying it. She said she knows Rico's two-timing her, but Rico will come back to her when she gets her figure back. I felt bad for her."

I was right.

Damn, Rico was bold, boning the shotcaller's lady while he was locked up. Wait til I told Chivas. He might even put the word out on Rico for this, solving all my problems. Well, not all, but some. Then I reconsidered.

Chivas might blame Esme more than Rico, and two little kids could end up without a mother and a father doing life. Maybe I was getting soft in my old age, but that was no way to grow up, all alone like that.

I had to play this real careful and not make any hasty decisions. I had to keep this to myself for now.

When we got home, Frank was sitting in the armchair staring into space, his hand wrapped around a can of Pops' beer. Frank hardly ever drank.

The coffee table was all crooked. The books that were its fourth leg were scattered on the floor. In the kitchen, a chair lay on its side and garbage can was overturned with coffee grounds and eggshells spilling out.

Zully gasped. "Dios mio."

I guessed what had happened. Pops found out about Lissy.

"Was it bad?" I asked Frank.

He nodded.

"Where is he?"

He thrust a thumb at the bedroom. Neighbor called the cops. I showed them my LAFD ID and got em to leave."

It must've been bad. No one called the five-o around here. "How's Lissy?"

"Not too good. I heard the screaming from downstairs and ran up. She'd locked herself in the bathroom and he was whipping the door with his belt, then he rammed it, tryna break it down. Moms was yelling at him to stop."

My arm-wrestling victory whistled into the air like a punctured balloon. I went to the girls' room. Lissy was stuffing clothes from a dresser drawer on the floor into bags.

She had red welts on her arm and neck. Zully was sitting on the bottom bunk looking serious.

"Papá got her with the belt," she said.

Lissy sniffed and continued packing without looking at me. My heart sank.

"You okay, sis?"

"Veronica said I can move in with her. She's coming to pick me up." Lissy's voice was thick. "I hate him. I fuckin hate him." Tears spilled down her cheeks.

I felt helpless, guilty for leaving her alone.

"My bad, sis. I shoulda been here for you."

"Ain't your fault we got a sick, drunk monster for a father." Lissy's cell phone buzzed. She checked it. "She's here."

"I'll help you with your bags," I said.

She stood up. "I'll come back for the rest later."

"I don't want you to leave, Lissy." Zully looked like her heart was gonna snap in two.

"I got to. You can come visit me, okay?"

Zully nodded.

We trooped into the living room. Frank eyeballed the bags and jumped to his feet. "Where you gonna go, Lissy?" Worry sounded in his voice.

"Gonna stay with Veronica for a while," Lissy said.

He seemed to relax. "I don't blame you."

We all walked downstairs. A compact car was double-parked in the street. I tossed the bags in the back seat and took turns with Zully and Frank to hug Lissy.

"Take care of that belly," I said.

The car took off. Something wrenched inside me as we watched it disappear. Zully leaned on my shoulder. "It won't be the same without her."

We went back upstairs.

"I'm gonna clean up the room," Zully said.

Frank and me unfolded the couch into the bed. I pulled off my shirt and unbuckled. Frank did the same. We got into bed.

Frank punched his pillow into a ball. "Why the fuck did she have to get herself knocked up by that crankhead?"

"Paco, one day you're gonna fuck up, too."

"I can't fuck up because I have to give a shit about this family. If I didn't, who would?"

The question hung like a hook over my head. "All's I'm saying is shit happens. It just does. No sense tryna figure it out or wishing it didn't."

"We're barely staying ahead as it is. Now I can never move out with another mouth to feed. Kids are expensive, all the shit they need. Nobody ever thinks about that, huh? Who's gonna pay for that kid? She ain't gonna get jack from that fuckin cholo. He's gonna be in and out of el bote or dead in a couple years."

I'd heard his cholo speech so many times, I could say it in my sleep, but I'd never heard him talk about moving out. "You thinking of going someplace?"

"You don't think I might like to get married and have my own family one day?"

"Mi mamá'll be real happy if you marry Glenda."

"Well, my paycheck ain't gonna stretch over two households. I'm stuck here with fuckin Superglue."

Frank felt stuck? "I thought you were into being the man of the house."

"Someone's gotta do it, but I'm getting real tired." He reached over and switched off the lamp, staying with his back toward me.

I blinked into the darkness as guilt gnawed at me. I never thought about the sacrifices Frank was making, that they might be a burden. "I didn't know you felt like that."

"You come and go, free as bird. You ever think what woulda happened to us if I ran in the streets like you?"

In prison they stick you in groups and you sit in a circle and talk about the choices you made that got you locked up. I saw now that Frank was trapped by his choices, just like I was trapped by mine. I realized he resented me for my choice, like I resented him for his. Still, he wasn't the only one who'd made sacrifices.

I was suddenly baking under the covers and kicked them off. "You're forgetting what I did for the family."

"What did you do?"

"Remember when Pops hurt his back and couldn't work for six months and we were gonna be evicted? You quit school and got a job at the Food 4 Less?"

"Yeah, then Moms got a loan from her boss to pay the back rent and I went back to school."

Shit, he didn't know. I sat up. "It wasn't no loan. Her boss wouldn't give her a dime. *I* gave her the plata."

The sheets rustled as Frank turned onto his back. "You?"

"Yeah, me. When Moms told me we were gonna be on the street, I went out and jacked more rides than ever. I lied and held out on the clica's cut, too. A few months later, I got busted on a

GTA and sent down to juvie. And you know what? I didn't care about getting busted. I was worried about how the family was gonna make it without me working the street."

I got up and crossed to the window, leaning my arms on the sill, feeling the fresh air.

Frank finally spoke. "I didn't know that, bro, I swear. Mi mamá told me she got a loan."

"She had to say that because Pops wouldn't have took the money if he knew where it came from, but I thought she woulda told you."

Even when I did something good, I got cheated out of the credit. I stared down at the shadowed street.

"I guess I owe you one, bro," Frank said softly.

"Nah, nobody owes me a fuckin thing."

I was bellied up to the bar at El Gato Rey after work, tossing peanuts into my mouth and watching a dancer wiggle her ass in a green G-string, killing time before going to meet Paloma, when Blueboy slid onto a stool next to me. He signaled the bartender for a beer.

"You got visitors. Flaco and Jackie are in the alley. Tweety and Cojo are on the way."

I frowned. "Whatup?"

Blueboy shrugged. "They say they're coming in for a sitdown."

This was news. Ten minutes later, I heard a "'sup, homes?" at my shoulder. In the mirror behind the bar, I saw Flaco, Jackie Chan, Cojo and Tweety behind me.

"Ese." I told the mirror.

"Gotta a minute, Mags? We got something to say to you," Flaco said.

I took a long, slow swallow of beer, just to make them squirm for a moment, then I gestured with my chin to a corner table. We scraped back chairs and sat. I waited.

Flaco spoke. "It's like this, homes. We're all real sorry bout what happened at the meeting."

Tweety broke in. "Rico says the pisto is for Chivas, but he's styling in a brand new truck, and we're all hurting. Something ain't right."

"Another thing." Jackie Chan chin-nodded at Flaco to continue.

"When me and Cojo were leaving Elysian Park the other night, we saw a crew of 51s driving up the hill as we were driving down."

I wanted to laugh out loud. "They see you?"

"I don't think so. It was dark," Flaco said. "They had the light on inside their mini-van so Cojo made the tatts."

"That tranny called them," Cojo said. "She was smiling, saying something bout 'you boys ain't gonna be doin this much longer'."

I sat back with the satisfaction of being right. "What I fuckin tell you, fools? I told you the putas would complain and then the 51s would come back on this."

"We don't want a war," Flaco said. "If we get in a war, with Rico calling the shots ..." He shook his head.

"He's crazy," Jackie said. "He's gonna get us all iced."

"You should be calling the shots, Mags," Tweety said. "You're smart."

I studied them with narrowed eyes. "How do I know Rico didn't send you to set me up on something?"

Flaco leaned forward.

"We know who that girl was, the one that showed up at the bautizo."

"How do you know that?"

"Maribel got it outta Rico. He was making like she just came by to get something to take to Chivas, but Maribel ain't stupid. She told Yajaira that Rico's cheating on her with Chivas's old lady, and Yajaira told me."

"Boning the shotcaller's vieja while he's locked up is real low," Cojo said. "Even if he ain't the shotcaller, that ain't done to a homeboy."

The others nodded. "We're sick of this shit with Rico," Jackie Chan said. "It's one thing after another with him. And now he's politicking against you after you done time on his fuckin 211."

"We know you're still sore about us siding with Rico at the meeting, Mags. He was pushing us real hard. I guess we had a moment of weakness," Flaco said.

"So, why're you coming to me with all this? You ain't told me nothing I don't already know. There's nothing I can do about it."

"We gotta get to Chivas and tell him what's going down, so he makes you his man on the street. We'll back your play," Flaco said. "But it's gotta be you, you always got his ear."

"I can't just walk into Men's Central and ask to see a shotcaller on a 187."

"You could write him a letter," Tweety said.

"They're gonna be reading all his letters," Jackie said.

I exchanged a look with Blueboy, then said, "Gimme a minute with Blue here."

They shuffled over to the bar, and I turned to Blueboy.

"What do you make of all this?"

"I think they're straight up. We all been sick of Rico for a while."

"They ain't so sick of him they said no to his fuckin promises."

"You know how it is, bro. They gonna say no to a jale? They just went along with it, didn't think of nothing else."

"A moment of weakness."

"Yeah."

The truth was I could really use the homeboys on the business with Gato to earn more money. Then an idea occurred to me. If I told Rico I had a new business for the clica, I could get out of the smalltime tax collecting shit and stay off the street.

"You got your thinking face on. Spill." Blueboy knew me real good.

"What about cutting them in on the deal with Gato? If we got a crew, we can move more rides, make more pisto."

Blueboy nodded slowly. "I think they'll go for that. What about Rico?"

"I'll say I gotta new business for the clica at the next meeting. Why would he say no if he's looking to earn more?"

"Let's do it." Blueboy whistled. The homies trooped over and sat.

"Aight. Number one, I ain't making no moves on Rico, so get that outta your heads. I want peace so I can make some real plata." Heads nodded. "Number two, Gato and me are setting up a chop shop. I need a street crew and ..."

Jackie Chan cut me off. "I'm in, Mags."

There was a chorus of "me, too."

"That's good feria," Tweety said.

"Number three, if you want in, I gotta have one thing—loyalty." I said the word real slow and looked at each homeboy in the eyes. "Anybody stabbing me or this operation in the back is gonna take a one-way ride out to the desert. I ain't getting played no more."

"We with you, homes," Flaco said.

"Number four. I'm going to bring this up to Rico at the next meeting. Everyone's gotta back me up or you're fuckin out."

There was a moment of silence as everybody digested the plan.

Tweety's head darted around the table. "Any more numbers, Mags?"

I tried to hide my smile. "No more numbers, Tweety."

Jackie Chan cuffed him gently on the side of the head. He smiled.

"And we don't gotta tell Rico the exact amount we're pulling in," Flaco said.

"You're thinking smart, Flaco," Cojo said.

"And if he hassles us, we got the lowdown on Chivas's vieja to shut him up," Flaco said.

"Now you really thinking, homes," Jackie said.

"I like all this thinking," Tweety said.

We bagged up. Tweety had a fat smile on his face, happy that he made everybody laugh even though he didn't exactly know what he said that was so damn funny.

SIXTEEN

I had pep in my stride as I entered Gato's office Monday morning. He was sitting at his desk with his coffee and newspaper, as usual.

"I got a full crew, Gato. We good to go soon as you say the word."

He looked up.

"Chévere. I told those cabrones in-laws to fuck off. We'll start this week."

"Ready when you are, jefe."

Gato put his hand out and we shook. "I got a wreck coming in a bit. You can work on the Nissan til it gets here."

Later, I was dismantling the rear quarter panel off a totaled SUV when Gato walked into the shop. "Rico's here asking for you."

I frowned. "The fuck he want?"

"He didn't say."

Did someone spill about the chop operation already? I wiped my hands on a rag and went down to the entrance. Rico was standing outside his truck, his hands on his hips, looking around at the place like he was planning to buy it. Mouse stood next to him.

"Ése! This is a lot better than the clown suit. You moving up in the world. I need to parlay with you."

"I'm working, Rico." Gato was standing in the doorway of his office, watching us.

"I'll make it fast."

"Come into the shop," I said.

We sat down on the car seats. Rico took off his sunglasses and looked around, nodding. "Nice setup."

Mouse fidgeted with his Hot Wheels car.

"What's on your mind?" I prompted.

"It's about your sister. Lissy." I tensed. "Chivas saw her in the visit room this weekend, and he don't like who she was visiting."

I played the innocent. "Oh yeah?"

"A fool named Payaso Santana, know him?"

"Can't say I do."

"5150."

I rubbed my nose. "I ain't her keeper, man."

"You know the code, Mags."

Rico grinned. He was enjoying nailing me after the arm-wrestle. Motherfucker.

I had to think how to handle this. To play for time, I went to the tool bench and grabbed a Snickers. I offered it to them. Mouse shook his head, Rico ignored me.

"Outta respect for you, Chivas wanted me to talk to you before taking it to the clica. What you wanna do about it?"

I took a bite of the candy bar and chewed slowly as I thought fast.

I was going to have to use the ammunition I had—Esme. I swallowed.

"I don't know if you want Mouse hearing what I got to say."

Rico glared at me, trying to figure out what I had on him. I yanked another piece off the candy bar.

Mouse looked at Rico for instructions. Rico jerked his thumb at the door. Mouse left, closing the door.

"Aight, fool." Rico folded his arms.

"I know what you got going down with Esme, the whole fuckin world knows. So, you tell Chivas he was mistaken bout my sister, and I don't pass the word that you're boning his ruca. Let me tell you, chisme spreads fast inside. People ain't got much to talk about."

Rico's eyes burned as he digested my threat for a minute. "You're making a lotta fuckin waves since you been back."

"Better put on your life jacket then." I sat in a car seat, stretching out my legs and crossing my ankles like I was going to catch zees in a beach chair.

Rico leapt to his feet. "You stay the fuck away from Esme."

I took the last bite of my Snickers, and crumpled the wrapper into a ball, which I tossed into a garbage can. "No argument from me."

Rico flung open the door and stepped out. "Mouse! You playing with that fuckin thing again? Gimme that!"

Something cracked loud against the wall. I crossed to the door. Rico and Mouse were marching to the truck. Mouse's Hot Wheels jalopy lay on the ground, its wheels broken. I picked it up, curling my fingers around it as I watched Rico reverse out of the yard, tires squealing.

After work, I picked up Paloma at a bus stop on Venice Boulevard. It was her day off and we were going to take another drive. I wanted to make up for the last disaster. I checked over the Nissan's engine before leaving Gato's, but stashed a gallon of water in the trunk, just in case.

When she got in the car, I reached for her fingers and braided them in mine. Her touch made me feel bigger than the sky. "You look beautiful, nena, like a movie star."

"You're full of shit," she said then kissed me. "I hope we ain't gonna break down this time."

"We won't."

"That's why I didn't wear heels." She squeezed my thigh to let me know she was joking.

We picked up McDonald's and Paloma fed me cheeseburger, fries and chocolate shake as we crawled south down the jammed freeway toward Palos Verdes. Gato told me it was a real nice place to take my girl.

The sun was getting low as we started on the winding road along the cliffs. The road was boxed in with real tall trees, their bark peeling off in big strips, then it opened up and we had a view of the ocean. I pulled into a lookout point. We got out and walked a ways, the wind lashing our faces. The surf crashed onto the rocks below and sent sprays into the air. Paloma clasped her arms around my waist, and I sheltered her in mine as we watched the sun glide below the horizon.

We walked back to the car in the dark and made out. Paloma's hand slid beneath my belt, sending ripples through my body. We moved to the back seat, thinking the dark was safe. We were in full action when a sharp rap sounded on the window and a light shone in. Paloma yelped and grabbed a handful of clothes to cover herself.

"I'll give you one minute to get dressed and get out of here or I'll give you a citation." The cop walked back to his idling patrol car.

I struggled to unstick myself from Paloma. We scrambled to get our clothes on and move to the front seat. The cop was waiting, his headlights beaming right on us.

"Hijo de la gran puta," I said. "We weren't bothering nobody. Nobody's even around."

"Forget it, Mags. Let's just go."

We pulled out and headed north. The atmosphere inside the car had turned sour. I rolled down the window as if the fresh air could clear it, but the night had been ruined.

Paloma broke the silence. "I'm sick of this shit sneaking around, keeping a big secret. You gotta tell Blueboy, Mags. Soon. I can't take this no more."

"I know, nena. I'm just tryna find the right way to tell him, the right time, the right words."

"You been saying that for two months now."

"It ain't that simple."

"You're just a pussy. That's all."

She had pressed her thumb right on the sore spot. "Yeah, I am a pussy!" I yelled. "You know why? Because I have to choose between you and Blueboy, and I don't want to choose. I want both of you!"

"Who says you gotta choose?"

"I know him, nena. You don't know half the shit we been through together. He ain't gonna take this like it's nothing."

"I know him, too. He's my brother."

She didn't understand. He was my brother, too and a betrayal like this ... I suddenly felt sick to my stomach. I had never thought of it as a betrayal, but that's what it was.

"Let me ask you this, Mags. Who *would* you choose if it came down to it?"

"Shit, don't ask me that."

"No, really. Tell me, who would you choose?"

I saw a streak of yellow hurtle by in the commuter lane. The rear of a pickup truck disappeared into the traffic. My insides flipped. Rico? I calmed myself. There must be hundreds of yellow trucks in LA. Paloma took my silence to mean Blueboy was my answer.

"So, you'd choose my brother over me."

"Paloma, I love you, you know that."

"Then it shouldn't be so hard to tell Blueboy."

"Like I said, it just ain't that easy."

"That's an excuse. You really haven't grown out of kicking it in the street with Blueboy."

I was getting mad. She wasn't even trying to see my point of view and now she was talking shit. "We're going round in circles. I don't want to talk about this no more."

We drove the rest of the way in silence. Paloma turned her head away from me, looking out the side window. When I dropped her off at the restaurant, I took her hands in both of mine.

"Paloma, you're the most important thing in my life. Everything I'm doing is for our future. Just gimme a little time."

She looked at me like she didn't believe me. Then she opened the door and got out. "Paloma!" I yelled. She didn't turn around.

I pounded the dashboard with my fist, an animal cry tearing out of my throat. The buttons on the radio popped off. Fuckin rustbucket. I sat back in my seat. She was mad at me and I hadn't even done anything. I was trying as hard as I could. Why couldn't she see that? I just needed some time to work things out, that's all. I took a deep breath. Fuck it. I still had to go see Lissy and warn her about Rico and Chivas. I drove to Veronica's, making a pit stop for a couple candy bars on the way.

Veronica lived in a semi-detached apartment in an old Spanish-style building. It was painted a peach color, which must've been nice at one time. Now it was kinda grey with dirt.

I climbed the steps to the porch and picked my way to the front door through a jumble of junk—a doorless mini fridge, bicycle handlebars, a bashed up dog kennel.

People around here collected discards from alleys and sidewalks in case there was something that could be fixed up and sold or used. Most of the stuff just sat around rusting out. I wasn't going to have somebody else's trash at my house. I wanted everything brand new.

Veronica answered the door. She was short and plump and married to a pendejo who I hoped wasn't home.

"Hey, I stopped by to see Lissy, she around?"

"Who is it?" The pendejo was home.

"Lissy's brother," Veronica called, then turned to me. "She's in the back."

She led me through the living room. I greeted the idiota, who was sitting in an armchair watching TV. He acknowledged me with the barest of nods and scratched the underside of his bearded chin.

We entered the kitchen, where dirty dishes were piled on a counter.

"Lissy, Mags is here." Veronica pointed to a doorway then returned to the living room.

I entered Lissy's room, if you could call it that. It barely fit a bed and a side table. It looked like it had been a closet at one time. "Whatup, sis?"

She tossed down her magazine and jumped up from the bed to hug me. A roll of toilet paper sat on the floor next to a pile of wadded up paper.

"How you doin, girl?"

"Okay. Veronica and Freddy fight a lot, so I just stay in my room."

I had to sit on the edge of the bed so I wouldn't fall into the hollow in the middle of the mattress.

"Feels like forever that you been gone, but it's only been a couple days."

"Feels long to me, too," she said.

"You gonna come back home?"

She shrugged. I checked out her neck and arm. The red marks from Pops' belt had faded, but I guessed the memory hadn't.

"I came by to tell you something, sis. I got a visit from Rico today. Chivas saw you in the visiting room with Benny this weekend." Her hands leapt to her face, covering her nose and mouth. "Don't worry. I told him to tell Chivas he was mistaken, that it wasn't you. He wasn't happy, but he went along with it. I got something on him that I used."

"Putaaaa."

"It was gonna happen sooner or later. You better tell Benny to watch his back."

"He's getting out day after tomorrow." I hiked my eyebrows in a question. "He got a deal—time served and probation."

"Sweet. So what you gonna do now?"

"Benny's clean. He kicked the habit in lockup. He says he wants to be a real father, make a real family."

I doubted he'd stay clean after he hit the street. I'd seen it time after time. Junkies would get clean inside because they had no other option, but when they'd get out, the first thing they'd do was smoke, snort, or shoot up. I thanked God I never got hooked on that shit.

"That's real good," I said. Tears welled in her eyes. "Why you crying?"

"Everybody's mad at me."

"I ain't mad, Zully ain't mad."

"Mamá, papá, Paco."

I waved my hand like I was waving away her worry.

"When they see the baby, they'll come around. Moms is gonna love being abuela. Now where's that baby at? Show me that barriga."

She smiled and pulled up her top, showing a curve to her stomach.

I rubbed the swell and put my ear to it.

"This one's a fighter, I can tell. Just like his moms." I pecked her belly button with my lips. She sniffed and giggled.

I'd put a smile on her face. It seemed like I'd been doing that my whole life. Sometimes I wished I had someone doing that for me.

"Everything's gonna turn out fine," I said.

"Wish I believed you."

"Believe me. Now quit crying."

"You told Blueboy bout you and Paloma yet?"

I sighed. "No, and she's mad about it."

"There ain't never gonna be a right time. You just gotta do it, like I had to tell mi mamá."

I looked at my hands, one sliding inside the other like they were somebody else's. "We kinda had a fight about it."

"You better tell him cuz she might do it. You gotta be the one. He's gotta hear it from you."

"Yeah, I know."

"Maybe you could tell him together."

"Maybe."

"Know something, Mags? You give good advice to other people, but you don't follow it yourself."

"I guess that's the hard part."

SEVENTEEN

I was raw at how Paloma walked off and left me in the car. I didn't want her to think she had me in her pocket, so I decided to let a few days go by and see if she came to me. It was hard to go without seeing her, but I also had to get the chop shop up and running. After that, if she still hadn't come to me, I would go to her, but I wanted to show her that I wasn't waiting on her to move on with my life.

Rico was now a bigger hurdle than before coz I'd threatened to rat him out to Chivas. My plan was still to give him a cut of the chop shop so he would stay off my back and let the homeboys work with me. But now that I was holding Esme over him, he might go on a power trip and cockblock me on the chop shop to call my bluff. It was better to have peace with him, even if I had to buy it. I decided to give him some cash upfront. I knew he wouldn't turn it down.

I called the homeboys to a night meeting at the salvage yard. It was an eerie place in the dark, the parts sitting like hulking shadows. The locos sat around the shop on the car seats, looking at me, waiting for me to talk. I leaned against the work bench and crossed my ankles and arms.

"We're starting tonight, dogs, like a trial run. We gotta get some feria to throw to Rico so he'll go along with this."

"What if he says no?" Jackie said.

"We'll deal with that when we come to it, but if there one thing Rico likes, it's green, even more than pussy. This is the plan. Tonight, we gonna start off easy with K-town. Look for an old model Honda or Toyota. They're cake. Jackie, you're wheelman with Tweety in the Nissan. Blueboy and Flaco, you gonna jack the ride. Jackie and Tweety, you post up til Blue and Flaco got the ride in hand, then come back here. Cojo, you help me on the chop. Any sign of trouble, just book. Don't get reckless and run risks. It ain't worth it. Once we get up and running, we're gonna have two, two-man teams hitting a different part of town or a different city for each job, like one in Compton while another works the Westside. That's gonna confuse the five-o."

I reached behind me for two license plates I snagged from a wreck and threw them to Jackie. "Switch these out on the Nissan."

From a bag, I took out prepaid cellphones and tossed one to each homie.

"These burners are only for business, not for calling the ruca. Carry them 24/7, but don't be giving out the numbers. I got you all on my phone under numbers—Blue, you uno, Cojo, dos, Flaco, tres, Jackie cuatro, me, cinco, Tweety, seis. The numbers go in alphabetical order so they're easy to remember. You do the same with your phones. We gonna use em for a week or two, then change em up."

"You should be número uno, Mags," Tweety said.

"Five is my lucky number, Tweety. When you got a ride, you dial five and say, 'The steak's on the grill.' Then when you get a block away, call and say, 'The steak's ready,' so we got the gate open when you pull up.

"Now if shit goes sideways and you get popped by the five o, what're you gonna tell em?"

"Nothing," Flaco said.

"Right. The only word you gotta say is ...?"

"Lawyer," Flaco said.

I nodded. "I know you heard it before, but I'm saying it again because everyone makes this mistake. Ninety percent of people locked up wouldn't be there if they just kept their damn mouths shut. You don't have to say shit to cops. That's the law. They're gonna get mad and try to trick you. They're gonna say you must be guilty coz only guilty people want lawyers. They're gonna try to bluff you, say your homie's rolled on you, offer you a deal to snitch. They gonna get right up in your face coz they fuckin hate it when we know how to play them. Don't believe a fuckin word outta their mouths, just keep saying you want a lawyer. Lemme tell you the first and only thing that cops say when they get busted—lawyer."

I looked around and they all nodded with serious faces.

"Tools, Mags?" Flaco said.

I slid open a drawer in the toolbox. "Pick your screwdriver. Slide hammers and slim jims right here. Only one man per team carries the tools in case of a bust. Take turns with each job so you share the risk."

After Jackie switched out the plates, they piled into the Nissan. Cojo opened the gate and they entered the night. We were on. Watching the red taillights disappear, I knew I had turned a corner. No more cheapass street shit for me. This was real business.

The job went smooth as cream. It didn't take long before I got the call that the steak was on the grill, then the next call that it was ready. Less than three hours after that, me and Cojo had a Honda Accord in a pile of parts.

I called Gato. He came with his truck, we loaded it, and he took off. Where he took the parts was none of my business.

It was still dark out when I got home. I got a couple hours sleep, then went back to work. Gato was there, with his newspaper and coffee—and a grip of cash. I was ready for Rico.

I rolled into the garage for the clica meeting. Blueboy was already there, smoking a cigarette. I greeted him but he just looked at me with eyes like tombstones. The fuck was up with him? I was about to ask but the others filtered in, and Rico started the meeting.

The homeboys tossed the feria from collections and corner slinging onto a chair beside him. Blueboy said nothing. He seemed sunk deep in himself. I kept throwing him looks, but he ignored me.

The collection was finished. Rico picked up the pile of money and tidied it into a neat stack. Everybody watched, waiting for their cut. Then I threw a roll of bills, with a rubber band around it, onto the chair in front of him. Rico looked at me from under his eyebrows.

"I got a new business for the clica," I said.

"Yeah? Whass that?"

"Gato's got a chop shop going. He wants me to handle the chops.

I need a crew to work the street."

"The homeboys got collections."

"It's big feria, Rico. That's just a taste." I gestured with my chin at the roll. "Young 'uns like Mouse can take over collections. We can earn more with older homies working the rides, but if you ain't down with it, I'll give Gato back his advance."

Blueboy was studying his feet pushing around a pebble. Everybody else was eyeballing Rico, who was looking at the bills he was shuffling in his hand. I knew he was weighing my suggestion. He finally picked up the roll.

"Long as the clica gets its cut," he said.

"That's how it goes."

"Meeting over," Rico declared.

The homies gathered around, all happy and shit. They knew they'd earn big on the rides. I looked around for Blueboy, but he was gone already. Then I caught Rico staring at me. His face broke into a real smug smile. A chill ripped through me. I knew then what was up with Blueboy. I told the homies I'd meet them at Gato's later, rolled into the alley and broke into a sprint. I had to get to Paloma before Blueboy did.

I heard a crash as I entered the driveway to their house. I poured on speed and burst through the front door. Paloma lay on the floor. Blueboy was yanking her up by a fistful of hair.

"Tell me the truth!" he yelled.

The coffee table was overturned, a dark stain spread from a spilled glass.

"Let her go!" I shouted. "I'll tell you everything!"

His head shot round. He released her and stood, chest heaving. Whimpering, she scrambled to her feet.

"Paloma, get outta here," I said. She didn't move. "Go!" I yelled.

She ran to her room as Blueboy's fist slammed into my jaw. I staggered back. He clocked me on the left cheekbone. Then an uppercut under the chin. My head spun.

"Fight me, you fuckin hijo de la gran puta!" he yelled. "Fight me!"

He was pacing, breathing through his mouth, shaking his arms loose. His eyes flared. A bull ready to charge. I threw a right, but he blocked it with his left forearm and punched my gut with his right. I jackknifed and he got in a kidney shot. Pain bolted through me from different angles. Bent over, I swayed, but managed to steady myself. He rested, waiting for me to straighten.

I raised my sightline enough to see his legs and head-butted him, grunting as I rammed into his belly. He groaned, then seized my ears and yanked my head up. His knee rammed me under the chin. My teeth felt like they'd smashed into the crown of my skull. He let go and I fell back, hitting my head on the table corner. I was dazed.

He tumbled on top of me, punching my face side to side like a bag. I cuffed his wrists with my hands. He struggled, but I pressed his arms to the right. I counted to three then I bucked the left side of my torso with as much force as I could muster as I kept pushing his arms to the right. He toppled onto the floor. I quickly shoved him face down and straddled him, spreading my knees so they each pinned an arm and held his head against the carpet. He made a muffled noise. I pushed his head harder, harder. The noises grew more frantic.

"Magdaleno, stop!" Paloma pulled at my shoulder.

I let go and slid off Blueboy. I sat with my arms flopped on my bent knees, breathing hard. Paloma turned her brother over. His face was red and patterned from the carpet pile. He stared vacantly, his eyes frozen like blue ice.

My breath caught but then his chest moved up and down. My head dropped with relief.

"You almost killed him!" she said. "Blue!"

She shook him. He turned his head toward me.

"You ... come near ... me ... or my sister ... again ... I will fuckin kill you," he rasped. There was nothing more for me to do there. I staggered to my feet and stumbled home.

The light shone under the girls' bedroom door. Zully was still up. I tapped at the door as I leaned heavily against the threshold. "Zully," I whispered. She opened and gasped at the sight of beatup face. "Shhh."

"What happened to you?"

"Just get me some ice, aspirin, anything."

She dashed to the kitchen, and I made my way to the bunk lowering myself carefully onto the bottom bed and lay down. I could feel my face puffing up, I could hardly see. My head hurt like a motherfucker.

Zully returned with two bags of frozen peas. I covered my face with them. The cold felt real good.

"Mags, you're bleeding. Turn over." She pushed me gently to one side. "You got a cut on the back of your head." It must've been when I hit the table on the way to kissing the floor. "Wait."

She left the room again, and returned with a towel, a glass of water and ibuprofen. She tilted my head up to take the painkillers, then rolled up the towel and positioned it under my head to catch the blood.

"You should be a nurse," I said.

"I get a lot of practice round here. You get in a fight?"

"You could say that. I'm gonna sleep in here tonight, okay?"

"Yeah. You okay now, want anything else?"

"I'm good." She took my shoes off and turned out the light, then climbed up to her bunk. "Thanks, sis."

The pills didn't do much for the pain. I couldn't sleep coz of the pain, but also my mind was clearing and the picture of one person emerged from the fog. Rico.

The motherfuckin hijo de la gran puta. He must have suspected it was Paloma and me behind the shed at the bautizo, maybe followed me to check it out. The day we went down to the coast. It sure looked like his truck that I saw on the freeway. Then he told Blueboy as payback for me using Esme on him. Which I shouldn't have done, but I didn't know how else I was gonna save Lissy. Rico was slipperier than a cunt slathered in KY.

I would get payback on Rico for damn sure, but he could wait. Paloma and Blueboy couldn't. I had a real mess on my hands, and I could blame Rico all I wanted, but it was on me.

I'd given Rico the opening because I'd been a pussy. I shoulda told Blue. I shoulda listened to Paloma, to Lissy. Why did I think I could get away with it? Everybody found out everybody's business in the barrio. Why did I think I would be different? Why did I think I would be smarter?

My whole body throbbed. I groped on the floor for the ibuprofen, shook out a couple more pills and gulped them down.

"You okay, Mags?" Zully said.

"Just thanking God I got you, lil sis."

EIGHTEEN

A stranger looked back at me from the bathroom mirror the next morning. My face looked like somebody had crushed blueberries all over it. My body was swollen and ached. Blueboy worked me over good. I hoped he felt satisfied.

Moms caught me coming out of the bathroom. She was used to me showing up with bruises and scrapes over the years, but I guess this was too much even for her.

"¡Dios mio, hijo!" She clapped her hand over her mouth.

"I just got in a fight. I'm okay."

She tried to fuss over me, but I wouldn't let her. I had to get to work, I told her.

I called Paloma soon as I got in the car. She didn't pick up. I debated whether to swing by her house, but remembering Blue's threat, I figured it prolly wasn't the wisest idea. I headed straight to the yard.

Gato stared at me as I practically crawled out of the car. "You could tell me you won, but I'd know you were lying," he called.

I waved at him as I made my way to the shop. "Tell you later." I'd have to think up a cover story. I didn't want to tell him that me and Blueboy got into it. I didn't want to tell anyone. Rico would tell the homies, that was for sure. I tried Paloma again. Still no answer.

I shuffled back and forth all morning in the shop, swallowing ibuprofen like candy and calling Paloma every half hour. I was getting antsier with each unanswered call. Had something happened to her? Was she mad at me? Didn't want to see me anymore? I started calling every ten minutes. She had to pick up some time. At noon, I called Lissy on her lunch break. She was the only one I could talk to, but I didn't get as much sympathy as I'd hoped.

"What did you think Blueboy was gonna do, bro? You woulda done the same thing."

"Yeah, I guess."

"You gotta put yourself in his place, Mags. What you did was pretty big and him like a brother to you all this time. And then he finds out from Rico? Talk about a knife in the back."

Her words were like stones sinking me in a swimming pool of guilt. I tried to climb out. "Not on purpose. I mean, I fell in love with his sister. That's my fault?"

"Whose fault is it gonna be? You gonna blame God or fate or something? It was you and her."

She was right, as much as I hated to admit it. "So, what should I do?"

"You gotta talk to him."

"I'm tryna talk to Paloma, but she ain't picking up her phone. I'm getting worried."

"She'll call when she's ready. Give her some space. She's stuck in the middle between her brother and you. I'd be pissed if you kept calling me."

I hung up, feeling worse than ever. I really had let Blueboy down.

But what was I supposed to do? Walk away from Paloma?

I didn't even know if I coulda done that. I just wanted time to get myself set up, make some money to start a business with Blueboy and Paloma away from the clica.

Fuckin Rico. I hurled a wrench at the calendar babe on the wall. Just when I thought everything was going good, it all fuckin crashed.

I heard the fall of footsteps.

"So. You gonna tell me what went down?" Gato stood in the door, hands in his pockets.

"Personal beef, Gato, nothing to do with the business."

"I got some of Migdalia's arroz con pollo if you're hungry."

"Thanks, man, but my whole face hurts. Anything I'm eating today is through a straw and maybe not even."

"Está bien. You good to roll tomorrow night? I got a special order."

"We're good." He left.

It was late afternoon, almost quitting time, when Gato returned to the shop. "So, it was over a girl."

"Huh?" I was bent under a hood.

"What do I tell her?"

"What're you talking about?" I pulled out from the hood.

"You here or not?" He pointed outside.

Paloma stood by the dogs near the gate. I dropped the wrench and jogged down to her, ignoring the pain that shot through my body with each step. She gasped when she saw my face. "Oh, baby."

For just half a second, the sunshine radiated around her head like a halo. I wondered if I was hallucinating, but I guess it was just relief that she was there.

"Yeah, I'm gonna be real ugly for a while," I said.

"We gotta talk."

I led her to the shop. I was suddenly embarrassed that the car seats were covered with dust and dirt and grease stains. I grabbed a rag and tried to clean one off but it had fresh oil on it so that didn't work. "Shit," I said, staring at the streak it left.

"Don't worry about it." She sat on another seat, me next to her.

I rubbed my thighs, unsure of what was coming. She picked up my grease-stained fingers and smoothed them, then leaned forward to smush her lips against mine. An explosion went off in my chest. In a second, we were wrapped in each other's arms.

"What are we gonna do?" she said after we pulled apart. A strand of her hair was stuck in the whiskers on my chin, a thread joining us. I let it stay there. "Blueboy left after the fight and he ain't been home since. Mi mamá is getting worried. I had to tell her everything."

"Shit, what did she say?"

"She doesn't care about you and me, but she said we should've told Blue."

"He's prolly shacked up with some girl smoking blunts. He'll come back when he runs out of mota. Then I can have a sitdown with him, get him to see this ain't no smalltime thing between you and me."

She searched my face with cotton-soft eyes. "What are you saying exactly?"

The words rushed out like a river straight from my heart. "These past few days without you, they been killing me." Her eyes shone, then tears slid down her cheeks like crystal beads off a necklace. I kissed them away, tasting her salt on my lips. "Listen, nena, I'm serious. I'm getting pisto together and we're gonna leave LA. It ain't just a dream. Te lo juro."

She buried her head in my shoulder. "When?"

"When I got enough to set us up good. I got everything going smooth now and I only got another month on parole."

"I can't lose Blueboy, Mags. He and my mom are the only family I got. My dad took off to New Jersey when I was little. He's got another family out there, doesn't give a shit about me."

I smoothed her hair, soft and clean. "I'll find Blueboy and talk to him. He'll come round." Deep down, I knew it wasn't gonna be as easy as I made it sound.

I slid my hand under the waist of her jeans and felt her thong strap. She pressed into me a little harder and raised her face to kiss me. Her hand rubbed the vee of my lap with a predictable result. I got up and closed the door to the shop. When our bodies joined, I felt like I'd fused with Paloma, that we were truly one being. Then something real weird happened, tears came into my eyes. I tried to hide it from Paloma by turning my head, but she saw and held my chin to bring my face back to her. She didn't say anything, just hugged me real tight, and I let the tears drip into her beautiful hair. I never felt so close to her so maybe it was good.

After Paloma left, I felt like a party balloon pumped up with the promise of the future, a real future. I felt like I could do anything I wanted.

I picked up a screwdriver and switched on the radio. Rubén Blades was singing "Pedro Navaja." I cranked it and sang along as I pried off hubcaps.

Gato's voice boomed over the music. "So Casanova, she's still with you, huh?"

I sang the chorus at him. "*La vida te da sorpresas, sorpresas te da la vida.*"

Gato joined in, singing with his arms spread open like he was on stage. We sang til the song ended. Life really was full of surprises.

NINETEEN

I rolled by El Gato Rey that night but Blueboy wasn't around. I asked Maite, the dancer he'd hooked up with, if she seen him. She said no, but I couldn't tell if she was lying. I decided not to lean on her yet, give Blueboy more time to show up on his own.

"If you see him, tell him I'm looking for him," I said. Then I added, "Just to talk," in case he thought that maybe I wanted another round in the ring with him. Which I didn't. I went to the table in the far corner, which was now the Cyco Lokos table, to wait for the homeboys.

I asked them to stop by to clear the air right away about me and Paloma and Blueboy. I was sure Rico woulda told them and I needed to know where I stood with them. Since I violated code, they had the right to beat me down, make me pay a bigass fine, demote me to shit work, or all three.

The homies soon shuffled in and took seats. I ordered a round of beers, which came with a bowl of peanuts. Everybody looked like they were going to a funeral, plus they didn't comment on my black-and-blues, which meant they knew what went down.

I took a deep breath and plunged in. "Aight. You all know I got a beef with Blueboy over Paloma."

"It's kinda written all over your face, Mags," Tweety said. Cojo shot him a sharp glance and he shut up.

"Rico told us," Flaco said.

"I figured he would. Listen up. What I did ain't right by the code, but it's right by me and Paloma. The way I look at it, this beef is between me and Blue. It ain't got nothing to do with the business or the clica. Anybody got a problem with that?"

A second of uneasy silence ticked by, then Flaco spoke.

"Seems like the code's gone to shit ever since Chivas got locked up so that ain't the issue. Everybody's doing what they damn well please. But what you did was a major disrespect to Blueboy, Mags. Ain't no way round that."

I nodded. I deserved whatever was coming.

"You're right."

"But we don't like what Rico did neither. He shoulda come to the clica first, not rat you out to Blueboy on his own account. And he got his own violations," Jackie Chan said.

Flaco continued. "So, we figure if we ain't taking action gainst Rico, we can't take action gainst you. You and Blueboy gotta handle your own situation, long as it doesn't fuck with the business."

"Look like Blueboy already handled it," Tweety said.

"That's what we told Rico, Mags," Cojo said. "He wasn't too happy, but he accepted it."

"That's fair." They weren't playing favorites.

"Besides, we owe you one for that vote on Elysian Park," Cojo said.

The others nodded.

"That too," Flaco added.

I relaxed, relieved. I knew Rico had to be pissed off that the homeboys were still with me, though he'd succeeded in driving a wedge between me and Blueboy. "Preciate it, homies. Now I gotta find Blueboy. He ain't been home since last night. Anybody put eyes on him?" They shook their heads.

"Aight. Get the word out. If anybody gets the 411..."

Tweety held up his burner. "I'll call you right away, homes, and say the dog's on the grill."

Everybody groaned. Jackie threw a peanut at him, then we all did the same.

Tweety laughed as peanuts flew at him, loving every second of it.

TWENTY

A week later, Blueboy was still AWOL. Me and the homies had roamed the streets looking for any sign of him. We checked bars, party houses, dealers. I checked the abandoned house about a dozen times to see if he'd showed up or maybe was squatting there.

I put the squeeze on Maite, but she seemed to be telling the truth when she said she hadn't seen him. I was desperate to find him, not for myself, but more for his mom and Paloma.

I wanted to make it up to them for causing his disappearance by bringing him home, but it wasn't happening. He'd fuckin vanished.

I knew I did Blueboy wrong and maybe he'd never forgive me, but I just wanted a chance to explain things to him. I stood in the middle of the junkyard a couple times, staring up at the vault of the sky, talking into the blue like I was talking to his eyes. "Just gimme a chance, bro, just hear me out."

I told him about my dream that we would be a family together someplace else. He was under that same sky somewhere—maybe he'd get my message. But there was only silence in return.

Fuck, why did it have to be *his* sister? Why couldn't it have been one of Jackie's sisters? He had five of em.

But it had to be Blueboy's sister I fell in love with. Maybe that made sense. It did have to be her because they were kind of the same, and that's why I loved them both. Ay Dios, why did you have to make things so damn difficult, a big circle with no beginning and no end and no way out?

Paloma and Doña Flor were getting frantic. Every night, Flor checked intake at the emergency room at the hospital where she worked. One of the nurses even called the morgue for her, but there were no twenty-year-old, blue-eyed John Does on ice.

After a week of nothing, Flor and Paloma filed a missing persons report. The cop at first said adults were within their rights to disappear from their families. Even if he was found, he might not want anything to do with them. Then she looked up Blueboy's record and said she'd pass it along to the gang unit.

I thought that was prolly bad—getting the five-o, especially the gang unit, involved in anything was never good in my opinion, but it was already done, and I didn't want to piss off Paloma.

As the first week rolled into the second and there was still no sign of him, I realized searching for him was pointless.

Blueboy didn't want to be found. He was playing hide-and-seek to punish me, but what about Paloma and his moms? They were worried sick. How long was he going to keep this up? I no longer felt guilty.

Now I felt mad. I had to get my life back to the business, which I had pushed aside to look for Blueboy.

Gato was getting antsy, saying shit like I wasn't serious, and he'd have to start looking for a new crew.

The homeboys were ready, too. They needed the pisto, and Rico was gonna be crawling up my ass soon for his cut. He'd been staying on the downlow this whole time, which only proved what a fuckin punk he was.

I called the homeboys to the yard.

"We're going out for rides tomorrow night and the next few nights to make up for lost time. Tonight, we gotta do something else before we get any deeper into this shit."

"What about Blueboy?" Jackie Chan said.

"He's gonna come walking into Gato's one night, like nothing ever happened, you'll see," Flaco said.

"That's what I think, too," I said. "Aight, everybody grab a tool and come over to the back wall."

They picked up tools and followed me.

"Something Chivas taught me was to never act overconfident and always take care of your back. If it ain't the five-o right behind your shoulder, it's the competition. He said you always gotta have an escape route. If they're coming in the front, you go out the back, or the side, above or below."

"So, where we going, Mags?" Tweety said.

"Out the back. We're gonna break through this wall to make an escape route. It's cinderblock. It won't be hard to bust through. We'll cover the opening with an old toolbox."

"What about Gato?" Cojo said.

"Gato don't need to know right now."

We bashed a four-foot hole through the wall.

It opened on to a space about a foot wide between the building and the back chain link fence that bordered an alley.

"What about the fence?" Tweety said.

"I got a plan for that," I said.

"That's what I like about you, Mags. You always got a plan."

"I'm trying. Someone get me the wire cutters on the tool bench."

We cut the fence so it could be pushed open real easy, then rolled a couple old oil drums out into the alley and stacked them in front of the cut.

The escape route was ready if we ever needed it.

A couple days later, I stopped at Paloma's house after work. Me and the homies had an ace week with the rides, and I had a pocket full of pisto.

I was gonna take Paloma to a real nice dinner on her night off, but when I walked in, it was like stepping into one of them houses built of ice at the North Pole.

Doña Flor was putting her jacket on.

"I'm going to church to light a candle to San Antonio. Do you know who that is, Magdaleno?" she said without saying hi or nothing.

"Uh, no."

"The patron saint of missing persons. Because that's the only thing that's going to bring my son back now--a miracle."

I didn't know what to say so I said nothing. She shouldered past me and banged the door shut.

I felt bad that she blamed me for Blueboy's disappearance, but what could I do if he didn't want to be found?

I sat on the couch and waited for Paloma. She came out, looking beautiful as ever, and sat next to me. We cuddled for a minute.

"Anything new on Blueboy?" she said. I shook my head. "There must be some place you ain't looked, Mags."

"He'll show up when he's good and ready. He's holed up somewhere. I bet you anything he's just fine."

I slid my hand under her T-shirt. My groin tingled. I was just about to scoop her up in my arms and carry her to the bedroom when she pulled away from me, looking at me straight on. "So, you're giving up then."

I threw my hands up, annoyed. "I don't know what else I can do. I've done all I can."

"Seems like you should be doing more, seeing as this is on you."

She'd lobbed the burning ball of blame at me, and it scorched. "What about you, Paloma?" I raised my voice. I couldn't help it. "Maybe you're forgetting, I wasn't in this by myself."

"I said I'd tell him, but *you* said *you'd* do it, and you didn't."

"Lemme remind you of something. If you didn't make Blueboy take you to Rico's bautizo and got so drunk and horny, Rico never woulda suspected us in the first place."

Her eyes narrowed. "I didn't see you saying no at the time."

"You wanna blame me? Go ahead. I'm the bad guy. It's all on me. That make you happy? I made a mistake cuz I ain't perfect. And I got news for you—you ain't either. Nobody is."

I leaned forward on my knees. The anger was coming off me in hot waves. "I didn't want to tell him because I knew I would lose him, so I didn't tell him, and I lost him anyway. How you think I feel? I got caught in a no-win situation."

"Yeah, but it ain't just you who lost him, it's me and Moms."

"How was I to know he was gonna jet outta here? But don't you see? He'll come back to *you* coz you're his family but he ain't gonna come back to me. Even though we always said that shit bout being brothers and all, we're not. We ain't blood when it comes right down to it. That's just the fuckin bullshit they feed you in the clica to make you feel like you obligated to do shit for them, like doing their fuckin time."

Paloma looked stunned. I lowered my voice.

"I'm not anybody's fool. I see things for what they are and what they're not. And now I'm seeing something else. I'm losing you, right?"

A knife point pierced my chest as I voiced my deepest fear. I looked at her. Even when she was mad at me, she was so fuckin beautiful. My eyes burned and I closed them, lowering my head. Then I felt Paloma take my face in her hands, her lips assault my eyelids, eyebrows, forehead, cheeks so's I could hardly breathe. I didn't want her to stop. She straddled me and pressed her mouth to mine. I opened my eyes and found her gazing at me. We kissed with anger, at each other, at Blueboy, at the whole damn world, until she pulled her T-shirt over her head and unhooked her bra, spilling her chichis in my face. We made fierce love on the couch, passing blame back and forth with every thrust. When we collapsed on one another, breathless after coming together in a giant shudder, I knew we were through it, and I still had Paloma.

When I got home, I found Pops holding his head in his hands at the kitchen table and Moms comforting him. She gave me a look saying, "Don't ask."

I turned on my heel and knocked on the girls' room instead. Zully opened the door a crack.

"Whatup with Pops?" I mouthed to Zully.

She motioned for me to come in and shut the door. Lissy, her belly the size of a pumpkin, was sitting in a chair with her feet on the lower bunk. The air smelled of nail polish.

"Lissy! What are you doing here?" I hugged her.

"Ssh!" Zully said.

"Just visiting. Pops came home early so I'm hiding out in here."

Zully picked up a bottle of blue polish and went back to painting Lissy's toenails. I sat on the bunk. "You're getting real big. He's gonna be a bruiser."

"I went to the doctor yesterday. Had an ultrasound. Check it out." She took out a black rectangle of paper from her purse and handed it to me. "It's a boy."

All I could see was a grainy blob. "Kinda looks like a science experiment." Zully punched my arm. Lissy laughed. "He looks real good." I handed the picture back to her. "You show Moms?"

"She had to sit down. She never saw one of these before," Lissy said.

"Whatup ...?" I cocked my head toward the kitchen.

"He came in all pale saying, 'I saw him, I can't believe he's here en el Norte," Zully said. Then he was talking real low to mi mamá. All I heard was, 'la mano blanca.' And then she put her hand to her mouth and said, 'Dios, no puede ser.' Then they talked real low again and I couldn't hear."

"The White Hand? Gotta be something from Salvador," I said.

"He's been sitting there like that for a while. It's kinda creepy," Zully said.

"I wish they'd tell us what went down over there," I said.

"They want to forget, I guess," Lissy said. I tickled the sole of her foot. She jerked it away with a half laugh, half cry. "Take off your shoes and I'll give you a foot massage."

"No way. I know what you're gonna do. You ain't putting that shit on me," I said.

We bagged up. "Remember the time we painted Frank's toes when he was sleeping?" she said.

"He didn't even notice he had red toenails til he was in the shower," I said.

"Man, did he yell!" Lissy said.

Zully pointed at the door and we quieted down. Moms and Pops shuffled by in the hall. Their bedroom door clicked shut.

Lissy turned to me. "Blueboy?"

I shook my head. *"Nada."*

"He'll show up when you ain't expecting it."

"That's what everybody keeps saying. Doña Flor blames me."

Zully rubbed my shoulder. "It's not your fault."

Lissy was silent. I looked at her.

"Go ahead, say I told you so."

"You know something? At least, everybody knows now. It ain't a secret anymore."

"So, Rico did me a favor, that's what you're saying?"

"Yeah, kinda." Sadness glistened in her eyes. I knew she was thinking of her situation with Benny.

"How's your ruco doing?"

"Good. He's talking bout going over to the other side for a while."

"México? Why's he gonna do that?"

"He got people in Michoacán."

"You going with him?"

She looked down and shrugged. That meant yes.

"Don't go, Lissy!" Zully said.

Lissy jabbed a finger at her. "Don't you say nothing to nobody, Zully, hear me?" Then she looked at me. "You neither."

I zipped my lips with my fingers, but my nose was twitching. Nobody rolled over the border for nothing. People usually went lamming it, but Benny's charges were done. Maybe he was going to be a 5150 pointman with the cartel over there. That didn't make sense neither. He didn't have rank in his clica, that I knew of anyway. I didn't give a fuckin rat's ass about Benny Santana, but whatever he had going down, he had better leave my sister out of it.

It was late. Lissy decided to stay over and leave early the next morning. I pulled out the couch and lay in bed with the lights off, the TV on and the sound mute. The flickering from the TV washed out the color from my legs, turning me into a grey ghost. A black-and-white Mexican movie was on—Cantinflas was doing his fast-talking to get out of trouble by confusing the cop. I'd seen it before. I'd seen every Cantinflas movie since I was a little kid. The Spanish-language stations played them all the time. I found a peanut butter cup smushed in the side of the couch. I chewed while I watched Cantinflas escape as the dumbass cop scratched his head. If only life was that easy.

Something crashed against the door, then it burst open and Frank stumbled in. He flopped onto the mattress, half on top of me. I rolled him off, smelling booze, and switched on the light.

"Bro, what the fuck?" He didn't answer. He was out cold, his mouth gaping like a goldfish.

I pushed his bulk to his side of the bed. He didn't even stir. I felt the hard rectangle of his wallet in his back jeans pocket. I took it out to toss it on the coffee table, but I flipped it open out of curiosity. Driver's license, LAFD card. A photo of Glenda, like a formal portrait. Another one of her lying naked on a bed in a sex kitten pose. Damn. By the creases in photo, it looked well used. So that's what he did on his nights at the fire station. I slid it back, then stared at the license. Frank and me looked alike. People always called us out as brothers. An idea crystallized in my head. A person making a quick check would think that photo was me, no problem. I could use Frank's ID as my get-into-jail card to see Chivas. I bet it would work. I tucked the license in my sneaker and tossed the wallet under the bed. I would go see Chivas in the morning and settle this shit

with Rico for once and for all.

Frank was still sleeping it off when I woke up early. With any luck, he'd still be zonked when I got back from the jail. If I couldn't get the license back in his wallet without him seeing, I'd throw it on the floor like it fell out and pretend to find it.

The air was chilly and the sky thick and cloudy, like with a layer of cotton balls over it. The day laborers were gathered at street corners, waiting for pickups to roll by, drivers signaling how many workers they needed by holding up fingers. Then it was a stampede and a battle to swing a leg into the truck bed. The taco trucks were parked nearby, selling coffee and breakfast burritos.

The visitors' line was already long when I arrived at Men's Central. I looked up at the tall cement oblong with tiny slits of windows, surrounded by razor wire coils. Just looking at it gave me the heebie-jeebies. The place was a hellhole. Buses marked "Los Angeles County Sheriff's Department," their windows blacked out and barred, pulled out of another gate, taking inmates to their court hearings. I remembered being on one of those buses, trying to snatch peeks of the world.

The line shuffled forward—wives, girlfriends, mothers. I was one of few men. I pulled Frank's LAFD baseball cap down on my forehead and balled my hands inside my hoodie pocket to hide my tatts.

My turn came at the check-in desk manned by a female officer. "Inmate name."

"Armando Borregos."

"Spell the last name."

I spelled it out.

"ID."

I handed her the license. My armpits were as wet as a dog's nose. But she didn't even check my face against the photo, just typed in Frank's name and waited. I prayed Frank didn't have a secret I didn't know about. He didn't. She gave me back the license. "Next."

I was in.

My heart hammered. I emptied my pockets into a plastic bowl and stepped through the metal detector into a waiting room where the visitors waited for their inmate to arrive from the cells. Latina girls in skinny blue jeans bought potato chips and soda from the vending machines to feed toddlers. Black women hollered at kids running around the hard orange plastic chairs. An older white couple nervously looked around, scared all these brown people were gonna jump them. I hoped Chivas wouldn't be thrown off by the name, "Frank." Hopefully, he'd recognize the last name and figure out it was me.

"Armando Borregos," a voice called.

I stood. The officer directed me into the security visit room, where I sat on a bolted-to-the-floor stool in front of a glass partition.

I almost didn't recognize Chivas when he came through the steel door. His midnight black hair was now dirty grey. His orange jail suit hung like a coathanger on the pointy bones of his shoulders. His eyes skimmed the row of visitors. When he spotted me, he threw his head back at the surprise. He grinned as he walked to the window and sat. We picked up the phones. We had to be careful what we said. Conversations were probably recorded.

"I wondered if it was you," he said. "You were always the smart one, *Frank*."

"How you doing?" as if I couldn't tell. His cheeks were potholes, his complexion rough as a taco shell. His eyes were the most alive thing about him.

He nodded like jail life was the bomb. "You? When you get back from vacation?"

"A while ago. I stopped by to see Esme the other day. Kids getting real big."

"Yeah, she told me. That's the hardest thing about this shit, not seeing the cipotes grow up."

"You gonna beat this, homes." I had to sound optimistic.

"The lawyer says we got a chance. They got nothing except a blood spot. How's work?"

He was asking about the clica. "A lotta beefs with the boss. He ain't doing us right."

He frowned. "Howzat?"

"He ain't thinking things through. He's getting into a beef with the competition over smalltime business. But he's got a brand-new truck, so he's doing real well for himself." I paused, allowing a second for this to sink in.

"Listen, I know you got shit with him, but just roll with him for now. He's just doing what *his* boss says, feel me?" His eyes bored into mine.

So, the crown had been fitted to Rico's head. I nodded, hoping I didn't look sideswiped. Maybe I had to give Chivas the intel about Rico's heroin sideline. He wasn't gonna be down with that. "Check this. I'm hearing he's got a side business on his own account, shit that was always off limits."

Chivas's face hardened into cement. He leaned into the window, almost touching it. Even though the glass separated us, I shrank back. "I don't know what shit you fuckin talking bout." His breath fogged the window. He was gripping the phone real tight. "What he's doing ain't nothing with you. You just forget all that."

His words were like bitchslaps. He knew about the smack. He was fuckin in on it.

"No sweat, man. I just thought ..."

Chivas raised his left arm to wipe the mist off the window. Then I saw them on the inside of his arm—a bunch of small bruises and needle tracks. I looked up at him, stunned. His eyes met mine and flickered. He knew what I saw, then he sat back, mouth snaking into a smile.

"Thinking can be dangerous. Hey, I thought I saw your little sister in here the other day visiting."

"Like you said, thinking can be dangerous."

He puckered his lips tight as an asshole, then he gave a half-smile. "You always got the smart answer."

There was nothing more for me to say. "I gotta bounce, man, go to work." As I waited for the door to slide open, I glanced through a window over the heads of a visitor and an inmate.

Chivas was standing at the door on his side, looking back at me. Our gaze met and he chin-nodded me with a warm smile. I did the same. For a flash, it was like old times, but I knew those days were over, whether he beat the murder or not.

His door opened. He shouldered through it sideways as if he couldn't wait to get out of there.

I drove to Gato's in a blur, my mind buzzing.

Chivas. On the fuckin needle. Hijo de fuckin puta.

I never would've believed it if I hadn't seen his arm. I once saw him shove a fool out of the car in the desert on a summer night, telling him he had to come back clean or not come back at all.

We never saw him again. Another time he smoked a cabrón right between the eyes after he found out he was hooked and that's why he was selling underweight.

"Fools like that, they put the whole fuckin operation at risk," he said. "Once you got a habit, your life's fucked anyway."

So, what the fuck had happened to him? But Esme was shooting up, too, so maybe he was on the needle before he got busted.

Maybe that had something to do with why he got busted. He got careless. That was why he had strict orders against us homeboys doing anything stronger than mota. What did Flaco say, that the code had gone to shit? He was sure right.

With my mind so busy, I missed my exit on the 110. Shit. The concrete spaghetti of freeway ramps, overpasses and interchanges was coming up. I switched into the lane for Imperial Highway for no particular reason. I was reminded that this was the stretch where I'd seen the yellow truck when I was with Paloma that day.

Rico. Suddenly everything became clear. Rico was the source of the smack. That's why Chivas made him the street boss. It was in return for supplying Esme and smuggling the shit into lockup. Chivas and Rico prolly had a booming business going. Prices on the inside were triple than on the outside, and you could cut the shit every which way til it was practically dust and fools would still buy it, they were so desperate.

That's where Rico got the feria for the truck. And he and Chivas kept it a secret so they wouldn't have to cut in the homeboys. Chivas and Rico were playing everybody, except Chivas sure as shit couldn't know Rico was boning Esme. "Mother-fuckers," I said to myself as I hit the steering wheel with the heel of my hand.

Traffic thinned as I reached the end of the highway at Dockweiler Beach. I hadn't visited the beach in a real long time. The clicas always came down here for bonfire parties that ended up in a lot of couples on the sand and sometimes in fights with rival barrios. I always loved the bonfire parties cuz I knew I'd get pussy.

Cuddling around a fire did something to girls. One time I got boned twice in a night. I was sixteen and thought life couldn't get any better than that.

I parked and walked down to the water. I took off my shoes and socks and felt the wet sand squish between my toes.

The Pacific Ocean was like a sparkling carpet that stretched on forever, the sun a burning white hole in the sky. I wished I could sail out in a boat, away from all this shit, hit some tropical island where women went around wearing nothing but grass skirts and flowers in their hair.

People cycled by on the bike path, some with babies strapped into seats. Teenagers skateboarded, their bodies waving like they were made outta rubber. Little kids dug in the sand with their plastic spades. A ripped lifeguard wearing his skin like a bronze suit arranged equipment. A whole other world.

I sat on the sand and wrapped my arms around my bent knees as I watched the waves—swelling, rising, crashing, running. They never stopped. I let the froth swirl around me before the water pulled back into the sea, making me feel like I was part of the tide.

It seemed like I came home a couple years ago instead of a couple months. I'd been so deadset on staying outta the life, but here I was, lost in the jungle of it again.

The joke was on me. I didn't try hard enough to stay away from it. I gave up too damn quick for the promise of easy money, being around my homeboys, the chance to get payback on Rico because I was mad at him and jealous of him. And now I was in too deep to get out, that's when I finally saw the truth.

There was nothing to envy in Rico, la vida loca, being down for the barrio, la familia. It was all fuckin hollow. Everybody was out for themselves and used everybody else, including my homies. I was guilty of it, too. It was about money and nothing else.

I picked up a broken piece of a shell and rubbed it. I shoulda applied to transfer my parole and not even come back to LA, gone somewhere far, like northern California.

But this was my home. I wanted to be with my family, my girl, my homies. Was that so wrong? Even if I went somewhere else, I couldn't escape my tatts. People would know what I was.

I pitched the shell into the water. The only thing I could do was stick to my plan—save money, finish my parole and get the fuck out, leave behind the mess with Chivas, Rico and Blueboy. I'd have to leave my homeboys and my family, too.

But so what? The homies sold me out once, they could do it again. My family didn't really give a fuck if I was around or not. Mamá had hidden the fact that I had saved the family. Pops hated me. Frank wanted to make his own family. Lissy was going to

Mexico with her ruco. Zully would meet some guy and go off, too. I had Paloma. She was all the family I needed. I sat for a while, feeling the cool of the water on my lower half and the warmth of the sun on the upper half. Then I stood, brushed off the sand and walked back into my life.

TWENTY-ONE

Everything was going smooth. The rides were coming in and going out, and we were earning bigtime. That made everyone happy, including Rico, who was getting his slice and staying away.

Only one thing was missing—Blueboy. His disappearance was like a cat winding around my legs. I had to be careful not to let it trip me up.

I was in the shower with Paloma one afternoon. She was soaping my back. "Where d'you think Blueboy's at? I mean, really. It's been weeks now."

Talking about Blueboy was the last thing on my mind. I was still somewhere between Paloma's thighs.

"Ni idea, nena. My guess is he's far from here. If he was around, we woulda heard by now."

She turned me to lather my chest. I closed my eyes and let the water fall on my face. "You think he could be RIP?" she asked.

The thought had crossed my mind lately. Bodies can stay hidden for a long time if the responsible party knew what they were doing. But I couldn't say that to Paloma. "Nah. You woulda got a call from homicide by now. He's alive."

I had to change the subject. I took the soap and glided it down her arms. "I want to bring you over to the house for dinner, introduce you to la familia. Like a formal thing."

"Really?"

"We ain't gotta hide now."

Her face cracked into a smile. "I'd like that." I ran the soap between her legs. Her smile widened.

We had the dinner on a Sunday night when Pops was home and Frank was off. I wanted everyone there, just like it was with Glenda. Moms made pupusas and a tres leches cake for dessert. Frank brought Glenda and I insisted Lissy come, even though she didn't want to. I went to get her so she wouldn't chicken out.

"Do it for me, sis. Pops ain't gonna do anything with all of us there," I told her as she lay on her bed refusing to move. "Besides Moms is cooking and you gotta feed that kid some good Salvi food." I pulled her up off her bed. "I'll give you five minutes to get dressed."

I stood outside the door, unsure if she'd go along with it, but then she called that she needed a few more minutes to put on makeup. As we sat down at the table, I looked around at everyone. Moms slapped Pops' hand away from the tortilla basket so she could offer it to the guests first. Paloma, Lissy and Zully compared nail polish colors.

Frank rubbed Glenda's thigh under the table, and she gave him a "not now" look. For the first time that I could remember, I felt like I was really part of the family. No matter what happened in the past, I belonged at that table. Maybe Moms was right when she said something about having a girl put you in place.

When I took Paloma home later, I lifted her hand to my lips as we sat in the car. "They liked you, nena. I could tell by the way everyone was talking to you. My mom looked real happy, and Pops was on his best behavior."

"She told me in the kitchen she was real glad you were settling down, and I was what you needed." She laid her head on my shoulder. I put my arm around her as I felt a burst of happiness inside me. Moms said that about me? Things really were turning around.

"You looked way prettier than Glenda, nena."

"You're always competing with Frank."

"I noticed him looking at you."

She was as radiant as an angel, and I was in her glow.

TWENTY-TWO

Gato had decided to make his club the payday place. I had to hand it to him. He knew the vatos would spend some of their dead presidents before they got out the door so the cash would go right back into his pocket. That was the kind of smart I wanted to be.

We met in the windowless back room that he used for card games, paneled with fake wood and set up with a round table and chairs. The music from the dance floor beat like a muffled drum through the walls.

The crew was all smiles as they folded their bills and stuffed them in their pockets.

"Aight, I guess that's it," I said.

Everybody started to rise from their chairs. "Mags, I got one more thing," Flaco said.

We all sat again.

"Spill."

"Remember how me and Jackie saw them 51s going up to Elysian Park that time?"

"Yeah."

"They ain't done nothing gainst us, no comeback."

"A grip of em got locked up. Maybe they ain't got the manpower," I said. "Or they don't know it was us."

Flaco shrugged. "Just saying is all. Kinda weird."

It was a good observation. Flaco was smart, trustworthy. Now that I didn't have Blueboy, I needed someone as my second. Flaco could fill the slot.

"We good?" Cojo had his hands on the table ready to push back his chair.

"Yeah, get outta here, but don't spend all your feria on the sharks that pass for girls out there," I said.

Everyone made for the door. "Flaco." I cocked my head in a gesture for him to stay. He hung back till the rest had filed out.

"Get the door." I sat down at the table as he closed the door.

"Check this, homes." I told him about Chivas, the needle tracks, him telling me to leave Rico be, how I figured he and Rico were piping chiva into county.

"Putaaaa." Flaco rubbed his chin. "You know who runs chiva in county?"

I shook my head.

"The 5150s."

I slammed the palm of my hand on the table. "Chivas cut a fuckin deal with them. Elysian's gotta be part of the deal and that's why Rico wasn't worried about payback or nothing."

"Motherfucker," Flaco said. "He musta got some sure pipeline into county the 51s can't get to."

"Know what else, homes?" I told him about Chivas seeing Lissy in the visit room with Benny Santana and Rico stepping to me about it. "I turned it right back on him, told him he better tell Chivas he was mistaken, or I'll get word to Chivas about him and Esme. But Chivas mentioned Lissy to me at the visit. I denied it was her, but he knew I was lying. But if everything's smooth with us and the 51s, why's he even giving a fuck?"

"He's gotta keep up the game or he wants you to think he has shit on you. Maybe he's just testing you."

"Yeah, maybe. Benny Santana's back on the street now. Got a deal for time served."

Flaco's eyebrows shot up. "Sweet."

"Maybe too sweet."

"What you gonna do about all this, Mags?"

"Nothing. Shit burns me up, but taking on Rico, Chivas and the 5150s is suicide. I just want to do my business with the rides, discharge parole and get outta the life. I don't want to get caught up in all this fuckin drama all the time."

"Problem is you know too much now." My eyes darted at Flaco.

"You gotta watch your back, Mags, know what I'm saying?"

Fuck. I wished I hadn't even gone to the jail now. I had overplayed my hand. But how was I to know Chivas was fuckin over the clica and a junkie? It was the last thing I would've figured.

The din of the club was getting on my nerves. "I'm booking," I told Flaco. "I gotta headache."

I went home. As soon as I entered the front door, Moms rushed out of the kitchen. "Zully? Oh, m'ijo, it's you."

"Yeah, just me, mamá."

"Zully's gone."

"What do you mean gone?"

"I had a big fight with her. She wanted to go with Belinda to a party, but I said she's too young for parties. She must've waited til I went to bed then sneaked out."

"Where's this party at?"

She wrapped her shawl tighter around her shoulders. "No lo sé. I'm getting worried. It's late and she's not back."

"¿Y papá?"

"He came home drunk. That's when I discovered Zully was gone. I went to get her to help me with him."

"Lemme think for a minute."

Lissy might know where the party was. I took out my phone and punched in her number. The phone rang and rang. Voicemail. I dialed again. *Pick up, goddammit.* Finally she did.

"Whatup?" Voices and laughter rippled in the background.

"Is Zully with you?"

"No."

"Shit." I told her the situation.

"I'll ask if anyone knows of a party tonight." There was a muffled conversation, then she returned to the phone. "There's a big house party on Hoover and Washington."

I hung up and told Moms where I was going. She closed her eyes and started praying.

I ran down the stairs.

I was going to give my sister hell when I found her.

The street was empty except for a couple drunks fighting, Indians from Mexico or Guatemala by the sound of their dialect. I used to love roaming real late at night. I felt like I owned the streets, and anybody I crossed had to answer to me. But now the night wasn't sitting right. It was edgy, like a finger on a trigger. Darkness disguised danger, and I didn't want my little sister out there.

I took off in the Nissan, slowing as I came up on Washington and Hoover. I looked for people bubbling on the sidewalk, listened for party music. I made a right and crawled along. The address "Hoover and Washington" could mean any number of streets around here. A bunch of slingers was kicking it on a corner. I pulled up next to them. One of them slouched toward me, hands in pockets, hoodie on his head. I chin-nodded as a greeting. "You know where the house party's at?"

"Two blocks over." He pointed west.

"'Preciate it."

I headed in that direction, but two blocks later, I still didn't see any party. Fuck. A couple staggered down the sidewalk. The girl was leaning heavily into the guy, like she was real drunk. He had his arm around her waist, propping her up.

They passed under a streetlight and I caught a flash of candy pink pants. I knew those pants.

I slammed the car into park and barreled onto the sidewalk after them. "Zully! Let her go, cabrón!"

The dude turned. I stopped like a bullet hit me between the eyes.

"Rico?"

"Tranquilo. It ain't what you think, homes."

"Fuck you. Zully, get over here."

Then I saw. She was holding together her torn blouse. The top of her pants was ripped. Blood stained her nose and mouth. Her hair was messed up. Tears streaked her face.

"It ain't like that. Rico saved me." Her voice was slurry. "These guys ..." She burst into sobs. Rico pulled her to him. I pushed him away.

"Leave her alone."

"Zully, tell him," Rico said.

She sniffed back her tears. She reeked of alcohol and smoke.

"I was at the party and I was talking to this guy and all of a sudden I got real woozy. I couldn't stand up. He took me outside to get some air and ... and then he was pushing me. I tried to say I wanted to go back to the party, but I couldn't really talk. I couldn't make my body do nothing." She choked up. "He said he was gonna take me home and he took me to his van. There was another guy there."

Dread balled my stomach into a knot. "What'd they do to you, Zully?" She hung her head. "Zully!" I was practically shouting.

She looked up, and I saw the answer in her broken, brimming eyes. "I tried to fight back but I couldn't." She sobbed.

I pulled my shoulders back and roared at heaven as the vision of what happened jelled in my mind.

"Chill, Mags," Rico said. "We're gonna find these motherfuckers."

"Where the fuck do you come into this?"

"I was walking by and I heard noises coming from the back of this van, like a girl crying and moaning, slaps. Didn't feel right so I tried the door and it opened. I saw this vato with a girl on the floor. I yelled at him to let her go, then I leaned in to grab her. He tried to shove me out and close the door on me, but I fought back. Then he pushed her out and booked, threw her clothes in the street. I was helping her get dressed, and I realized she was your sister."

I swallowed hard. My head was spinning. *This wasn't happening.*

Zully wiped her eyes with her hand. "I wanna go home."

"I was just taking her to my truck," Rico said.

"I got her." I cradled Zully in my arm to lead her to the car, then a flood of gratitude overcame me. I stuck out my hand to Rico. We made a fist and pumped.

"I'll come by later. See how she's doing," Rico said.

I folded Zully gently into the car. She was a limp as a rope. My baby sister, gang-raped. I almost broke down then and there, but the thought of revenge pulled me together. Whoever did this was going to pay and there would be no mercy.

Moms tripped out when she saw Zully. "Dios mio, what happened?" Zully buried her head in her chest. "Perdóname, mamá, perdóname."

I told Moms what happened. Her face paled. "Gracias a Dios, she's alive," she said about ten times. When she'd thanked God enough, she bundled Zully into her bedroom and told me to stay with her. "I'm calling Frank," she said.

Zully reached for my hand. "Why didn't he kill me, Magdaleno? I can't live after this."

"Shhh. Don't say that."

"I feel so ashamed. It's all my fault."

"It ain't your fault, Zully. He was a sick hijo de puta."

"But it was my fault. I shouldn't have gone to the party."

"He's the one to blame, not you and I will find him. I swear to God, I will track whoever did this down."

Moms came in with a mug of chamomile tea, her answer to any kind of trauma, and made Zully sip it. Frank marched in shortly after in his firefighter T-shirt, pants and boots, followed by a ginger-haired whiteboy holding a medical bag. His arms and face were full of freckles like he was dusted with cinnamon. Frank introduced him as James. He told me and Frank to wait in the living room. Frank sat on the couch, leaning forward on his knees with his head in his hands. His shoulders shuddered. I looked away. I'd never seen my brother cry and I didn't want to. I stalked around the living room, clenching and unclenching my fists, thinking of what I was going to do that scumbag when I found him.

James came out of the bedroom. He put down his bag and took out a bottle of hand sanitizer, which he squeezed onto his hands and rubbed it in. "Sounds like she was slipped a roofie. There's some bleeding. You should get her the Rape Crisis Center to check if there's any internal damage. The closest one's at Samaritan." James put his hand on Frank's shoulder. "You want me to call an ambulance?" Frank was dazed. His eyes were rimmed red.

"I'll take her," I said.

James left. I called Lissy, who said she'd be right over, then went into the bedroom where Zully was gripping Moms' arm like it was a life buoy. "I don't want to go. Don't make me."

"Zully, you gotta get checked out," Frank said. "They're real nice at the crisis center. They're not gonna hurt you or nothing."

She shook her head wildly. "I just want to stay here. I don't want no one to see me."

"You gotta see a doctor."

She nestled her head in Moms' chest. "No, no," she cried hysterically. "Mamá, don't make me."

"Hija, you have to see the doctor." Zully shook her head again and clutched Moms tighter.

"She needs a doctor, mamá," Frank said. "The crisis center knows how to deal with ..., these cases."

"Paco, it ain't you who got raped," I said.

"She needs medical attention!" he yelled.

"Both of you, out!" Moms ordered.

The commotion even stirred the old man out of his blackout. "¿Qué pasó?" He stood supporting himself in the doorway of his bedroom. Me and Frank rushed over and pushed him back into bed. He wasn't in a state to fight back.

Lissy arrived, breathless and rushed into the bedroom. A couple minutes later, she emerged. "I got Zully to go to the crisis place. We gotta go now before she changes her mind."

Frank went back to the fire station, making me promise to call him after the hospital. I took the girls and Moms to Good Samaritan. I stood in the parking lot, fingering my glow-in-the-dark rosary, feeling jagged shards where my heart used to be. Why did it have to be Zully, God? How the fuck did you let this happen?

TWENTY-THREE

The next morning, I woke up to the smell of coffee and tortillas. Moms was scrambling eggs while Zully sat at the table picking at her plate. Her lip was as big as a chorizo, her cheek a purple blossom.

I sat down. "How you feeling, sis?"

She nodded without looking up.

"You remember anything about what them fools looked like?"

She shrugged.

Moms slid a breakfast plate in front of me. I shoveled the food into my mouth like I was filling a grave with dirt and went to take a shower. I made it extra hot and extra long to try to wash the night off me.

Wrapping a towel around my waist, I crossed the living room to grab clean clothes from the dresser.

A familiar raspy voice ground like a cement mixer in the kitchen. I looked in.

Rico sat at the table with coffee and a plate of eggs in front of him. He grinned.

"Sup, homes?"

El Rey Rico Maximus now had a superhero's cape to go with his crown.

The goodwill I felt last night vanished. Of all the fuckin people who had to find her. Zully's face shone as she looked at him. Moms handed him a basket of warm tortillas.

Maybe his picture was going on the TV set next to Frank's, too. I gave him a stare that could've split wood.

"Just stopped by to see how sis is doing." He took a tortilla from the basket and folded it.

"We gotta talk," I said.

"Take your time. Get dressed." He tore off a piece of tortilla and popped it in his mouth.

I went to get my clothes now I had the superhero's permission.

By the time I was dressed, he'd finished his breakfast. We went up to the roof and sat on a couple wooden crates kept there as seats.

The sky was grey. By noon the sun would scrub off that color and it would be a sea of clean blue.

I looked out at the crowd of skyscrapers downtown, over the apartment buildings and trees that stretched their limbs like they were gasping for fresh air.

It was the usual Sunday quiet as the neighborhood slept off its Saturday night.

Rico spoke first. "They were 5150s, Mags."

"You know this how?"

"I seen em at the party."

"You didn't tell Zully to get the hell outta there?"

"I didn't even see her. I was just stopping by on my way to see Maribel. Soon as I seen the 51s, I bounced. I didn't want no trouble."

"You recognize them?"

He shook his head. "I seen the tatts, though."

I picked up a piece of gravel and chucked it over the side as I thought.

"You think they knew Zully was a Cyco sister?"

Rico shrugged and fired up a cigarette. "Maybe. Somebody mighta said something."

"Or maybe they're just scumbags who like raping little girls. They put some shit in her drink."

Bricks of rage piled one on top of the other inside me. "Like they can't get a girl without doping her up? What kind of fuckin shit?"

Rico took a drag. "The 51s are always pulling that crazy shit. They're always fuckin high on whatever they can lay their hands on."

Smoke spurted in puffs with his words.

That was true. The 5150s liked to crazy it up to live up to their placa. They took their name from the penal code section 5150 that gave cops the right to hold mental cases for three days. Their clica also didn't run with the no-dope discipline that we did.

"You don't think it coulda been someone else?"

"The vatos I seen in the van were the ones at the party." He picked a tobacco shred off his tongue. "What you wanna do about this?"

I studied the treetops. "I wanna cap them hijo de putas' asses."

"We gotta move on this pronto. I was gonna do a job tonight, but it can wait."

"A 211?"

His eyes narrowed slightly. "How d'you know that?"

"That's your shit, right?"

Rico loved stickups. He got off on anything that revved his adrenaline, put him on the edge. He gazed at the skyline. "I'm gonna hit a bank soon. I'm sick of the smalltime."

"That's a federal offense, the FBI and shit."

"They'll give me one of them names, like the Latino Bandito or some shit, and put me on a wanted poster." He cackled, then drew on his cigarette and blew out fuzzy smoke rings. "Know what I like about holdups, Mags? It ain't the money. It's the power. For those couple minutes, I am God. I got people praying to me, begging me, cuz I'm the one in control. I decide if they live or die? I-am-su-preme!"

He jumped up and screamed into the sky, punching it with his fists and his words.

"And I think of that puta, mi mamá, holding my head under the faucet as the sink filled with water, burning me all over with her cigarettes, kicking me into the closet, and I laugh. Now I got the power."

For an instant, I felt sorry for Rico. Just an instant. You couldn't feel bad for him for too long because he didn't let you. He wanted respect and the only way he knew how to get it was being harder than anybody else. Resentment grew against him and turned into hatred, but Rico either didn't see it or didn't care. As long as he was el chingón, that was all that mattered.

The sun was blistering the clouds into rags. Rico flicked his butt over the side of the building. "I'm calling an emergency meeting.

Two o'clock."

After Rico left, I went over to Paloma's. I told her what happened, and she wanted to see Zully. We stopped at a truck selling peluches on a corner and I bought the biggest teddy bear, about three-feet tall, pearly white with a scarlet satin heart sewn on its chest.

When we got home, Lissy was stuffing the dresser with her clothes, her bags sprawled open on the floor.

"Whatup with this?"

"She's moving back in," Zully announced from the bunk ladder. She was arranging her stuffed animals on the top bed and seemed happier.

Lissy banged a drawer shut. "I ain't staying away no more. I gotta take care of her."

"Lissy can't climb the ladder so I'm moving back to the top bunk," Zully said. She turned and her eyes rested on the bear.

"This is for you. Paloma picked it out."

"Hey Zully," Paloma said.

I handed Zully the bear. She hugged it, burying herself in the fur. "It's almost bigger than you, sis."

"It's so soft. I never had such a nice one, thank you."

"You remember anything about the guys, Zully?" She shook her head and squeezed the bear to her again.

"The doctor said it might take some time for the shock to wear off," Lissy said.

Lissy's face was puffy as a blowfish. A maternity top tented her waistline. I wanted to ask her about the 5150s at the party, but she was too close to them. She'd spill to Benny even if I asked her not to. I wasn't naïve enough to expect her to put me and Zully above her man.

"We just stopped by to give you the bear. I'll check back to see if you need anything," I said.

Moms and Pops were drinking coffee in the kitchen. When she saw Paloma, Moms got up and insisted we have a cup. I started to make an excuse, but Paloma threw me a look like she didn't want to be rude, so we pulled out chairs. We sat in uncomfortable silence. Nobody knew what to say.

Frank walked in, his eyes like raccoons. I guessed he didn't sleep too good. He was carrying a huge Minnie Mouse, bigger than my bear, and a bunch of pink roses. I wanted to rip that Minnie Mouse apart and stuff the pieces down his throat.

"The captain let me go early. Zully in her room?"

Moms nodded. "Lissy's there, too."

When I heard Zully squeal, louder than she had with my bear, I had to get out of there. I drained my cup. "We gotta go, Moms." I eyed Paloma and she stood.

I raced down the stairs.

"Baby, you mad about Frank's Minnie Mouse?"

"That obvious, huh?"

"The bear is beautiful. She loved it," Paloma said as we got in the car. I tried to avoid looking at Frank's Chevy, shining like a fuckin blue beacon on the other side of the street.

"Yeah, but it ain't Minnie Mouse."

"Remember, you rescued her and took her to the hospital. Frank's just tryna make it up to her because he wasn't there."

"It was Rico who rescued her."

She yanked my chin to face her. "Mags, you went looking for her and you found her. You were there for her."

I felt a pop inside me, like the tension dissolved. I nodded. "That's why I love you, nena."

"Where are we going anyways?"

"I'm gonna take you home. I got some business to do. I'll come by later."

"Mags, don't do nothing stupid." Her forehead creased into worry lines.

"I won't."

TWENTY-FOUR

Anger always felt like something hot and alive. But this anger was different. It was cold, hard, sharp. And it had burrowed right to my core. Every time I moved, its blade nicked me. I knew I wouldn't be free of it until I avenged my sister's rape.

According to the code of the street, rapists were scum. Inside, many of them ended up in protective custody for their own safety. I remembered one time, after word got out that this white shitbag was a serial rapist, he had his balls sawn off with a sharpened plastic spoon. That was what I wanted to do to these motherfuckers.

I went to pick up Flaco to go to the meeting, stopping on the way to stock up on candy bars. Flaco lived in a motel-type apartment deal, two rows of little boxes all joined together where you could hear the neighbors' every piss drop, fart pop and mattress squeak. His little brother was outside in the courtyard, pouring water from a plastic cup on to the plants his moms grew in old coffee cans. Just washed clothes, hung out to dry on the chain link fence, sent water down the sidewalk like creeks.

Andrés was about fifteen, but Down syndrome kept his mind younger. He'd got big since I last saw him, fatter more than taller. I leaned over, unlatched the gate and called to him. "Ey, lil homie."

He dropped the cup and ran over, throwing his arms around me so hard, he pushed me back a step. "Homie!" he said.

He was soft as a marshmallow. "How you been? You been good?"

"Homie!" he said again into my chest.

I ruffled his hair. "Flaco inside?"

"Watching TV."

"Can you get him for me?"

Andrés didn't let go, just turned his head and shouted. "Flaco! Mags is here."

Flaco appeared barefoot and shirtless in the doorway. He was so damn skinny his stomach was a hollow beneath his ribs and his hip bones jutted like handles.

"Getting my shoes, homes."

"Can I come?" Andrés's eyes filled longing. For a moment, he reminded me of Zully.

"Not this time, homie, but I got something for you." I pulled a Payday from my pocket. His face lit up and he snatched the candy, ripping open the wrapper.

Flaco bounced down the steps, shoelaces flapping and pulling a T-shirt over his head.

"This is some bad shit, Mags," he said as he opened the car door.

"You heard, huh?"

"Yeah, Rico told me. Any idea what he's gonna say at the meeting?"

I took two more Paydays out of my pocket and handed one to Flaco as I steered into the street. "Here. You gotta put on weight. Rico says it was the 5150s, but I don't get it. If Chivas and 5150s made a deal, why are they going after my little sister?"

He chewed a minute. "They couldna planned it cuz they didn't know she was gonna be at that party. Or maybe the 51 shotcaller never told the crew, just like Chivas never told us."

It had to be random. Had to. If the 51s went for Zully cuz of me, I don't know how I could live with myself.

"Why would 51s be at that party anyhow? That ain't their turf."

"Ain't ours neither. Maybe they figured they were safe. Rico was there, right?"

Rico. He had a nasty habit of making guest appearances in my life. "I swear, this shit's got me so wound up I can't even think straight."

"I feel you. The times when them kids attacked Andrés, I felt the same."

A picture of Zully in the van flashed through my mind. I choked back the lump rising in my throat. "I want to find the motherfuckers who did this and make them suffer, if it's the last thing I do on this earth."

The atmosphere in the garage was sober as a graveyard. The homeboys all came up to me and asked how Zully was doing, said how they wanted to get these motherfuckers too. When Mouse and me pulled our chests together for the fist pump, I remembered I had his Hot Wheels car.

"I got something belongs to you. Come to the yard some time." His face was puzzled for a second then his eyes sparked. He knew what I was talking about.

Everybody took seats in the circle, and Rico started the meeting. "We cannot let this disrespect on a homeboy go unanswered. We gotta strike back hard and fast like the jaguars that we are. We're gonna do the mission tonight."

"Driveby?" Cojo said.

Rico nodded. "The corner where they're always slinging."

"A bullet's too easy on 'em," I said.

Rico's eyes glittered like the black sand beaches back in Salvador. "Not if we get a grip of 'em at once, and we keep going, picking off 51s one by one," he said.

"We'll take out the whole fuckin clica," Jackie Chan said.

"We need an RPG like terrorists, that'll do the job," Tweety said.

Flaco leaned forward.

"Rico, we don't know who the putos are, so we might light em up before we find out they're the ones we wanna give the special treatment to, know what I'm sayin? And if we ice any of em, the 51s could just put Mags' sister on them and the ones that done it will get away with it."

Flaco was on point. Rico's plan was too simple for exact revenge. But I liked it.

"They're gonna be beggin us to stop. We say we stop when they hand over the two putos that done this. This is coming from Chivas. He's on the same tier as the 51 shotcaller. Chivas gonna get the names, guaran-fuckin-teed."

I glanced at Flaco. Chivas and the 51 jefe on the same tier? Rico basically just told us they cut a deal on the chiva.

"If Chivas could get the names first, that saves us a lot of work," Flaco said.

"So you don't wanna put in the work? That's what you sayin?" Rico said.

"You know it ain't like that," Flaco said.

"We gotta make a hit first so we got the upper hand, so we can say we're gonna keep capping your locos til we get the names. Get it?" Rico yelled. "Mags, you ain't said nothing. What you got to say?"

"We gotta make a hit first to get our point across loud and clear." It was one of few times I agreed with Rico on something, but I appreciated how hard he was charging on this. I guessed it was cuz he'd seen Zully in the van. Rico leaned back, looking smug that he won.

"Aight." Flaco threw up his hands in defeat. "I didn't mean no disrespect. I'm just saying is all. You know me, I roll with the flow."

Rico looked at me. "Mags, you and me gonna get the hardware. Flaco, Jackie, you borrow the ride. We meet back here an hour after dark."

"Who's doing the mission?" Jackie said.

"Me and Mags," Rico said.

The meeting ended. I offered Flaco a ride, so he'd know I wasn't mad at him for what he said. We rolled to the car.

"Mags, you know I wasn't dissing you back there, don't you?"

"I know. It's good you ask questions, shows you're thinking."

"I just don't trust Rico. I know you're itching for payback, but we gotta double check everything he says. Drop me at that vacant lot. I'm gonna see if Ace is around."

"The bum?"

"Yeah, he does small shit for the 51s sometimes and they pay him with rock. He knows all them fools. He mighta heard something."

"Aight."

"Mags, I gotta say something." I shot my eyes at him to give him the go ahead. "One time long time ago, you told us never let shit get personal. The minute it's personal, you lose your judgment, and the shit goes all bad."

I pulled over at the lot. "Here's your stop, Flaco."

TWENTY-FIVE

I stuck my neck out the pickup's window. The wind hit me full face as Rico floored it to beat a yellow light, forcing my eyelids to close to a crack.

"We almost there," Rico said.

A piece of grit stung my cheek. I pulled my head in. "I gotta ask you something. How you communicating with Chivas?" Since Rico was feeling all warm and fuzzy toward me, I figured I'd take advantage to find out what I could.

"He got a cell phone."

I sensed this was what I needed to know. I tried to sound casual. "How'd he manage that?"

"Connects."

My ears perked. I tried to sound casual. "Inside or outside?"

"Inside."

A dirty guard. So that was his pipeline. Almost foolproof. No wonder the 5150s made a deal with Chivas.

Rico swung a hard left at a soul food place that had a barbecue chicken deal going in the parking lot. A bunch of people were ripping into legs and thighs and washing down the grease with quart bottles of Colt 45.

We pulled up in front of a house with a steel-bar fence. As we stood at the gate, Rico whistled. The curtain jerked back and fell. Then the door opened and a girl with a rack you could set a dinner plate on appeared.

Rico wolf whistled. "Dora, babygirl, you sure look fine tonight.

What I tell you, Mags? Prettiest girl in all LA."

"Cut it out, Rico. You ain't getting none and you know it." Despite her words, she was smiling at the compliments.

"You gonna let us in, baby doll, or we gonna play patty-cake out here all night?"

Dora unlocked the padlock on the gate, and we followed her heavy hips into the house. Her hair was mussed at the back from laying down, so the black roots showed under the bleach. Rico eyed her butt and raised his eyebrows at me.

"Wanna beer or something?" Dora asked.

"No, mami. I catch you another time," Rico said.

"Whatever." Dropping onto a couch, she reached for a half-smoked blunt and lighter resting in a fake skull that had an ashtray in the hollow of its crown. A Mexican shoot-em-up blasted on the TV. The sound of kids fighting came from a bedroom.

Rico was already walking through the kitchen. He pushed open the back door and switched on a light. We stepped into a yard filled with rusting appliances, door and window frames, a lawn mower, a foosball game. Rico went to a corner and rooted around in some crates. He straightened, holding two plastic bags. He unraveled the rubber bands around them and pulled out a .22 and a .38.

"I been saving these for a special mission. Already loaded." He stuck them both in his waistband.

Dora was blowing smoke at the TV. She patted the couch beside her. "Stay a while, Rico. I be missing you."

"I'll be back later, baby girl. I got business to take care of."

Rico bent down and kissed her. She threw her arms round his neck, showing off bitten down fingernails painted black. She wouldn't let him go when he tried to pull away. He yanked her arms off his neck.

"You promise you be back?" she said.

"I ever lie to you, mami?"

She gave a sarcastic smile and got up to let us out. He blew her a kiss as she padlocked the gate. We got in the truck and Rico stashed the cuetes under his seat.

"You got a live one there, dog," I said.

"She's aight when I ain't got no other action. She does me favors."

Rico drove like an old man to the garage, stopping at yellow lights, signaling when he changed lanes, not giving the five-o any excuse to pull us over.

A dark blue Corolla was parked in front of the garage. The homeboys came outside as the pickup pulled up.

Rico got out. "You fools couldn't find no SUV or mini-van?"

"We figured the color's good," Jackie Chan said.

"Do I gotta spell it out all the time? Aim is better from higher up."

"We can get another ride," Flaco said.

"Nah, we'll go with this one."

We pumped fists, the homies wishing us luck. Rico transferred the pieces from the truck to under the Corolla's shotgun seat, ready to be pulled out, and we hit the street. The mission was setting into my bones, pricking all senses into high alert, fluttering my stomach. A muscle thrummed in my right cheek. My palms were damp. I rubbed them on my pants. We said nothing, both of us steeling our minds for the job.

I eyed a corner store at the end of the block. "Wait. I gotta get some candy bars."

Rico pulled over in the shadows under a smashed streetlight.

"You wanna get wet?" he said. "Better than candy bars. Numb you right out."

I shook my head. "I don't need numb. I wanna stay mad."

"Aim is better when you got your adrenaline under control, homes."

"Nothing wrong with my aim."

"I hit that place a few months back. I'll wait for you here. Don't take all fuckin day. We gotta mission to do. Your mission, in case you forgot."

"I didn't forget. Be back in five."

I left Rico doing up his sherm and jogged up the block and into the store. I was choosing my chocolate bars when the sleigh bells on the door jingled. A moment later, I heard the thud of the refrigerator door, the pop and hiss of a can opening. Footsteps shuffled to a stop at my aisle. All the muscles in my back tensed up. I looked round.

Morales. Shit.

"Magdaleno, we got to stop meeting like this."

I grabbed a handful of candy bars. "Scuse me, Officer." I

squeezed by him to get to the counter.

"What you been up to lately?"

"Working." I slapped the candy on the counter in front of the slot in the steel-barred window and tossed some crinkled bills on top of them. I was itching to run outta there, just grab the candy and leave the change, but I knew I couldn't. I had to act real casual.

"Staying away from the homeboys?"

I willed the fool behind the counter to move faster. "Yep."

"Better be the truth."

The guy pushed the change and the candy bars through the slot. Finally. I scooped it all up and dove for the door, not looking at Morales.

The cruiser was parked outside. The other bluesuit stood on the sidewalk, hand resting on the Glock in his gunbelt.

I glanced down the street. The Corolla was gone. Rico must've booked when he seen la ley. Fuck.

I wiped a trail of sweat from my temple with my forearm. I had to jet before Morales came out. I walked the opposite way to where Rico been parked, being careful to take my time. As I turned the corner, I peeked back. The dynamic duo in blue were kicking it in front of the mini market.

I walked another block and called Rico, no answer. We weren't far from the garage, maybe a dozen blocks, so I went back, figuring Rico would prolly be there. He wasn't. The homies had bounced already too.

I crouched against the outside wall and chowed down a Three Musketeers, calling Rico. *Pick up, motherfucker.* Still no answer.

A chill tingled the base of my spine. I ate my way through the pile of candy bars, then felt sick. Either from eating too much candy or the unease chewing my nerves. Rico shoulda answered by now. I was about to try him again when a familiar whomping noise broke the silence.

The ghetto bird thumped louder. It was flying low, its searchlights slashing the darkness like blades. The five-o was looking for someone, close by too. I had to get home fast or I was going to end up doing the asphalt angel, kissing the street while Morales slapped on the steel bracelets.

I threw up my hoodie and walked fast, keeping to the shadows and alleys, holding myself back from breaking into a jog, drawing attention to myself, when I heard the sound of distant sirens.

I made it home in twenty minutes. Pops was snoring on the couch when I walked in. Shit. I was going to have to move him to pull out the bed. I shook his shoulder. He stirred, his eyes blinking. "Papá, I gotta get the bed out."

He pulled himself up and staggered to his bedroom, for once with no fuss. I made up the bed and lay in it, staring into the darkness, trying to slow my breathing to calm myself like they taught us in anger management inside, but it wasn't working. I was too fired up.

Something happened. Rico? Maybe not. I reminded myself that things were always happening in this neighborhood, but my gut told me otherwise. It was Rico.

I knew right then, way down inside, I'd made a mistake. I'd let the shit get personal. Something I always vowed not to do. And I realized something else. Your best fuckin homies make your worst fuckin enemies.

But it was too late now. I was in too deep. Way too deep.

And fuckin Rico knew it.

TWENTY-SIX

Yelling, clanking, buzzers, bright lights. I was back inside. I woke up with my heart racing and my pillow damp with sweat. I looked around. Pops' chair with the sunken cushion; Frank's photo on the TV. It was just a dream. I gulped, felt my heart slow. Then the memory of last night sped into the freeway of my mind and braked to a dead stop. I had to find Rico.

I was in the shower when I heard the scream. I threw a towel around my waist and barreled out of the bathroom.

"¿Qué pasó?" I stood in the doorway of the girls' room, dripping on the nubby carpet. Lissy rocked back and forth, doubled over on the edge of the bunk, her face all twisted with sobs. Moms and Zully sat beside her, rubbing her back, faces worried. "Is it the baby?"

"Benny got shot," Zully said. "He's in critical. They don't know if he's gonna make it. His moms just called."

It couldn't be. No way. I banged my forehead into the door threshold and rolled it from side to side. It felt cool and solid on my spinning mind.

Now I really had to find Rico. I ran back to the bathroom and threw on my clothes. I was tying my shoes in the living room as the girls came out holding their purses. Lissy, red-eyed, waddled like a penguin under the weight of her belly.

"Where're you going, Mags?" Zully said.

"Work." I kissed Lissy on the cheek. "Stay strong, sis."

The morning was crisp. Mothers with long black ponytails swishing down their backs walked kids to school and pushed toddlers in strollers. Men in baseball caps roped ladders onto the scaffolding of beatup pickup trucks. Everything was normal, except it wasn't.

My cell phone buzzed. Mouse. "Where you at?" he said.

"Just bouncing from home."

"Making eggs. Come by if you're hungry."

"Be right there." I headed for the garage.

Mouse opened the door as I pulled up and we went inside. He was the only one there. "The fuck went down last night?" I demanded.

"You lucky, Mags. It got fucked up. Bigtime." A storm whirlpooled in his eyes. "We lost Blueboy. He's resting in peace."

"Blueboy! What the fuck he got to do with this shit?"

"Rico said he had to leave you at the store cuz the cops showed. He was riding around waiting to come back to get you, then he seen Blueboy. He picked him up and told him about the mission. Blueboy said he just seen a 51. They found the vato and fronted him. The fool ran and Blueboy lit him up. The homeboy got off a round, and Blueboy got capped in the face. Rico said there was nothing he could do. He had to book before the five-o showed. He's laying low with his tío."

When I was eight years old at the park one time, a kid kicked a soccer ball right into my stomach and knocked all the air out of me. For an instant, my lungs wouldn't work. I couldn't breathe. That was how I felt now. Finally, I sucked in some air.

"That ain't all." I looked at Mouse. How much worse could it get? He squirmed. "A kid got iced."

"A kid?"

"Some lady was standing in a window holding a baby. The kid caught a bullet in the back."

I plonked onto the couch. Blueboy, Benny, Rico, a baby. Everything assaulted me like spray from a shottie. I couldn't think.

"You aight, Mags?" Mouse's voice echoed.

Paloma. I jumped to my feet. "Post up here, Mouse. Call me."

Everything seemed to be in slow motion as I drove. People on the street moved like wooden dolls. Vehicles crawled. It seemed like it took forever to drive a mile.

I banged on Paloma's door with my fist. She opened right away.

"Blue... Blue..." I was suddenly stuttering.

"I know. He was in a shooting. Mi mamá was working at the hospital when he came in. The doctors say he's unconscious but stable."

Que ¿qué? "You mean he ain't dead?"

"No, but the doctor says he's real lucky the bullet didn't go into his brain."

Words blurred together again. I shook my head. "You gotta explain this to me." We went in and sat. "Mouse just told me he was RIP. That's what Rico told him."

"Uh-uh. He caught a bullet in the eye. He's in ICU but he's gonna make it."

A tide of relief made me erupt into laughter until tears leaked out the corners of my eyes. After a minute, I calmed down and wiped my cheeks. Paloma was staring at me. Then I had a shitload of questions.

"Did they tell you what went down? Where's Blue been all this time? How come he just showed up like this?" I said.

She shrugged. "We gotta ask him. The cops said they found a car crashed into a pole, like a streetlight. Blueboy was unconscious, his face all tore up. He got a couple broken ribs from slamming into the steering wheel, cuts and bruises."

Rico was driving. He musta given Blueboy the wheel.

"The detectives told mi mamá they think the ride was involved in a driveby down the street. A homeboy got lit up, and a baby got killed in the gunfire. They ran the ride. It was hot. They found a piece in the car, too. Now they're waiting for Blueboy to wake up. They said the homeboy might not make it."

Tell me it wasn't Benny Santana. My throat went dry. "They say who the fool was?" I croaked.

She shook her head. "I gotta get to the hospital, see if Blueboy woke up yet."

"The cops said anything bout who Blueboy was with?"

"No. They just told Moms Blueboy's looking at heavy prison time and it's in his best interest to cooperate." She studied me. "You know anything about this?"

"I wasn't there, nena, swear to God." I crossed myself and kissed my thumbnail. That much was true.

"Yeah, but you know who was, don't you?"

The freight train of the truth bore down on me. I told her about the revenge mission. When I finished, her eyes were heavy with sadness mixed with something else. I had to get to work so I said goodbye. As I walked back to my car, I realized what that something else was—fury.

I went to work. I grunted at Gato who was standing in his office doorway, holding his coffee and newspaper.

"What's wrong with you? Girl trouble again?" he called. I waved my hand at him and kept walking to the shop. "I got a job for tonight. Airbags."

I was changing the sparkplugs on Gato's SUV, but I couldn't get this driveby off my mind. Questions jabbed me like fuckin needles. Blueboy suddenly showed up as Rico was driving along the street looking for a 5150? And the 5150 they happened to run into was Benny Santana? Who was the shooter?

Mouse told me Blueboy lit up the homeboy, but Blueboy was found behind the wheel of the car, which had to mean Rico was the shooter. The wheelman didn't shoot. Did Mouse get it wrong? Or was that Rico wanted everyone to believe?

On top of all that, the baby. Shooting a kid, even by accident, was one of the most serious offenses in clica code.

Unless there was another scenario. I was so lost in thought, I straightened and crashed my head into the hood.

I backed out, rubbing my skull. I paced back and forth in the shop, my mind whirring through the events. Rico fires at Benny, who squeezes one off in return. Blueboy catches a bullet. The ride veers out of control and crashes. Blueboy's unconscious, gushing blood. Rico, maybe a little banged up but okay, figures Blue bit it. He flees into the night, and believing Blueboy's dead, pins the whole thing on Blue to save himself.

It was pure Rico.

I put myself on autopilot to get through the day, and then I called the homies to get the airbag job done early. I said nothing about my theory. I wanted to hear what Rico had to say first.

We agreed we had to get the story straight from him, but he wasn't answering our calls. I passed by the restaurant and checked in with Paloma.

Blueboy was in and out of consciousness so nobody had talked to him, but he was out of ICU.

When I got home, Zully was watching TV with the lights off.

"Any news on Benny?"

"He's in a coma. Doctors say he don't got much chance of coming out of it."

"They say how it happened?" I had a sudden gust of hope it was some other shit. There had to be a bunch of shootings every night in LA, right?

"A gang driveby. A baby got killed, too."

My spirit sank although I knew it was too good to be true to be something else. "Lissy?"

"She's at the hospital."

I went to take a shower, like I always did after banging. In the past, I turned the water as hot as I could stand. I'd soap myself til my skin squeaked, and I could almost see the stains wash off me, swirl round the drain, then be swallowed forever. But now, as I lathered up under the jet of hot water, I didn't know if I could ever feel truly clean again.

TWENTY-SEVEN

My sleep was restless. I arrived at work feeling worse than if I'd downed a fifth of tequila the night before.

"Good thing I got you a coffee this morning, Mags. You look like you could use it," Gato said.

We entered his office, where a cup sat steaming on his desk. "That's yours."

After a few sips, I started to feel the ping of caffeine. "Airbags work?"

He nodded. "We're going to do more of them. They're good money." He rubbed his thumb and forefinger together. His phone rang. As he answered, I scanned the front page of the newspaper on his desk. A big photo of a peanut-skinned baby with pinchable cheeks and a mischievous smile caught me mid-swallow.

Toddler Killed in Gang Driveby.

I spluttered into a coughing fit.

Gato hung up and smacked me on the back. "You all right?"

I nodded. "You done with the paper?"

He handed it to me. "Nothing in it anyway."

As soon as I got in the shop, I sat on a car seat and unfolded the paper, my throat tightening as I read.

An eighteen-month-old boy was killed in the crossfire of a gang-related driveby shooting that also wounded two suspected gang members, one critically, in a central city neighborhood of Los Angeles, city police said.

David Antonio Moreno was shot in his mother's arms shortly after 12 a.m. yesterday as she stood in the window of her second-floor apartment trying to comfort him to sleep, police Capt. Jaime Montenegro said at a press conference.

The baby was hit in a hail of gunfire fired from a passing vehicle aimed at a gang member on the street below the apartment, Montenegro said. A 19-year-old man was injured and is listed in critical condition. A 21-year-old man is listed in stable condition. Their identities have not been released.

"This is a tragedy in every sense of the word," Montenegro said. "We will do everything in our power to bring to justice the perpetrators of this senseless crime."

Homicide detectives are working around the clock to solve the case, the captain said. He asked anyone with any information to call the police department's confidential tip line.

Mayor Elena Rosendo-Wilson said the city is offering a $50,000 reward for information leading to an arrest. "It is time to stop living in fear in neighborhoods that are being held hostage by ruthless criminal gangs," she said.

Anti-crime community group, Take Back Our Streets, is planning to hold a rally at MacArthur Park tomorrow to protest gang violence.

"We're not even safe in our own homes, let alone on the streets," said Victoria Castillo, group leader.

The black-and-white print fuzzed before my eyes. The mayor. A rally. Pieces of this were flying everywhere. I tore off the page, folded it and stuffed it in my pocket. It was time to force Rico to talk.

That night, I gathered the homies, and we went to Rico's uncle's place. As we pulled into the driveway, we noticed two Harley choppers parked there, their chrome trim gleaming in a floodlight from the house.

"Rico buying bikes now or what?" Jackie said.

We went round the back. Rico, a shiner on his forehead and cuts on his face, rushed out the door before we even knocked. He put his finger to his lips for us to be quiet and closed the door real careful. He motioned for us to follow him and led us into the rooster shed. The birds squawked like crazy, so Rico chucked handfuls of cracked corn into their cages to simmer them down.

"Don't tell my uncle. They're only eating hard-boiled egg white for the fight coming up. They fight crazier when they're hungry."

"Them beaks look nasty, homes," Tweety said, staring at the birds lunging at the food.

"We sharpen them like blades, slice the opponents right up. Mouse, post up at the door." Rico was giving orders like he had called the meeting. Mouse cracked the door an inch and stood lookout. "We got deep shit," Rico said. "This is bringing down a lot of heat, and Chivas is real pissed cuz of the kid."

Whose fault is that? I wanted to yell. Instead, I took the newspaper out of my pocket and handed it to Rico. "He ain't the only one who's pissed."

He unfolded the page. After glancing at it, he handed it to Jackie Chan. "Read this out loud so everyone can hear."

Rico couldn't read so hot, I knew that, but Jackie wasn't much better. The words came out like he was riding the brake. After a couple seconds, Flaco snatched the paper and read it. I watched Rico's expression. It didn't change. He musta already heard that Blueboy survived. Flaco handed the paper back to me when he finished.

"The fuckin mayor, a fuckin rally!" I waved the paper. "The fuck went down, Rico? Why you went ahead with the mission without me? How'd Blueboy get in this? Who was the fuckin shooter?"

Rico folded his arms, eyes like asphalt.

"You, Mags, went to the store. We're going on a mission, and you want fuckin candy bars. The five-o showed. I'm in a hot ride so I had to jet. I came back round.

The bluesuits were chilling in front of the store and you weren't there. I figured you punked out."

I dove at him, shoving him in the chest. He staggered back

against the cages, causing a flurry of feathers and squawks.

Flaco and Jackie jumped on me, pulling me back by the shoulders. "Now ain't the time, Mags," Flaco said.

"Everybody chill. We gotta keep cool heads right now, aight? We got a situation to handle," Cojo said.

I shook my arms loose.

"I'm good."

"Like I was saying," Rico continued, staring me down. "I was riding round, looking for Mags then I saw a vato walking down the street. I thought maybe it was Mags, so I slowed up. It was Blueboy. I couldn't fuckin believe it. He got in. I asked him where he was at all this time. He said he was outta town. I told him what was going down. He said he just seen a 5150 so we went after the fool. I wasn't gonna pass up a chance like that. Blueboy hit him up, he booked and Blue got off a couple squeezes. The fool shot back, and Blueboy caught one in the head."

A bitter taste flooded my mouth.

"So, you saying Blueboy was the shooter, and you were the wheelman?"

"Blueboy was the shooter *and* the wheelman."

I woulda bet my soul he was lying, but there was no way to prove it til Blueboy could talk.

"Pretty convenient he showed up right then. You didn't have to do nothing at all."

Rico just blinked.

"That newspaper don't say nothing bout Blueboy being charged," Jackie Chan said.

"Maybe they don't got nothing on him," Cojo said.

"The .22 was in the ride," Rico said. "Cops just don't wanna say nothing bout the evidence they got."

"They're looking for witnesses," Tweety said. "Homicide been knocking on doors up and down that block."

"There ain't gonna be no witnesses. Everybody in the barrio knows better," Rico said.

"Yeah, but people are real riled up over this kid. Everybody's talking about it. Some fool might drop a dime," Cojo said.

"We gotta make sure they don't," Rico said. "Anybody know how Blueboy's doing?" He looked at me. He had to be worried about what Blueboy was telling the five-o, if he was gonna put Rico in that car with him. If Rico was the shooter or not, he could be charged with murder for the kid, attempted murder for Benny Santana and possession of firearms, just because he was in the car. Plus, the DA could tack on an enhancement for a gang-related crime to add more time to the sentence. Rico had plenty reason to be worried.

"The bullet took out one of his eyes. He's outta ICU, but he's still not conscious," I said.

"At least he got another eye," Tweety said.

"You get a message to Blueboy—he was alone in that ride," Rico told me.

"By the way, that 5150 was Payaso Santana. He's in a coma and it ain't looking good," I said.

Rico's face was a steel mask. "He ain't gonna be a witness then."

"No, he ain't. But if he bites it ..."

"Double 187," Cojo said.

"Don't forget the 5150s," Jackie said.

"War," Cojo said. "They gonna be looking for payback bigtime."

"This is real heavy-duty shit, fools," Jackie said.

"We gotta go lower than lopro, like underground. All business operations off," Rico said. "We can't risk nothing with this heat. The five-o's gotta figure it's a Cyco-5150 beef so they're gonna be looking to squeeze any of us to dime off on the driveby." Rico scanned the homeboys' faces. "We're in survival mode now."

When I got home, Lissy was making chamomile tea in the kitchen. She turned to me. "I been waiting for you." Her face and voice were stone. "What d'you know about this driveby?"

"I wasn't part of it. I swear on the soul of mi mamá." I crossed myself and kissed my thumbnail. I'd been doing a lot of that lately.

"Don't play me. You got guilty all over your face. You put the green light on Benny."

"Lissy, that ain't true." I went hollow like my insides dropped away.

"You told me you didn't care I was with him, you weren't gonna do nothing. You're a motherfuckin liar, Magdaleno. You shoulda gave me a chance to warn him. We coulda got away, gone somewhere." Her face crumpled.

"Lissy, I swear I didn't put no green light on Benny. I swear it. He was in the wrong place at the wrong time."

"Benny was just coming from here, if that's what you mean by the wrong place. I felt real sick and asked him to come over. He knew it was a risk coming into the barrio, but he took it for me, for his baby. And he wasn't packing. He wasn't no threat to nobody." She dissolved into sobs. "Benny ain't going to make it. He caught two slugs in the back of the head and the neck. He's on life support. The doctors want his moms to pull the plug. She's at church praying for a miracle, and his pops is on his way from Mexico. I know a miracle ain't gonna happen because there's no God. If there was a God, He wouldn't allow this gang shit to even exist. He wouldn't have gave me a brother like you."

I could take rejection from anyone else in my family, but not Lissy. Not her. I pressed my fingers against my eyes so hard I saw colors. I was losing Lissy. This couldn't be happening.

"I didn't want nothing to happen to him, you gotta believe me." My voice came out thick as mud.

"What am I gonna do without a father for my kid? He's gonna grow up never knowing where he came from. You ever think of things like that when you're shooting at people?"

"Por favor, hermanita, I never wanted this to happen."

Pops entered the kitchen. Seeing the overspill of emotion at hand, he turned around and walked out.

Lissy swiped her nose with her sleeve and sniffed.

"You can't apologize your way outta this one." She grabbed her mug and left. The bedroom door banged closed.

I unfolded the couch and lay down in my boxers, turning to face the wall as Pops passed through to the kitchen. Lissy was right. It was all my fault. I never should've come home. I should've stayed locked up. That was where I deserved to be, the only place I could stay out of trouble. I was good for nothing.

God, why the fuck you didn't take me instead of Benny? Why did you let me live? The neon rosary around my neck glowed in the dark, the cross shining bright, mocking me. Fuck you, Jesus.

I yanked it off and hurled it across the room. It landed in a pitter-patter of bouncing plastic beads. Fifteen minutes later, there was a crash and a string of curse words Spanish. I sat up. Pops was on his ass. He'd slipped on the beads.

TWENTY-EIGHT

I already had my scheduled parole appointment with Angel so when he called me to come in again, it seemed kinda strange. I asked him what for, but he said it was just routine paperwork. I figured it had something to do with my discharge. I only had a month to go.

He kept me waiting in his office, which wasn't like him.

I was wondering what this was all about when I heard the door open.

"You real busy, Angel," I said as I turned.

He wasn't by himself. Following him were a man and a woman in puke-colored suits. My skin itched like a three-day-old scab. I knew who they were even before I spotted the gold shields on their belts.

"Magdaleno, this is Detective McNab and Detective Lindgren. They've got a few questions to ask you." Angel sat down heavily in his chair and threw the folder he was carrying on the desk. Mine, I guessed. I never seen him so serious.

"We're from Homicide," Lindgren said. She had shoulders broad as a man's, dust-colored hair and a complexion lumpy as mashed potatoes.

I folded my arms, set my face. My leg started to bounce, but I stopped it. I couldn't show any sign of nerves. Lindgren parked her fat ass on the edge of Angel's desk, knocking over his pencil holder. She didn't seem to care, just stretched out her legs and crossed them at the ankles.

McNab stood next to her with crossed arms resting on his eighteen-wheeler-tire of doughnut fat.

"You're not in any trouble, Magdaleno," McNab said. "We just want to ask you a few questions."

"We're investigating this driveby a few days ago. A small child was killed. You know anything about that?" Lindgren shot words from her mouth like pellets. So, she was the hardass of the dynamic duo.

"Just what I read in the paper." I stuck to the rule—give the shortest answer possible and offer no information.

"You with the Cyco Lokos, right?" she continued. "Big enemy of the 5150s."

"I'm outta gangbanging."

"Where were you last Sunday night, Magdaleno?" Lindgren asked.

"Home." Heat crawled under my skin.

"Officer Morales said he saw you in El Azteca market around 11 p.m."

"I went to the store to buy candy."

"There are stores closer to where you live. Why'd you go to that store?"

"I went running then I went home."

"You always go running so late?" McNab jumped in.

"I go when the mood catches me."

Back to Lindgren. "Was anyone else home when you were there?"

"My pops."

A pause. "You know we got Rubén Aguilar in custody, right?" Lindgren said.

"I don't know no Rubén Aguilar."

"Blueboy," McNab said. "He's a homie of yours, right?"

"I know him."

"You know if someone else was in the car with him that night?"

"Nope."

"Were you in the car with him?" McNab asked.

"Nope."

They paused and looked at each other.

"All right. I think we're done here," McNab said. "We'll be close by, Magdaleno."

Lindgren stood and plucked a tissue out of the box on Angel's desk and handed it to me. "Here, you're sweating." I felt a drop trickle down the side of my face. "I find out you been lying, I'll sling your ass right back in a prison cell, homeboy."

They left. I screwed the tissue into a ball and dropped it on the floor. I wiped my forehead with the hem of my T-shirt instead.

"I hope you're not involved in this, Magdaleno," Angel said.

"The fuck was that about?" I rasped.

"You're a registered Cyco Loko. They know the Lokos are always beefing with the 5150s, and one of the victims is a 5150. Your name came up on the parole list, so you were easy to get to. You know the score, man."

"You shoulda gave me a heads up."

"You know I can't really do that."

"I got something to worry about?"

"Not unless you were involved."

I took a deep breath. "So, this really was just routine?"

"Pretty much. You really weren't involved?"

I ignored the question. "I'm discharged next month, right?"

"Stay out of trouble and you're a free man."

I left. When I got outside, my legs gave way as the reality of the situation slammed me. If the cops found out I knew about the driveby, that it was my sister's rape behind it, that I was supposed to be the shooter on it, that I went with Rico to get the pieces

I wobbled to the side of the building and leaned my ass against the wall, hands on my knees. I could be charged with murder, maybe conspiracy at the very least. I had to book out of L.A. Fuck finishing parole, I had to jet.

I took a deep breath to steady myself. More deep breaths, the panic faded and my mind cleared.

They had nothing on me. If I fled, I'd look guilty as fuck. I had to hang tight, finish parole, then it would look natural for me to leave town. Plus, if they got me for skipping parole, they'd have something to pressure me with on the murder. Right now, they had nothing. I had to keep it together, then grab Paloma and go. But I also knew things could move fast and beyond my control. I hoped I had a month.

I stayed shook up all day, so I called off an operation for that night and waited for Paloma to get off work after the lunch shift.

With all the heat, it wouldn't be a bad idea to scale back the business, for a while anyway. I had enough money.

She came out and slid in the car. Holding her was like a shot of penicillin. I suddenly felt everything was going to be all right. I wanted to hang on to that feeling.

Laughing, she peeled me off her. "Whatup with you?"

"Just missed you is all."

I couldn't tell her about the visit from the murder cops, not yet anyway. I drove off.

"Blueboy's awake. He got a big bandage where his eye used to be. He says he can get a fake eyeball." She sounded happy and that made me happy.

"He should wear a patch like Gato."

"Yeah, he's thinking about it. He likes that pirate look." She giggled then fell serious. "They charged him with GTA and possession of a firearm. He told them he boosted the car for kicks, ran into some gunfire. He didn't even know that .38 was in the ride, never touched it. And he told me that was the truth. He never fired a shot, he was driving. But the cops said the .38 had his prints on it. They're gonna go for maximum state time unless he cuts a deal. They're pressing him to roll about the driveby. They're transferring him to county tomorrow."

"You ask him where he was all this time?"

"He said he was in Arizona."

I twisted my mouth. "Who's he know over there?"

She shrugged. "I asked him, but he said he ain't talking about it."

"Huh." I didn't know what to make of that. "How's he acting with you? He say anything about me?"

"Real cool, like nothing never happened. He never mentioned you."

We pulled up at her house and went in. She'd brought two pork chop dinners from the restaurant, so we snuggled on the living room couch and ate as we watched a Brazilian novela.

After we finished eating, I lay down, resting my head in her lap. Her hand clutched mine. I stroked her palm and stared at the TV, but I wasn't watching. My mind was going a million miles an hour about the driveby. Things just weren't adding up.

The cops said they found a .38 in the car with Blueboy's prints but they didn't charge him with the shootings, just with possession.

That had to be because the .38 wasn't the gun that shot the kid or Benny. But Rico said at the meeting that the .22 was in the ride. So, the .22 musta been the piece that was used. Rico also said that Blueboy was the shooter, but Blueboy told Paloma he wasn't, that he'd never even touched a gun. He wouldn't lie to Paloma.

It hit me. Maybe Rico *meant* to leave the .22 in the car to set up Blueboy for the driveby. Maybe, in all the rush and confusion, he left the wrong gun. He left the .38. So, the cops figure someone else musta had the .22 in the car.

I played how it musta gone down in my mind. When they wrecked, the impact made Rico drop the .22 and pushed forward the .38 from under the seat. Rico picked up the .38 and wrapped Blueboy's hand around it, thinking it was the .22. Then he drops it next to Blueboy and goes to pick up the .38 and jets, figuring he'd just set up Blue with the murder weapon. Only he didn't. He actually picked up the .22. In the chaos he didn't notice he had the wrong gun until later. That had to be what happened.

I remembered what Lissy said, too. Benny wasn't packing. If that was true, then who the fuck shot Blueboy? I sat up, jolting Paloma. I needed to find some answers. "I gotta bounce, nena."

"Where you goin?"

I shrugged. "Just antsy. I can't stay still."

I strode into the late evening sun and got in my car. I felt edgy with pent up energy. I drove slowly around the streets to distract myself.

Men, wifebeaters stretched over basketball bellies, chilled with beers in their hands or worked on their cars at the curb. Women sat on the steps, fat oozing out of the waist and thighs of their shorts like jelly out of doughnuts, pushing strollers with their feet as they gossiped. Kids played catch, jumped rope.

I turned a corner. I was somehow on the street where I found Rico and Zully that night. Rico. Again.

The night that started this fuckin mess. Something bugged me about that whole thing. I still didn't know who were the putos who raped

Zully. I wondered if she could remember more now. She seemed better. Maybe if I brought her to the scene that would jog her memory. I floored it home.

Moms was picking up beer cans from the floor when I walked in.

Pops was snoring on the couch. I guessed he was too drunk to go to work that night. Every now and then that happened.

I knocked on the girls' room door and stuck my head in. Zully was lying on her bed reading a book.

"Zully, I gotta talk to you."

"So, talk."

"You remember anything else about that night?"

She looked down at her book and shook her head.

"You sure? Anything about them fools, anything at all?"

She squeezed her lips together and shook her head again.

"Zully, this is real important."

"I gotta read this for school."

I paused, wondering how I was going to get her attention. "You wanna take a walk with me, get some candy bars, doughnuts?"

"I don't wanna talk about it."

"I'm just tryna figure out what went down, sis."

A crash from the living room made us jump. "Esperanza!" Pops yelled.

We looked at each other. She snapped the book shut. When Pops woke up drunk, his mood was worse than a starving pitbull. The best play was to get out of his way.

"Doughnuts sound real good," she said.

We sped through the living room. Pops was sitting on the floor, struggling to get himself back on the couch. The coffee table was upended. He'd tried to use it as support and fell on the floor.

"Why did I end up with such lazy, good-for-nothing kids?" he shouted.

We slammed the door on him. I bundled Zully down the stairs and into the car.

"Can we go to Donut King?" she said.

"Yep, but we gotta make a stop first." I pulled out. In five minutes, we were back on the street where she was attacked. I parked at the curb.

"Now show me where the party was at."

Fear was in her eyes. "Don't make me, Mags."

"Don't get all scared on me. I ain't gonna let nothing happen to you."

She looked up and down the block then pointed to a house—a shabby bungalow with a yard full of weeds.

"You know who lives there?"

She shook her head.

"What went down? Tell me."

She took a breath then talked. "There was a lot of people smoking blunts and drinking. The music was real loud. Belinda disappeared. I think she went to a bedroom with some fool. So I was by myself and this guy came over and said, 'What's up?' I said hi and told him I was waiting for my friend. He said he lost his brother, too, and made a joke like maybe his brother and my friend were together. He had two beers in his hand, and he gave me the one he got for his brother. I drank a little bit of it and got real woozy, like I couldn't stand up. He took me outside to get some air." Her hands were twisting like snakes in her lap.

"Go on, Zully, you doing good," I said softly.

"He said I should go home and that his ride was down the block and he could take me. I remember I tried to say no, I had to wait for my friend, but it was like...like I was all over the place. He put his arm around me, like holding me up." Her voice faltered. "When we got to the van, he opened the back door. I thought it was weird we weren't getting in the front, but then he pushed me in. Then he got in and closed the door." She choked back a sob. "I heard another voice from the front and then they were both over me. I started to cry and yell. One of them smacked me in the face and told me to shut up." Tears skidded down her cheeks. "I tried to get them off me, but I couldn't fight back. Everything went all blurry."

A huge pain speared my chest. I wanted to string up those scumbags and cut out their organs. "When did Rico come?"

She wiped her eyes. I felt guilty for making her go through it all again, but I had to. "All I remember is the door opened. There was yelling and someone took me out. I thought ... I thought it was gonna happen all over again, but it was Rico, asking if I was okay."

I rubbed her hands between mine. "The fool at the party, what'd he look like?"

"I can't remember."

"Think, sis. You gotta remember something."

She closed her eyes. Her chest rose and fell. "He had like a little beard, just on his chin. And long hair, like a hippie or something. Kind of tall. Old, like Frank."

"What about the other fool?"

She shook her head. "He had long hair, too. I remember their hair falling in my face when…"

I hugged her, smoothing her hair. "Let's get some doughnuts." She sniffed and nodded.

I drove slowly, thinking over what Zully had just told me. They couldn't be 5150s because 5150s didn't wear their hair long, so why the fuck was Rico putting it on them? Could this be some set up of his? I needed to talk to other people who were at the party, who saw long-hair and his brother. Somebody had to know who they were.

I dropped Zully at home with a box of doughnuts and decided to pay a visit to her homegirl Belinda, who hadn't even come to visit Zully since that night. I also wanted to give her hell about taking my sister to the party and leaving her alone.

The Vizquels lived two blocks away on the fourth floor of a crapped out brick building. I took the stairs two at a time, past the sounds of babies crying, dishes clattering, TVs playing Spanish news, until I got to their apartment. I hammered on the door and lucked out—homegirl stuck her head out along with a blast of spicy cooking smells.

Her Bambi eyes widened when she saw me. "Magdaleno!"

"Soy yo, baby cakes. How you doing? Ain't seen you round lately."

Her voice and eyes drooped. "Mis viejos ain't letting me go out."

"Maybe that's a good thing, seeing as how you don't pick the best places to go, and then you run off to make kissy-kissy with any dude you meet, leaving your homegirl hanging."

She spun her head to check if anyone was listening behind her. She probably hadn't told mami y papi that particular part of the story. "Listen, Mags, I …"

"I ain't here to listen to your bullshit excuses. You see the vato Zully was talking to that night, long hair, tall, maybe with another guy with long hair?"

"I didn't see nothing."

A lie. I stepped to her face. She flinched. "Tell me or I'm gonna tell mami y papi you were getting down with every guy at that party."

Fear flickered on her face, and I knew I got her. "I seen two of them. They looked exactly alike, long hair, black leather jackets. I don't know who they were, I swear, Mags. I never seen them before."

That I believed. They didn't sound like nobody I knew either. "White, Black, Latino?"

"Latino, maybe white."

"You remember anything else, you call me right away, aight?" She nodded. "One more thing, you *ever* take my sister anywhere like that again, it's gonna be all over school that you love running trains, the more guys the better. Feel me, baby cakes?" She nodded again and shut the door fast.

Black leather jackets. They weren't homeboys. I ran down the stairs.

TWENTY-NINE

Twenty-four hours later, I was sipping an energy drink in the shop as Cojo and Jackie Chan worked the front panels of a Honda Civic. Tweety was taking off a door.

There was none of the usual joking and bagging on each other. After I told them about how I suspected Rico had set up Blueboy, everybody went quiet. I put on one of Gato's salsa CDs to break the silence.

Flaco walked in the shop, followed by Mouse. Flaco jutted a thumb at him. "He says you told him to come by to pick up something."

"In the drawer over there." I pointed to the tool bench. He rummaged in the drawer, then held up his beat up Hot Wheels car, a smile springing to his face.

Pocketing it, Mouse stepped toward me. "Mags, I wanted to ask you. Can I join your crew? Shit's kinda slow with all this heat and now Rico's gonna book."

"Rico's leaving town?" Everybody stopped working and looked at Mouse.

"He's gonna chill in Arizona til the heat's off."

I exchanged a look with Flaco. Blueboy'd been in Arizona. "Must be getting crowded over there," I said.

The homeboys put down their tools and gathered round Mouse, who looked scared at the sudden attention.

"Whatup in Arizona?" Flaco said.

"He got cousins there, from his tía Guillermina. They're in a biker club called Los Federales or some shit."

Bikers. Long hair. Black leather jackets. The chromed out Harleys.

The images floated like wisps of smoke in front of me, then blended together to form a picture.

Rico was behind the rape.

I fell back against the car, dumbfounded. I had to clear my throat to talk.

"Mouse, you seen these bikers?"

"They're twins, like clones, hair down to here." He put his hand against his upper arm. "The only way you can tell em apart is one has a lil beard. Rico said they were running a meth lab in the desert and it blew up, so they came here to lay low for a while. Guillermina ain't too happy about them landing on her doorstep. She says she never had nothing to do with that family. But they're getting ready to go back and Rico's going with em."

"They got Harleys?" Flaco asked.

Mouse nodded. "Yeah, real tight bikes."

The homies all looked at one another, realization all over their faces. Rico sent Blueboy to Arizona to work in his cousins' meth lab and when it blew up, Blueboy came back with the bikers.

"That cabrón knew where Blueboy was the whole time we were looking for him," Jackie said. "Motherfuckin hijo de la gran puta!" He pitched a wrench at the wall.

"We gotta find him, Mags, before he books," Cojo said.

I yelled and drove my fist into the Honda's window. I slammed the glass again and again. It cracked. Flaco and Jackie pinned my arms. My chest heaved.

"You gonna fuck up your hands, Mags," Flaco said.

I collapsed onto a car seat. Blood ran trails from my raw knuckles. "That ain't half of it. Rico set up my sister. Zully remembered what them guys looked like. Long hair, older, one with a goatee. Her homegirl said they looked exactly alike and had black leather jackets."

"Rico's cousins," Flaco whispered.

Tweety pummeled the car seat. We sat in stunned silence, broken just by Tweety's grunts and the thwack of his one-two punches. My stomach churned. I felt a giant heave and upchucked on the floor.

I'd just closed the front door when Lissy entered the living room like she'd been waiting for me. Her belly was a beachball through her nightgown.

"They took Benny offa life support tonight. I just wanted you to know." Her face was pale and hard. She drilled me with her eyes for a second that felt like forever.

I tried to say, "I'm sorry, sis," but I choked on a mess of guilt and sorrow. She went back to her room. I curled up in a ball on the couch. Everything was slipping from under me. It was like I was sucked up in some crazy tornado that was getting stronger and faster and I couldn't get out of it.

I saw some weird light under the dresser. I got down and looked. It was the cross from the rosary I threw against the wall. It was still glowing, like it was waiting for me. I picked it up and blew the dust off, apologizing to God for trashing it. Maybe it was a sign there was still hope I could make it outta this disaster called my life.

THIRTY

The next morning, the Nissan chugged when I turned the ignition key. "¡Puta!" I barreled out of the car and kicked the tire.

It was almost six and the sky was the color of dirty dishwater. I felt half dead after spending most of the night kissing porcelain. My stomach just wouldn't settle.

The plan was to pick up the homies and head to Rico's to confront him about everything. We figured we'd surprise him at the ass crack of the day, like cops do in their big takedowns, walking out dazed suspects in bracelets, bed hair and boxers. If Rico was half asleep, maybe he wouldn't be able to come up with a story fast, although lying came as natural to him as taking a piss.

Frank pulled up in his Caprice and saw my face. "You going to a funeral or what?"

"Fuckin starter busted."

"I can help you with it later."

"Yeah, just I gotta get up to the Valley right now."

He looked at the Nissan. "If you're just going up and back, take my ride. I'm gonna catch some zzz's. Three fire calls last night. I'm wiped."

I perked. "For real?"

"Just don't do nothing stupid. Bring it right back."

He grabbed his gym bag and got out of the car. I slid behind the wheel.

"Preciate it, bro. Thanks. A lot."

He leaned in the window. "Nothing stupid, hear me?"

"Don't worry." Frank rapped the roof and I rolled to Flaco's, making a pitstop for candy bars on the way.

Andrés was swinging on the gate when I pulled up. His face lit up when he saw me.

"Whatup with you out here so early, lil homie?" I said.

"I'm waiting for Rico. He's gonna give me a ride to school in his truck."

An alarm bell went off in my head. "Oh yeah, howzat?"

"I'm his homie now. Me and him got a secret."

I thought fast. "You want a candy bar?" I pulled a Snickers out of my jacket and offered to him. In a second, he had the wrapper ripped off. "So, what you doing with Rico, homiecito?"

"I did a favor for him last night," he said through a mouthful.

"Yeah? What kind of favor?"

"Rico said to keep it a secret." Chocolate was already smeared all over his face and fingers.

"Yeah, but you know we all homies. We don't keep no secrets."

He shook his head. "Rico said never to tell. I had to put something back where it belonged, but I didn't really put it where Rico said. A lot of dogs were barking, and I got scared."

The fuck was he talking about? "What was it? Where were you at?" He shrugged as he chewed. He most likely didn't know anyway. "Can you get Flaco for me, homie?"

He headed into the house. I couldn't blame him. All Andrés wanted was a homie, like everybody else. We all needed homies. Flaco came out, threading his arms in his shirt sleeves, Andrés trailing him. He was seemed to be half dressed when I picked him up. "Andresito, you go get ready for school," Flaco said.

"Okay, homie." He got to the doorstep and turned. Flaco made a shooing motion at him. He entered the house.

Flaco looked appreciatively at the car as he got in. "Sweet ride."

"My brother's. The Nissan died on me this morning." As we rolled out, I told Flaco what Andrés just told me about Rico. He shook his head. "What the fuck is Rico playing at, using my little brother for his bullshit?"

"All I know is Rico's gotta be desperate. They pulled the plug on Payaso Santana yesterday."

"Fuck. Double murder," Flaco said.

We picked up the rest of the crew and headed to the Valley. Flaco got the homies up to speed on Payaso and Andrés.

"Rico ain't gonna stop at nothing to save himself now," Jackie Chan said.

"You got that right," Cojo said.

I parked in front of Alfredo's house. The choppers were still in the driveway.

"They ain't gone to Arizona yet," Jackie said.

We trooped round the back. I opened the screen door and knocked. Guillermina answered, surprised at the crowd on her doorstep. I asked for Rico and said it was urgent.

"He left an hour ago with his uncle for a cockfight. Did you try calling him?"

"Yeah, but something's wrong with his phone. If you hear from him, could you tell him we really need to talk to him?"

"I'll tell him," she said.

"His cousins around?" Flaco asked.

She looked at him curiously. "What do you want with them?"

Flaco shrugged. "Nada. They got some tight bikes is all."

"They went with Alfredo."

Disappointed, we headed back to the car, walking past the motorcycles. The chrome on the motorcycles was so bright and shiny, it seemed like it was mocking me, like them assholes were mocking me.

I leaned into Cojo. "You packing your fila?"

He smiled, guessing at my intention, and took the blade out of his pants and passed me it. I crouched between the bikes and ripped the front tires of both. We walked fast to the car and jumped in. I floored it down the street as the homies whooped.

Revenge is getting back your power that someone took away. There's nothing else that gives you that feeling. So yeah, this was a small, petty move, but it was a move, and it felt fuckin incredible.

THIRTY-ONE

After dropping off the homies, I went home. Frank was sleeping so I left his car keys on the coffee table. I called Gato and told him about the starter. He said he'd give me a tow back to the yard as soon as he got rid of a customer. He'd be a while. I heated up some leftover rice and beans and was chowing down when Paloma called.

"You gotta get over here," she said.

"Whatup?"

"You just gotta come. It's serious." She hung up. What now?

Frank was zonked so I grabbed his keys.

Paloma opened the door as I pulled up, the pitbulls next door barking. She looked real worried as she waited for me to walk up. She grabbed my hand and pulled me to her bedroom and closed the door softly.

"Moms is sleeping." She handed me a manila envelope. "This was on the doorstep when I went out this morning."

The envelope was heavy. I looked inside. My stomach balled into a knot. I held the envelope upside down and the gat fell on the bed. A .22 semi-automatic. The double deuce that killed the kid and Payaso. Had to be.

Paloma sat next to me. "You know anything about this?"

"You touch it?"

"You think I'm a fool?"

"It's the piece from the driveby, that's what I think anyways."

Her hands flew to her face. "Ay, Dios mio, Dios mio." She was getting hysterical.

"¡Callate vos! I gotta think."

Andrés. This was what he was talking about. "It was Rico. He asked Flaco's little brother to plant it last night. The kid got scared by the dogs next door and he musta thrown it on the porch and ran. He was prolly supposed to hide it somewhere." Hide it so it could be found—by the murder cops. Rico prolly already dropped the dime, called the tip line. That's why he took off early this morning.

Paloma's hand was trembling. I threaded my fingers in hers. It helped steady me, too. My nerves felt like they were gonna snap.

"And the piece? What we gonna do with that?" she asked.

"We gotta get rid of it," I said.

"How?"

"I'll take care of it. Less you know the better." I pulled her to me and kissed her like I found water in the desert.

I walked back to the car. The cemetery for hot pieces was the sewer. Hundreds of murders and robberies were washed down its pipes. But I needed to wait until nightfall to avoid unwanted eyeballs. I tucked the envelope under the driver's seat and went home to wait for Gato.

It was the end of the day. I'd fixed the starter on the Nissan and done a million other things for Gato. I was exhausted, but more by stress than work. Worrying about the piece had me more wrung out than a towel in a spin cycle.

The phone buzzed. Flaco. "Remember Ace, the homeless dude?"

"Yeah."

"He showed finally. He was in county. He says he got the 411 about the 5150s, but he wants feria. I don't got pisto right now. I had to give my mom money for rent and it was Yajaira's birthday last week."

"He solid?"

"Yeah, he's good. He wanted a C-note, but I talked him down to fifty."

"Scoop me up in twenty." I hung up.

Fuck, I still had the gat. It was too risky to ride around with a hot piece right then. I had to stash it in the yard for the time being.

I wandered through a tunnel of stacked car doors and fenders. At the end, just inside the back fence, rusting engine parts were piled in a heap.

I threw them aside, tossed the .22 in the middle, then covered it up.

Ace had a mouth of missing teeth and grizzled hair and always wore a torn trenchcoat. He'd been on the pipe for years. He lived in a little camp he built himself in the middle of tall bushes on a vacant lot.

Me and Flaco pushed our way through a hole in the lot's fence. Flaco whistled.

The bushes rustled and a hand poked out, motioning us to come in.

We dove into the scrub, then found ourselves in a clearing, a couple tarps strung between trees as the roof. A rolled up sleeping bag and upturned buckets surrounded a fire pit.

"You got the paper?" Ace's irises swam in a sea of yellow spider-veined with red.

Flaco took out the fifty to show him, then shoved it back in his pocket. "Talk first," he said.

Ace sat down on a bucket, throwing back the tail of his coat like he was sitting down at a grand piano. We parked our asses on buckets, as well.

"So you wanna know bout Payaso Santana."

"What you got?" Flaco said.

A rat the size of a Chihauhua ran across the clearing. Me and Flaco raised our eyebrows at each other, but it didn't seem to bother Ace.

He rubbed the cleft of his chin.

"There was a green light on him. Word went round he was a snitch. He cut hisself a sweet deal when he got arrested in the takedown. He was the only one released on time served."

That was why he was talking to Lissy about going to Mexico. He knew he was green lit.

And Rico just happened to run into him that night?

I exchanged a glance with Flaco.

"So the 51s got their problem solved, and they ain't had to lift a finger," Flaco said.

"Word is some of the 51s ain't too happy how it got solved," Ace said. "They lookin at it like it's a Cyco move. They talkin bout payback."

"While you was in county, you hear anything about smack?" I asked.

"You got another Franklin?" Ace asked.

I frowned. "What?"

"The deal was a Franklin for intel on Payaso. You want more, you pay more."

I rolled my eyes. "Aight."

"I heard two Latino clicks took over the supply with a dirty guard," Ace said. "Might be some moves on em cuz they upped the price."

Chivas and the 51s. What we thought. I stood and handed Ace a hundred.

"Stay outta county, Ace," Flaco said.

"It was gettin cole, man," Ace said. "Cat cain't sleep out. I turned myself in on some bench warrants. Three hots and a cot, know what I'm sayin?"

We headed back to the car.

Ace marched down the street, his black coat flapping, already on the way to feed his glass pipe. A hundred bucks wouldn't last long.

"You thinking what I'm thinking?" Flaco said once we got in the car.

"Rico did the hit on Payaso for the 51s. Chivas and his new carnal, the 51 shotcaller, cut the deal." I slumped in the seat. "I was sposed to be on that mission, dog."

"It was a set up. Rico was gonna do something, so you went down for the driveby or the 51s took you out."

"So why'd he go ahead and do it without me?"

"He had to do the hit for Chivas so when Blueboy called saying Payaso was close by, he couldn't waste the chance. You were a side job. Personal beef."

"Then Rico sets up Blueboy when the hit goes bad."

Flaco nodded. "That's about it."

"But why wouldn't the 5150s take care of their own? Why hand off Payaso to us?"

Flaco shrugged. "Maybe Chivas owed them for something."

"What about that shit with my sister? Rico couldna known she'd be at that party."

"He was with his cousins at the party, saw Zully and figured he could use her to get back at you."

I nodded. "He put the rape on the 5150s because he knew he had to do the hit on Payaso. That's why he came over the next morning to see what Zully remembered bout the assholes who raped her, and why he was pressing so hard at the meeting to move fast on the driveby."

It all fit, except for one piece.

"I still don't know how Blueboy figures into this. You think he was in on it?" I stared out the windshield.

Flaco drew a deep breath. "I hate to say it, but yeah, I do. I don't think he couldna *not* known Rico was setting you up, maybe not on the rape, but for sure the 187 on Payaso Santana. I bet when he smiled when he heard it was Payaso—perfect payback for his sister."

It hurt to hear that, but Flaco was right. All this time, I was thinking I could make peace with Blueboy, but I been fooling myself. I hurt him way too deep. Still, he didn't deserve to go down for what Rico did.

THIRTY-TWO

Rico had booked.

We checked his house that night. The choppers were gone, and so was his truck. No one answered the door.

As we sat outside his uncle's, Flaco had his girl Yajaira call Maribel, who said Rico went to work with his cousins in Arizona.

"He'll be back, and we'll be waiting," Flaco said.

As we headed back from the Valley, I got a call from Paloma—the cops were at her house with a warrant. She was in a panic.

"Just take it easy. Don't show your nerves. They won't find anything," I told her.

We called it a night and went home.

Frank was lying in the sofa bed, watching a cop show when I came in.

"You home early on your night off."

I sat and unlaced my shoes.

"Me and Glenda are over."

"Damn, bro. ¿Qué pasó?"

"We had a fight. Some stupid shit I don't even remember. She says, 'Maybe we should take some time apart then.' I got pissed that she went there so quick so I said, 'Yeah, maybe we should just break up.' I didn't really mean it. Then she goes, 'If that's the way you want it,' and left. That was that."

"Give it some time. She'll calm down and you'll calm down and you'll be all lovey-dovey again."

"I don't think so."

"Bet you anything. You'll see."

I pulled the pillow up behind my head and tried to watch TV, but I had too much drama of my own running through my mind.

"You going to Benny's funeral?" I asked.

"Nah. Moms and Zully are gonna go with Lissy."

A deafening boom suddenly sounded, rattling the windows.

"That was an explosion." Frank jumped out of bed, reaching for his cell. "Sounds like a gas line blew," he said into the phone. He gave the address as he shoved his legs into his pants.

I ran to the window, but I couldn't see anything but the alley. I grabbed my jeans. Everybody came out of their bedrooms.

"What was that?" Zully said.

"I'm gonna check it out," I said.

"Be careful, m'hijo. That was close," Moms said.

"If it's a gas line, we might have to evacuate," Frank said. "Be ready."

I shoved my feet into my shoes and jogged down the stairs with Frank and into the street.

Flames were shooting from a car parked on the opposite curb, great licks of orange and yellow. Metal fragments painted electric blue glinted on the street.

I stopped short. It couldn't be.

"Nooo!" Frank yelled.

He ran toward the inferno, then braked and shielded his face with his forearm. I ran after him. The heat was intense.

Sirens whined. A fire truck pulled up, red lights flashing in a circle. Firemen ran toward the fire dragging a hose. A cop appeared and ordered everyone to move back.

Within a couple minutes, the flames fizzled out.

All that was left of Frank's Caprice Classic was a black twisted hunk of metal. Smoke hung in the air, stinging my nostrils. Frank was frozen, staring with a slack jaw at the wreck.

"Is that your vehicle, sir?" a bluesuit asked him.

Frank nodded. I headed back into my building. I didn't need to be around for cops. The possibility that Rico was behind this entered my head. But why would he blow up my brother's car and not mine? Had he ever seen Frank's ride?

Then it hit me. I had driven the Caprice to Rico's uncle's house. Guillermina must have lied when she said the twins went with

Alfredo. They'd seen the Caprice and, after discovering the slashed tires, asked Rico where I lived.

I sank onto the bottom step of the staircase. This was on me. But maybe it wasn't. The fire could've been caused by an electrical short or something else.

The thought allowed me to pick myself up and climb the stairs to the apartment. The rest of my family followed.

We all sat in silence around the kitchen table, waiting for Frank. Moms made coffee and poured us each a mug. The only sound was the teaspoon digging into the sugar jar, the clinking of the spoon stirring, the sliding of the jar as it moved around the table. It was 3:38 a.m. when Frank finally came in.

"Come and have coffee, m'hijo." Moms got up to get him a cup as he sat at the head of the table. She slid the mug in front of him, then the sugar jar.

"They said it was intentional. Somebody blew up my car," he said.

I dropped my head.

Moms gasped. "Who would do such a thing?"

Frank turned a metallic gaze to me. "Do *you* know, Magdaleno?" My eyes peeked up. Eight eyeballs were trained on me like rifle sights. A hot flush spread under my skin.

"Uh, no, I don't, Paco." My voice squeaked.

"You had the car. Where did you go—the Valley, wasn't it?"

"Yeah, but that ..."

Lissy broke in. "You're a lousy liar, Magdaleno. You got guilt all over your face. Just like when Benny got hit."

"I didn't have nothing to do with that or this." I sounded desperate even to myself. Somehow it was easier to lie to cops than my family.

"You brought a lotta bad luck on this family lately." Frank stayed calm and cold, which was worse than yelling and punching. That I knew how to respond to. This I didn't. I wanted to get up and jet, but I was glued into the chair. I wanted to shout and make a scene, so he'd back off, but my mouth was paralyzed. Everything I'd ever done caught up to me in a giant rush and lay there like a big stain on the table. I couldn't fake my way out of it anymore.

"What's next?" Frank continued. "Who's the next one to be hurt by you, Magdaleno?" Lissy. Frank. Zully. I couldn't deny the truth of what he said. "Maybe you got to move on. Keep a distance from us. Then you can live your life the way you want, but we ain't involved."

Was he kicking me out of the house, *out of the family?* In shock, I ran my eyes around the table. Not even mi mamá looked at me. Their silence echoed in my ears. I never felt so damn small. Tiny. I found my voice and it was tiny too.

"I guess you don't want me in the family no more, and I can't blame you. Alls I'm gonna say is I never meant to hurt nobody. I would never hurt any of you." My words snagged on the jags inside me, making me choke a little. "And in case you think I never did anything good for this family, you can ask mi mamá where she got the money to pay the rent that time when mi papá hurt his back. Ask her for the truth. It wasn't no loan from her boss."

I walked over to the closet, took out my duffle bag and unfolded it. I crossed to the dresser and tossed clothes into it. I moved slow. I was waiting for one of them to say, "Magdaleno, it's okay. No te vayas. Don't go." But no one said a damn thing. Not even Moms.

Slinging The duffle over my shoulder, I opened the door and paused to look back. The only one watching me was Papá. He was gazing at me clear-eyed, as if seeing me for the first time. I walked out and closed the door.

THIRTY-THREE

I woke up Paloma by tossing pebbles at her window. When she let me in, I hugged her so tight she had to pry me off her.

"What're you doing here so early?"

I told her about the car and Frank kicking me out. Her face grew stern as a school principal's.

"I don't know, Magdaleno," she said when I finished. "For a smart vato, you sure make dumbass mistakes. It's your own damn fault. You shouldn't have done that shit to the motorcycles. What did you think was gonna happen? You know those fools don't play around."

I recoiled. "You got la regla or something?"

Her tone got even snippier, so I guess that pissed her off. "I got the early shift, that's what I got, and I don't want to be late."

I just got booted from my family. I thought I deserved some sympathy. "I'll give you a ride. I don't want you being late cuz of me."

"I gotta get ready."

"I shouldna come." I was talking more to myself than her, but she heard me.

"Yeah, maybe you shouldna." She walked into the bathroom twitching her hips.

On the way to work, she sat in the car, quiet, not touching me, looking straight out the windshield. Even mad, she looked beautiful—her nose with its tiny upturn, her lips pink and plump as the pad on a cat's paw.

"You okay?" I didn't want to stay pissed off.

I could hear her blowing out air through nostrils. "I'm tired of this shit all the time with you. It's just one thing after another. When you came home, you said you were leaving the life and now you're in it deeper than ever. You said you were gonna tell Blueboy and you didn't. Now you got this shit with your family and it was your fault."

She was right. I was a fake, a pretender, but I didn't mean to be. "I know, nena. I'm tired of it, too. I got just a lil more time til I discharge parole, then we can book. Things are gonna change, I promise." The words sounded dry and twisted as I said them. Would I really be able to keep my promise to her? Not even that long ago, I was so sure of myself, my future. Now I wasn't so confident. As much as I wanted to lay it on Rico, Pops, el fulano de tal walking down the street, it was on me. I knew that. The only one I had rights to be mad at was me.

I pulled up at the restaurant beside a parked car. Someone behind me leaned on their horn. I ignored it. Her hand on the door, Paloma turned to me, her eyes sparkling with water.

"You're full of shit. I'm thinking life with you is always gonna be 'soon, nena, soon,' and me being there for two things—booty and your cry pillow. That's all this relationship is. I don't want that kinda relationship. I don't want the kinda guy that's always gonna do shit and always got an excuse for never doing it." She got out and slammed the door.

"Paloma!" She didn't turn around. An earthquake erupted in my chest. First my family, now my girl. A sob fought to get out of my throat. A horn blew behind me.

The driver slowed as he passed, giving me the stinkeye as he flipped me the finger.

"Fuck you, motherfuckin hijo de la chingada gran putaaa!" I screamed as loud I could. I turned back. Paloma was gone.

I drove to the salvage yard. Duque and Duquesa trotted to greet me, wagging their tails. At least they were glad to see me. I unchained them, grabbed my bag and they followed me into the shop. I breathed in that dirty smell of oil and felt a lil calmer. Being a grease monkey was what I was good at, a world where I fit. I threw down the duffle onto the car seats and plopped beside it, tearing off a Milky Way wrapper. The dogs laid their heads in my lap. I rubbed them behind their ears.

When Gato arrived, I asked him I could crib at the yard a while. "Shit with the family," I said by way of explanation.

"Come stay at my place."

"Thanks, but I don't want to be around people right now. I'll be okay here."

He patted my shoulder. "Shit always happens in families, but they're always your family."

"I guess that's the problem," I said.

I put on salsa music and forced myself to pick up a screwdriver to work on a wreck Gato bought at an insurance auction. Just when I was so close to getting my life together, it fell apart. Everything I did backfired, hurt the people I loved. And now I had no one. I felt like I had nothing left inside me anymore.

THIRTY-FOUR

For the next few days, I had to force myself to work. I had no energy. Could barely even talk. I lay awake all night then moved like a zombie all day. When Gato went home, I let the dogs loose to keep me company.

Feeling their body heat and their breath was the only thing that made me feel I was still living.

The homeboys tried to cheer me up and get me to go out with them. They all invited me to stay at their places, but I knew I'd just be a burden. Flaco and Jackie asked what we were going to do about Rico. I shrugged. He didn't seem so important no more.

"He's got me beat. No matter what I do, I fail. He won, dogs," I said.

Cojo and Tweety told me I should buy Paloma a ring or a necklace.

"Girl love that sparkly shit," Tweety said.

"Yeah, the minute she opens the lil box, she'll be all over you," Cojo said.

I shook my head. "She'll think I'm just tryna buy her."

She hadn't even called. Every time the phone buzzed, hope pricked in me that it was her, and then I crashed when it wasn't. I wondered what she was doing, who she was with.

I looked at the clock and imagined what she had to be doing at that time—going to work, taking her break, watching her novela as she painted her nails.

I tried everything to get her out of my head. I held the boombox against my ear and blasted the volume. I rammed my skull against the wall. I ran laps around the yard, the dogs at my heels, til I doubled over in pain. But as soon as I stopped the music, the ramming, the running, she was right there, in my mind again.

I cursed myself for going over there that morning. I cursed her for not waiting to say what she had to say, for telling me on the day my family kicked me out. Then I remembered how she would hold my hand and pump me up for the future we planned together, and I bawled til my eyes felt like raw eggs.

Zully was the only one of my family to call and ask me how I was doing. I said I was doing fine, and nobody had to worry about me again.

It was a Friday night. We'd boosted a ride, and the homeboys helped me chop it. With all of us working on it, it was done in an hour. Then Jackie counted to three. Two of them grabbed my upper arms and the other two scooped up my legs. They carried me out the door.

"The fuck is this?" I said.

"You're going to Gato's tonight," Flaco said.

"But first you gotta take a shower and shave. No offense, Mags, but you stink," Tweety said.

"I been washing," I protested.

"Ain't the same as a shower," Cojo said.

They bundled me into the back seat of the Nissan, Cojo and Tweety flanking me like guards. Jackie drove to his house, where he took me into the bathroom and switched on the shower faucets. He stood waiting.

"I think I can still take a shower by myself," I said.

The hot water felt good. I washed my skin raw. I shaved. I was startled to see a gaunt face with dark hollows looking back at me from the mirror. No wonder the homies had dragged me out. Flaco tossed a clean shirt and pants in through the door, and I put them on. When I came out into the living room, they looked up from the TV and nodded. I had to admit, I felt better, less than half dead, anyways.

"I gotta warn you. If you're taking me to Gato's, you gonna be carrying me out cuz I'm gonna be off the hook," I said.

They whistled, clapped and cheered.

It was a regular night at El Gato Rey. Jackie rapped the bartender, but wasn't working any magic, judging by the thin line of her mouth. Flaco and Mouse ogled the dancer bending over in front of them on the stage. Tweety and Cojo managed to score seats at a table of girls. I sat at the bar, chugging my second beer. It was hitting me fast since I had hardly eaten in days. It was a good place to come cuz it was somewhere I never shared with Paloma, which made it easier to distance her in my mind. I ordered a third beer. The waves of alcohol lapped inside my head, lifting me out of my problems like saltwater.

"Hola sexy." A breathy voice gushed in my ear. I swiveled on the stool. A jaina beamed at me with one hand on the bar, the other on her hip. She was wearing a gold sequined bikini, with loops of rhinestones draping her stomach and thighs. Her eyes were dark dots in nests of blue eyeshadow. "You don't remember me, Magdaleno?"

I squinted at her. She did look kind of familiar.

"Yvette, from Mr. Choi's store?" she said.

I did a double take. "Whoa, yeah. Yvette. I didn't recognize you. You working here now?"

"Just started this week. Choi cut back my hours, plus I got sick of his bullshit and this pays a lot better."

"Damn, that seems like a lifetime ago."

"You been busy, huh?"

"You could say that. You wanna drink?"

"I gotta go on in a few minutes. You sticking around?"

Maybe it was the beer or the dim light, but she was a lot prettier than I remembered.

"I ain't going nowhere." She held my eyes for a moment then pushed herself off the bar. "Catch ya later, then."

Jackie leaned over. "Who's she?"

"Just a girl I used to work with," I said.

The music pumped up, and she walked on stage with her hips thrust forward all sexy-like. As she gyrated and writhed, rubbed and rolled, she never took her eyes off me.

When her number was over, Flaco slapped me on the back. "If you don't jump on that one, I ain't never talking to you again, homes."

Jackie toasted me with his beer.

A couple hours later, Yvette was riding me like a bucking bronco, her skin silky with sweat. The girl could sure move. Our bodies stiffened and she arched her back and neck then rolled off me. We lay, chests heaving, staring at a damp-stained ceiling lit by a naked light bulb.

Yvette lived in an apartment where the rooms had been partitioned off with plywood panels to make cubicles and squeeze in as many tenants as possible. Frank was always complaining about these places being illegal firetraps and the city never doing anything about them.

The room was wide as my outstretched arms and just long enough to fit a cot and a rickety stool, which held candles in jars decorated with pictures of saints and a couple plaster saint figurines. Clothes bulged from hangers on wall pegs. At least she had a portion of a window that she shared with a neighboring cubicle. Yvette pushed up the window, letting in a blast of cool air, and collapsed back on the bed, putting her head on my shoulder. I moved it back onto the pillow. We weren't that cozy yet. Somewhere a toilet flushed, a guitar strummed, a drawer banged shut. You could hear everything.

"I can't stand this place," she said. "I found a spy hole in the bathroom wall the other day. I plugged it up with toilet paper. I forgot to lock my room door the other night, and some drunk creep came in and tried to get in bed with me. I screamed and he left."

"You gotta get outta here, girl. Where's your people at?"

"Long story. I been alone a while now. I can take care of myself. But with the job at Gato's, I think I'll be able to move out pretty soon. One of the girls there is talking about a couple of us getting a place together."

I decided not to ask her more questions. I didn't want to know her mess because I didn't want to talk about mine. It was cleaner, simpler like that. I could see her for what I saw. Bringing the past into it would make it more complicated.

"How bout you?" She trailed a finger down the valley of my chest. "You got people?"

I sat up. "I gotta bounce."

"Hey, don't trip out on me. Forget I even asked."

I was already grabbing my pants from the floor. "I just remembered something I gotta do."

"See you at Gato's tonight?"

"I'll be in and out." I threw on my shirt and shoes. "Don't forget to lock the door," I said as I closed it.

THIRTY-FIVE

I went home with Yvette the next night and the next and the next. It became a regular thing that I'd meet her at the club, and we'd go back to her place. It was like lotion on my bruised ego to have someone waiting for me, greeting me with a smile, losing myself in steamy sex.

Even though her bed was cramped, it was better than sleeping on car seats. I made it clear to her that questions were off-limits, about the past, present and future. We existed in the moments we were together, nothing more.

I heard nothing from Paloma. I kept seeing her in every swish of long hair on the street, every pointy profile through car or bus windows. The pain in my heart subsided to a dull ache that I couldn't get rid of, but I was able to live with.

I checked Gato's newspaper every morning, but there was nothing about the driveby. Rico was still underground. Just as well. Too much had happened too fast. I needed time to recoup, to let things settle, allow skin to grow over my wounds. And it did. But it was a different skin, metal hard. I wasn't going to let anyone under my tatts again. They were my armor.

The chop shop was running smooth. The homies were bringing in rides almost every night. My biggest hassle was where I could stash all the bills I was hauling in.

I bought some palm trees in big-ass pots, bundled the feria in plastic bags and buried them under the dirt. I lined up the trees in a row outside the shop and told Gato I was making the place pretty. He thought that was real funny.

It hit me one night when I was alone in the shop that joke was on me. What was really funny was now I had the pisto to book and just days to go on parole, but I didn't have Paloma or Blueboy. I laughed until I cried.

But I didn't need them. I didn't need anyone. From now on, it was just me.

I was laying in bed with Yvette one night after we'd had an argument with her neighbor over the shared window. Usually, she came home so late the guy was already asleep, but that night it was early since it was her day off. She wanted the window open to get some air, he kept closing it.

I finally got up and banged on his door.

When he saw the tatts on my bare chest, he backed right down, pretend-smiling at me with one of them stupid gold grilles that indios love putting on their front teeth.

When I got back in bed, she snuggled up to me. I adjusted the pillow and felt something. I drew out a puffy little bag tied with a red string.

I half-smiled. "Is this what I think it is?"

She snatched it and tucked it under the mattress corner. "It's for good luck."

I smiled at her. "It's a love potion. My sister got one one time from some bruja. So, who you tryna get to fall in love with you, girl?"

She punched my chest lightly. "Who'd you think? I got it at the botánica downtown when you were still working at Choi's. I had to sleep with it under my pillow for forty nights."

I laughed.

"I saw you going into that place. You really believe in that hocus-pocus shit?"

"You're here, ain't you?"

My cellphone buzzed. I pulled the phone out of my pants on the floor.

Flaco.

I sat up as I answered.

"It's Blueboy, Mags." He paused. "He got shanked in county last night, bled out in the shower." It took me a second to take in what he was saying. "Mags, you there?"

Ice spread through my gut. Blueboy was dead. "Noooo!" I yelled. The cell phone slid from my grasp. Yvette sat up and encircled my shoulders. The fleshy globes of her melones pressed against my back. "What happened, baby?"

I ignored her. In my mind, I saw Blueboy lying pale and naked on a concrete floor. His tattoos slashed wide open as water washed his life down the drain. The killers woulda kept everyone outta the showers, including the guards, for enough time so he would lose so much blood, there'd be nothing medics could do. He woulda been conscious for a while. He woulda known he was dying, feeling himself getting weaker and weaker. Then he woulda passed out, his heart stopping when there wasn't enough blood left to pump.

No matter what went down between us, Blueboy didn't deserve to die like that. Tears ganged up on my eyes. I shook off Yvette. I had to get outta there, be alone.

I stumbled out to the car and called Flaco back. He said Ace had flagged him down on the street as he was rolling out of Gato's and offered the 411 for a C-note. "He told me the word on the street was the hit was 5150 payback for Payaso Santana."

"What d'you think, homes?" I said.

"I think it was Rico and Chivas. Smoke Blueboy then there's no witness to ID Rico as the shooter, even put him in that ride. Case closed. Rico skates a double 187 with the law, and the penalty for lighting up the kid with the clica. He keeps scoring chiva for Chivas and boning Esme. Rico needs to make it look like it was 5150 payback."

"I told Blueboy to watch his back, homes, I told him." My voice cracked like an ice tray under warm water.

"Don't be tripping on that, Mags. It ain't on you."

But I couldn't shake the feeling that it was. I spent the rest of the day chewed up by guilt.

If only me and Paloma hadn't got together, if only I'd told him about us, if only I hadn't stopped for candy bars the night of the driveby, if only Morales hadn't walked in that store at that moment. I got myself so twisted in the pretzel of if onlys, I worked my way back to "if only I hadn't been born."

But since I had, it was a useless train of thought.

Pictures of Blueboy flashed through my mind: his crazy one-shoulder shrug, the desert sky of his eyes, his hee-haw laugh, the frog-like hoods of his eyelids when he was high. It was all gone. Stolen. I needed Paloma, to feel her breath mingle with mine, to wrap her hair around my hands. By late afternoon, I couldn't take it no longer. I had to see her. I knew what I could do to make amends. I could pay for his funeral. I threw down my tools and dug up a wad of cash from a palm tree pot and headed over to her place.

Paloma stood in the doorway, her face droopy with sleeplessness, her hair a jungle, her eyes cold as marble.

"Hey, nena. I heard. I just wanted to see how you were doing."

"How'd you think I'm doing?"

"I want to give you this, to help out with the funeral and all." I held out the bundle of cash.

Her face tightened, then she batted the wad out of my hand. It flew across the porch.

"Blood money, that's what this is!" she screamed. "You think you can buy off your guilt with this, that money makes up for my brother being dead, that this is what his life is worth? Fuck you! You know what the detectives told us today? The bullet he caught in the eye was from the same gun that iced the 5150 and the baby. His own fuckin homeboys tried to kill him, and when that didn't work, you murdered him in jail! They stabbed him up twenty-seven times with a hairbrush handle made into a blade. You know what kind of death that is? You know how much pain he was in? I am so fuckin sick and tired of your homeboy shit. That's all you are—mierda, pura mierda! We are done, over!"

"Listen, when you calm down, come see me. I'm staying at the yard."

"Like I'm gonna come crawling to you? Fuck you!" I turned on my heel. There was no point in staying. "I don't never want to see you again, Magdaleno! My brother's dead because of you! Youuuu!"

I got in the car, shaking as her screams echoed in my head. I should never have went. I'd made everything worse, as usual. Somehow I drove. I didn't know where I was going. I was on autopilot, turning right here, left there, past the school, halting at the stop sign. The trees along the street suddenly looked familiar.

I realized I had driven home—what used to be home, at any rate. I really had no home.

I slowed to a crawl, scanning the sidewalks for Zully, Moms,

Lissy, Frank, even Pops. I wanted the comfort of seeing them even if I couldn't talk to them. Then a smudge of a familiar banana yellow crossed my hazy vision. I zeroed in on it.

A pickup was pulling out from the curb at the end of the block. Rico! What the fuck was he doing here? Whatever it was, I knew he wasn't bringing no flowers and chocolates.

I slammed the car into a space in front of a fire hydrant, galloped up the stairs and burst through the apartment door. Zully was watching TV, holding a cushion on her legs curled up on the couch. She looked shocked to see me.

"Magdaleno! What you ..."

Two empty glasses sat on the table. "Was Rico here?"

"He just left."

"What'd he want?"

"He came by to see how I was doing."

"He ask where I was at?"

"Yeah, but he said he didn't come for you, he just wanted to see how I was, if I ever needed help with anything, to call him."

"You tell him I ain't living here?"

"Yeah." My heart flopped.

"What'd he say?"

"He said, 'I guess he's shacked up with Paloma.' I said I didn't know where you were at."

"He say anything bout Blueboy?" She shook her head. "He say anything else?"

She picked at the fringe of the cushion. "He said maybe I'd like to go for a ride with him some time."

"And you said yes."

She toyed with the fringe. "Kinda."

"Zully, he set you up for the rape! Those putos were his cousins. You stay away from him! He's a dangerous motherfucker! He's playing you, just like he played me." I was yelling so hard, spit was coming out my mouth. Zully burst into tears. I paused staring at her, but not seeing her. My mind snapped clear. I knew why he really came over. He wanted to pin the murders on me, put *me* in that car with Blueboy.

"Where was he at in here? He go into the kitchen, bathroom, bedrooms, where?"

"He ... he sat here. Then he went to the bathroom."

I ran into the bathroom. I swept everything off the top of the toilet tank with my hand and took off the lid. I didn't know what I was looking for, but he could've planted any fuckin thing.

I plunged my hand in the water and felt all around. I got on my knees and checked the back of the toilet, under the tank, the sides. I stood and tore back the shower curtain, threw down the shampoo bottles.

Then I picked them up, unscrewed the tops and looked inside.

I chucked them in the tub. I cleared out the shelves of the medicine cabinet. Everything crashed into the sink.

"Stop it, Magdaleno! What're you doing?" Zully stood in the doorway.

I pushed her aside and stopped in the entrance of the living room. When she went into the kitchen to get the drinks, he coulda hid something in here. My eyes hunted for any sign of disturbance. Nothing seemed out of place, but Rico was smart. I tossed off the couch cushions, dug my hand into the cracks at the sides, emptied the dresser drawers onto the floor, looked on the sides of the drawers, inside the dresser.

Zully pulled at my shirt.

"Magdaleno, this is crazy! Stop it!"

I swatted her off like a mosquito and kept going. I had to find it before the cops arrived with a warrant. I wasn't going to let him win this one. No fuckin way. I got on my hands and knees, looked under the furniture.

I pulled out the books holding up the coffee table, which upended with a crash of the glasses, and flipped through the pages. I threw them aside. I pulled apart the frame of Frank's photo on the TV set, tossed that.

The door opened. "¿Qué es esto?" Moms held onto the doorknob, her eyes wide and her mouth open.

Zully ran over and cried into her chest. "He's gone loco, mamá. He won't stop."

I looked around and saw what Moms was seeing. A lamp and some knick-knacks lay broken on the floor. The armchair was upside down. Clothes were strewn over the whole living room. Moms stared at me with a horrified question mark on her face.

I couldn't talk so I ran. I raced up to the roof and sat hunched on a crate, just like I used to do when I was a kid to get away from

Pops. The sun was bleeding its last rays across the mountains.

In the distance, the Hollywood sign was already lit up. I felt all twisted inside. I didn't know who I was anymore, who anyone was. It was like the borders of myself were disappearing. Maybe I really was going crazy.

I heard a noise behind me. Moms sat beside me, saying nothing. Her silence was worse than a thousand scoldings.

"Lo siento, mamá." I grabbed the braid hanging down her back and pressed it against my nose, inhaling that strawberry scent of her shampoo. "Blueboy's dead. Stabbed up in jail. Paloma broke up with me. My family don't want me. I ain't got nothing."

She gasped. "¿El Blueboy está muerto?"

I nodded. She cradled my shoulders. I bent my head onto hers, feeling on my cheek the crown of her hair hot from the sun.

"Que en paz descanse. I worry the same will happen to you one day, that'll you die before your life has even started."

She sighed.

"You were such a happy little boy, Magdaleno. Paco was always serious, but you always had a joke ready to make everyone laugh. And you had a big heart. You gave a bag of groceries to a homeless man on the street once, remember?"

"You and mi papá got mad. I wanted to give him the fridge, too."

"You cried and cried when the neighbor's dog got run over. The Mother's Day cards you made me in school were the nicest from any of you kids. I still have them." I'd forgotten those things. "I don't know what happened to you, how you got so hard." She grabbed my hand and rubbed my tattoos with her thumb.

"I ain't so hard, mamá, believe me. I just kicked it with the wrong crowd. Now I'm in too deep. I can't get out."

"Getting out is always harder than getting in, but if you seek the way, you will find it."

I wasn't as sure as she was. I had to ask her the question that was bothering me. "Mamá, why didn't you tell mi papá I gave you that money when he hurt his back?"

"He's proud and stubborn, as you know. It would have killed him to take money earned illegally by his teenage son. Maybe it was wrong of me not to tell him, but I needed him to take it. I had to put food on the table for six people and keep a roof over our heads. He's been humiliated enough. Telling him would've humiliated him even more. It was nothing against you, hijo, and yes, you saved us. Gracias."

I knew it was the truth. Something loosened inside me. I straightened, picking up a stray branch and hurling it off the roof. It lodged in a treetop with a ruffle of leaves. "How was he humiliated?"

"He was somebody in El Salvador. He was a guerrillero famed for his bravery. He was even in the newspapers. People knew his name, talked about him. Then things happened, and we had to come here. Now he's less than nobody."

I remembered something. "What happened that day, a little while ago, when he was a wreck in the kitchen and talking about la mano blanca?"

"It was a new guy at work, otro salvadoreño. Even after all these years, he recognized tu papá. Then your father remembered who he was. He was a member of La Mano Blanca. That was the military's clandestine death squad. Your father was at the top of their death list."

"So what happened?"

"Tu papá was worried sick that he would have to quit his job, maybe even leave Los Angeles. He didn't know if the guy still bore a grudge against him or maybe he had been sent to finish the job."

"But the war ended years ago."

"The rifts ran deep. There was a lot of hatred and bitterness on both sides, even peace can't heal that right away. Tu papá decided to stay as far away as possible from the guy, but one day the jefe assigned them both to unload a truck. Your father had no choice but to do it. When they were taking out the boxes, the man told him that he knew who he was, and tu papá said he knew who the man was, too. They stood looking at each other. Tu papá thought the guy was going to pull out a gun or something. But then the man said he had a family and a new life now. The past was over and that he hoped your father wouldn't create problems for him."

"What did mi papá say?"

"He said he was hoping the same thing."

"They were both scared of each other."

"Yes, then they shook hands."

"So, they're friends now?"

"Not exactly. This man would've kidnapped, tortured, murdered anyone who sympathized with la guerrilla. Tu papá can't forgive that so easily, but he can let the past stay in the past. There's no point in bringing it into the present or making it the future." She squeezed my hand. "I better get dinner. Coming?"

"I don't think so."

"Come home, hijo. Everybody's calmed down now."

I shook my head. "Frank's right. I just bring trouble on everybody."

She stood. "At least come get some food to take with you. You can't live on candy bars."

I nodded absently.

I wanted to be alone, think on what she had just told me. I could see now that I had to do what Pops did—cut the string to the past and let it go, let it fly away like a loose kite. That was the only way to build a new future, otherwise I was destined to keep repeating the past.

That was what had happened since I came home from lockup because I hadn't wanted to cut that string.

I *thought* I wanted to, but deep down I wasn't willing to make the sacrifice like Pops—becoming a nobody, leaving everything I knew, everyone I loved.

That had saved Pops from getting caught in his past, but I didn't want to end up like him—drunk, bitter, struggling. Maybe I didn't have to, maybe I could be different.

I stayed on the roof till the egg yolk of sun vanished. I went to Gato's and then called Yvette.

THIRTY-SIX

It was the day of Blueboy's funeral. I figured if I went, it would be inviting another tirade from Paloma, and I didn't know if I could take that. The homies said they weren't going neither.

I told them it was my beef with Paloma, not theirs, and not to disrespect Blueboy like that but they said if I wasn't going, they weren't going.

Instead, we went to Dockweiler Beach and sat in our own thoughts on the sand under a sky like a rug of deep blue and bright white.

As I looked up and let the sunrays beat down on my closed eyelids,

I hoped Blueboy was in a place he could find happiness.

"What she said to you ain't right, Mags, Paloma putting Blueboy on you," Cojo said. "We all know what being all involved means when we sign up for it. Shit happens on the street, can't be helped."

That was a mouthful for Cojo to say. "I never knew you were a philosopher, Cojo," I said.

He cracked a sheepish smile. "I ain't no whatever-you-said. I'm just a homeboy."

"Besides, maybe Blueboy set you up with Rico, Mags," Jackie said. "Rico used Blueboy for his own selfish interest, like he used me and everybody else," I said. "I wanna remember Blue for the good in him, the good times we had."

Flaco turned to Mouse with a frown. "You ain't heard nothing from Rico?"

Mouse shook his head. "Nada."

"Somebody's gotta be lying. Somebody knows where he's at. Rico's got that business in county with Chivas. He can't walk away from that," Jackie Chan said.

I looked out at the sea. It was real calm and gentle. I'd told the homies about Rico being at my house. They got fired up and made another round of checks at his uncle's and his women.

I didn't go with them. Since the day on the roof with Moms, that hard nut of resentment, envy and desire for revenge inside me had shriveled to nothing. I'd lost my drive for hunting down Rico.

"We're going round in circles. Maybe it's time to end it," I said.

"End what, Mags?" Tweety said.

"I ain't got the hate in me no more. All we're doing is hating."

"You wanna give Rico a free pass, that's what you're saying?" Jackie said.

"It's more like giving *us* a free pass. So we can get to where we're going."

"Where we going, Mags?" Tweety said.

"Wherever we want to. You wanna win a belt, right? That's where you're going."

"We're gonna look like punks," Flaco said.

"I ain't no punk. I'm just tired is all, real tired."

We fell into an unsettled silence. I knew the homeboys were tryna figure me out.

Jackie broke the quiet.

"Remember when Cojo had to pull Blueboy outta that window?"

Cojo laughed.

"Yeah, we were doing a liquor store. The owner came in just as Blue was going through the bathroom window and grabbed his legs. Blueboy was holding on to the edge of the window, yelling. I got him under the shoulders and pulled. The fool was pulling him from the other side. We were going back and forth til the fool let go, and Blue came flying out and landed on top of me.

"We fuckin booked. The fool ran outta the store, cussing us up and down, but he couldn't catch us."

"What about the time when Blueboy got the hots for girl?" Flaco said.

"Yeah, what was her name again?" Jackie said.

"Stephanie," Tweety said. "I knew her so Blueboy was always

tryna get me to find out where she was gonna be so he could show up and run into her by accident. Second time, she saw right through it. She got mad at me and wouldn't talk to me no more." He chuckled.

"Then she decided she liked him, but after they got together one time, he didn't like her no more. Then she was running after him, and he was tryna avoid her," Jackie said.

"And she kept asking me for Blueboy," Tweety said. "Fuckin loco." We laughed again.

"She got caught in them blue eyes," Flaco said.

"We all got caught in them eyes," I said.

"I'm gonna change my fighting colors," Tweety said. "From now on, I'm wearing blue for Blueboy."

We told stories about Blueboy til the wind blew through our clothes and the sea turned grey. I dropped the homeboys at their cribs to eat and rest up for the job for Gato later that night and headed to the yard to do the same.

As I expected, the gates were closed. Gato'd went home. I got out of the car to open the padlock, but there was no lock. Was he still around? I pushed open the gates and drove through. The yard was in shadows, except for the floodlight that lit the central area. Gato's SUV wasn't there and the office was dark. No Dobermans came running to greet me. I whistled and called them. Silence. Then I saw their chains lying on the ground like long worms.

Maybe something had happened at home or at the club and Gato had to leave in a hurry. For some reason, he took the dogs. Since he knew I was coming back soon, he didn't worry about the padlocking the gate or calling me. Trying to ignore the prickling in my spine, I walked to the shop, pushed open the door and threw the light switch.

The first thing I seen was dark, wet spots on the hood of the Dodge I'd been working on. What the...? I took a step closer to examine them, then a drop plinked in the puddle. I looked up. Duque and Duquesa hung by the necks from the engine lift chains. Blood trickled from neat round holes in their foreheads. Shock paralyzed me.

Something clicked behind me. I wheeled. A tall dude, hair pulled into a ponytail and wearing a biker's cut and a goatee, aimed a cold smile and a gun at me. His clone, except for a Fu Manchu dripping down the sides of his mouth and a mane of flowing black hair, stepped out of the shadow. Rico's cousins.

I had to move fast to regain the element of surprise. I dove at Ponytail's knees. He fired but the shot went wide as he went down. The gun clattered on the floor, spinning under the car. I jumped up, but Fu Manchu tackled me from the side. I threw an elbow back, catching something hard. He grunted, stunned, and I took advantage of the moment to jump onto the trunk of the car. I felt a vise around my ankle and a forceful yank. I crashed onto my chin, sending shockwaves of pain through my jaw. I reached across the trunk and over the side to grip the wheel well as one of them pulled my leg. Fu Manchu was in front of me. He grabbed my head and whammed it on the hood. Lightning bolts flashed across my vision. I drew back my free foot and sprung it in an upward kick. It connected. Ponytail yelled and let go of my leg, which gave me a slight forward push. I released one hand from the wheel well and punched Fu Manchu in the huevos. He staggered back, groaning.

I scrambled onto the roof of the car and grabbed the chain with Duque hanging from it. Ponytail swung at my legs with a ballpeen hammer. I jumped, tucking my legs under me, and swung out on the chain Tarzan-style, kicking Fu Manchu, recovering from his blow to the balls, in the forehead. He tipped backward. I landed in front of the file cabinet, heaved it aside. A burning pain pierced the middle of my back as I shouldered through the escape hatch. I gasped and kept going. The gun. I had to get the .22.

I squeezed through the narrow space between the fence and the shop wall and came out in the maze of car parts. The darkness was thick as tar. As my eyes adjusted, I could make out vague shapes. The pain in my back sparked with every muscle movement. I crawled into a tent-like alcove formed by two piles of hoods propping each other up. Now that I was still, I could smell the strong, coppery scent of blood. I felt my back. My shirt was soaked. My fingers found a knife handle. I could just get my fist around it. I gritted my teeth, arched my back and pulled. A blast of agony, and it was out.

On hands and knees, I poked out my head. All clear. I scrambled out and crouch-ran along the back fence. I had to find the pile of old parts where I buried the .22. My pant leg caught on something sticking out. I yanked it free, but the movement jogged a pile of parts, causing a loud scrape of metal. Fuck. I froze, but there was no sound. I kept moving. I spotted a messy mound head. That was it.

I kneeled and removed the parts as quickly and quietly as I could. My breath was coming in ragged pants. A crash startled me— they were close by. I started chucking the parts to the side. I needed that gun. Finally, I cleared the space in the middle and scrabbled the ground with my hands. Nothing. Fuck. It was the wrong pile.

A cold click sounded right behind my ear. "Hands in the air and get up real slow, motherfucker."

They tied my hands and feet, gagged me and threw me into the back of a van parked on the street. The same van they had raped Zully in. They drove fast. As we turned, I rolled like a boat on a choppy sea, and my head rammed the sharp corner of a metal box. Blood trickled down my neck and dread lodged in my stomach.

Judging by the dull windshear roar, we were now on a freeway— the 110, the 105? It was a waste of energy trying to guess. I was going to be tossed as roadkill on the side of a fuckin desert highway. Didn't much matter where. Was Rico behind this? Or were the twins doing their own payback on me after they found out they hit my brother's ride not mine? Gato would freak when he found the Dobermans. I added him to my civilian casualty list. He'd blame me and that would be the end of that business. Would Paloma cry for me when she found out I was dead? Would Pops care? Lissy would regret what she said to me, but Frank would shake his head and say I had it coming.

We drove for what seemed like forever. Finally, we got off the freeway and slowed down. A little while later, we stopped. I heard the crunch of gravel, then the van doors flew open.

Cold, pure air rushed in. I breathed deep as they hauled me out. The silhouette of a single large building loomed in front of us. Above it, the sky was stitched with stars. We were out in the country.

One of them was looking inside the back of the van. "Fuck, he got blood all over the place."

"Cuz can clean it up. This is his shit. Hold the gun on him while I get his feet."

He untied my ankles and shoved me hard in the back. "Walk, asshole."

I stumbled and crashed on my face into gravel. It felt like a bed of nails.

They wrenched me upright and frog marched me into the dark building. It smelled musky. I knew that smell, but I couldn't place it. The floor was soft, dirt or sand. A barn.

A light switched on. I blinked. A metal barrier a couple feet high formed a circle on the floor. Bleachers on both sides. Sawdust on the floor.

They pushed me into the middle of the ring and told me to lay down on my back. I tried to resist and got whacked upside the head with a piece of wood. I dropped to the ground. One of them held down my shoulders with hands tight as clamps, while the other spread my legs, tying them at the ankles to rings on the metal barrier.

Then they slashed the rope binding my wrists. I tried to fight my way free and got another blow to the head. They stretched out my arms above, lashing my wrists with long ropes to the barrier. I was spreadeagled. Finally, they shoved my head into a burlap sack that smelled of grain. I opened my mouth to breathe better and scratchy bits fell in. I spat and shook my head to dislodge them.

"Wait," one said. "There's one thing I gotta do first."

He stomped on my huevos. I yelled as my vision turned to flashing splotches of color. They laughed.

A door banged. "Whatup, Mags?" a familiar rasp called out. "Bet you wish you had a Snickers right now." I didn't know why I was startled. I should've figured. Rico cackled like a fuckin lunatic.

"You motherfuckin hijo de la gran puta!" I strained at the ties. The bag grew hotter with my breath trapped inside. I told myself to calm the fuck down and sucked in all the air I could with an open mouth. The rough cloth flattened against my lips as I inhaled.

"Your problem is you don't got no respect, Magdaleno. You don't ever wanna play by the rules. That's what fucks you up every damn time." His voice was close but shifting. He was pacing around me. I lay still. "And you think you're smarter than everybody else, *but you ain't smart enough!*" His voice rose into a high-pitched scream. "I gotta say I was surprised you and the homeboys weren't at Blueboy's funeral. I dropped by to pay my respects. Paloma's a real fine girl, Mags, can't blame you for fuckin her. I wouldn't mind some of that pussy myself. Now that you outta the way ..."

"Motherfucker!" I shouted.

"Now your little sister, she's real pretty, but since my cousins had her, I don't know, she's kinda used up, know what I'm saying?" They laughed.

Anger shot through me. I clenched my teeth and pulled against the ropes with every muscle in my body. I pulled til my veins felt like bursting.

I groaned out of frustration and lay back, feeling sweat itch my face. Even if I broke free, it would be three on one. It was useless.

Rico guffawed.

"My cousins used to tie up cattle on a ranch. You ain't breaking outta them ropes. The truth is Zully's the only part of this I feel kinda bad about. But people have to be sacrificed sometimes. Even you. I had to get you out of the way so I could get a chance with Chivas, so I threw down that piece with the robbery on it. I knew when Chivas saw me for the loyal soldier that I am, I could win him. He could never see that cuz you were always in the fuckin way. Then him going down on the 187, well, that put me in a real good position. Then lil Mags comes skipping along the garden path getting in my way again."

He was fuckin insane, like his moms.

"Chivas sends saludos, by the way. He respects you, Mags, but you shouldna went to see Esme. He didn't like that, you getting all up in his business."

"He's nothing but a fuckin tecato junkie. Esme, too. He's cutting deals with the 5150 to get chiva into county with a dirty guard, and to ice Payaso Santana for snitching."

"True, true and true. My plan was to make you take the hit for Payaso. But it didn't work out that night, thanks to you and your candy, and we had to move fast. The fact that Payaso was your sister's ruco, that worked out real sweet, specially for Blueboy."

"You were the shooter, Rico. You shot the kid and Payaso. You thought Blueboy was RIP when the car wrecked. But you fucked up. You left the wrong fuckin cuete in the ride. So, you got Flaco's little brother to plant the hot piece at Blueboy's and dimed off the five-o. Then you disappeared, and Chivas ordered the hit on Blueboy in county to protect you and his business. After Blue got stabbed up, I was next on the list. You showed up at my house, looking for me. Zully told you I was cribbing at the yard, and you sent your cousins."

He clapped his hands slowly, applauding me. "Like I said Mags, you're real smart. But just so's you know, I didn't light up Blueboy, and Payaso never fired shit. My bullet musta ricocheted and come back through the window. I was crouching low by the door or it woulda nailed me. Bullets do weirdass things sometimes.

"I needed Blueboy cuz he was pissed down to the bone at you. But since the driveby didn't go to plan, he had to be sacrificed. The 51s hit him in county since they owed us one for Payaso. And you know who told me you were cribbing at the yard? Your little white dove Paloma. Man, she's one pissed off bitch. So, you see, you ain't figured it all out. You ain't all that. Bring em in!" he called sharply.

Metal clanked, birds squawked, feathers fluttered. I realized then what this place was—a cockfighting ring. That smell was Rico's uncle's rooster shed. The sack was yanked off my head. I gulped air as my eyes focused. A twin stood on each side of me, holding roosters. I caught a something glinting on the birds' legs—the steel gaffs. I struggled against the restraints out of reflex. One of the twins squatted beside me and ripped my shirt open so my chest was bare. He stood up and backed off.

"¡Dale!" Rico yelled.

They threw the birds in the air. The cocks landed on my stomach and chest in a flurry of feathers. They started pecking me, gouging my flesh with beaks like razor sharp jackhammers. I bucked my hips and shoulders to get them off. They jumped a couple inches, wings flapping, then landed again, and drilled and tore at me like they were eating me alive. The gaffs slit my skin every which way. I was swallowed by pain.

I screamed in agony, twisting my body, but that only made them dig more into my skin. I could see chunks of bloody flesh in their beaks. They stabbed my neck, my shoulders, my face, fast as AK-47 fire. I shook my head like a wild man, scrunching up my eyelids as hard as I could to protect my lids. I felt the sting of a gaff slicing my nose, a stab in my lip. Blood salted my mouth. The bird buried its beak into my lip, tugging at it. The other cock attacked my ear. I prayed. *Por favor, Dios, make them stop. Lord, have mercy. I'll do anything, please make them stop.* But they didn't. I was going to die, this was it. This was the end. Everything blurred. *Please let me die please.* I felt myself slipping into merciful blackness.

THIRTY-SEVEN

I came to in a fuzz. Where the hell was I? Was I dead? My chest clutched as I remembered the roosters. Panicked, I swiveled my head from side to side. No birds. No Rico. No cousins.

I relaxed, then every nerve pulsated with an electric current of pain. I was alive all right.

I smelled grass and made out the silhouette of leaves, a yellowed light beyond them. I was in a bush. I inched myself up to a sitting position. Every move hurt like a motherfucker. My chest, stomach and arms were raw hamburger.

I shivered. My ripped shirt was on the ground next to me. I pulled it on, wincing in pain, and staggered to my feet.

The surroundings looked familiar. I recognized MacArthur Park. Home turf.

I had to get outta there before the five-o made their next pass. They'd have too many questions. I patted my pockets for my phone just in case Rico left it on me. No such luck.

Fuck.

The deserted streets told me it was the wee hours of the morning.

I hobbled into the vacant shopping area. A drunk snored in a doorway, bottle next to him. A couple yelled at each other on a corner.

"Hey," I called. "Can I borrow your cell phone? I need help. Please." They looked at me in fright. The guy grabbed the girl's arm and bustled her into a car.

I walked, hoping to find someone who would lend me their phone so I could call Yvette or one of the homeboys. Then I remembered. Their numbers were all in my phone. I didn't know them by heart, and El Gato Rey would be closed by now.

My best option was to walk home, and hope Moms or the girls would help me one last time. But I didn't know if I could make it. The pain was worsening with every step, blood was dripping off me. I felt weak and lightheaded. I could barely shuffle one foot in front of the other. I rested against a wall, despair flooding me. I wished I had a gun. What was the use of living anymore?

Tears stung the cuts on my face. I looked up. A red-bulb cross blazed in a store window across the street. Moms' church with the ex-cholo pastor. Hope flared in me. Steeling myself again, I shuffled as fast as I could to the cross. I banged on the glass, sending shock waves up my arm.

"Please, help me."

Desperation tore at me. I kept banging. He had to hear me. Light flooded me as a bulb over my head switched on. I fell against the glass in relief. The lock rattled and the door opened a crack.

"¿Quién?"

"Esperanza's son, Magdaleno. Remember me?" As he looked at me, alarm sprang on his face. "You better come in."

THIRTY-EIGHT

It was late afternoon when I woke up, pain throbbing through a groggy haze. The room was warm with in yellow sunlight. I was lying on a narrow bed. I looked around. Next to me was a pine wood table holding a Bible and thick book, "Alcoholics Anonymous," and some first aid supplies. Milk crates were stacked on their sides, the cubbyholes filled with neatly folded clothes and books. A shade covered a small window.

I remembered. The cross, Moms' church. My head felt big and clumsy as a pumpkin. I patted my face with my fingertips. It was bulked with bandages. I threw off the covers. I was naked except for more bandages. I vaguely recalled voices, and a sensation of pricks, tugging, pulling.

A head poked round the door. "You awake, sleeping beauty?" The pastor. I couldn't remember his name.

"Man, what happened?" I croaked.

"I should be asking you." He disappeared and returned with a glass of water that he handed to me. I drained it and felt clearer.

He brought in a chair and sat on it backwards, nodding as he surveyed my bandaged body. "Fernando did a good job. Took a while. You were real cut up. He had to clean you up, put in a lotta stitches."

"You took me to a doctor?" Julio, that was his name.

"Fernando's a nurse, well, used to be. He got hooked on pills and got caught stealing from the hospital pharmacy. He's a compa from AA. Don't sweat it, he's cool, won't say nothing. He's done stuff like this before."

"Julio ..." I swallowed. "I'm real sorry I walked outta your misa that time."

"I figured you might come back one day. Sometimes it takes a while til people hit that bottom. Sure looks like you hit yours. You got real jacked up."

"They put los gallos on me."

His eyes went wide. "You mean roosters did this?"

"Yeah, they tied me down and sicced fighting cocks on me."

"That's a new one. An enemy clica?"

I shook my head.

"Beef with a homeboy." He gazed at me. I knew what he was thinking— what had I done to deserve that? "Long story," I said to answer his unasked question. "You didn't call mi mamá or nothing?"

"You want me to call her?"

"No. I brought enough trouble on my family. I don't want them to know about this."

"You got somewhere to go?"

"My homeboys." Pain boomed in my back. I felt a bandage and winced. I remembered I got knifed by a twin in the salvage yard. When the hell was that? Last night. Felt like ten years ago already. "You got any painkillers?"

"I'm a recovering addict, man. I don't even take aspirin. But Fernando left you ibuprofen and some sleeping pills. Just drugstore stuff." He chin-nodded at the bedside table and stood. "I'll get you some more water and some soup. You should eat something. Then I gotta get the room set up for the AA meeting."

He crossed to his milk-crate dresser and tossed me a T-shirt and sweatpants.

"Your clothes are in the wash. Bathroom's next door. Sounds like it might be better for you to lay low for now. You can stay here a couple days, rest up til you get your strength back. Fernando's stopping by later to check on you."

I was overwhelmed with relief and gratitude.

If Rico was the devil, Julio was some kind of angel.

"Julio ... gracias."

He smiled. "This is what I do."

I swallowed a couple pills and dozed off again. At some point, I dreamt a flock of gallos was attacking me, pecking out my eyes and leaving me blind.

I woke up, my heart racing and clammy with sweat. Seeing nothing but dark, I thought I really was blind til I found the light switch.

A while later, I heard dish clatter and smelled coffee. There was a knock on a door and voices, then Julio entered the room, holding a mug that he set down on the bedside table. "This is Fernando."

A Filipino the size of a girl with eyelashes to match trailed him. A prettyboy maricón. He smiled at me. "How do you feel?" He had an accent.

"Better." I did feel a little stronger. I sipped the coffee.

"Good. We have to change your dressings, keep the wounds clean so they don't get infected." He sat on the side of the bed and peeled off the bandages. "Julio told me it was gamecocks that did this to you. I was wondering what happened. Some of the wounds are like something chewed at you. Some are punctures and there's a deep cut on your back."

"That was a knife. The roosters had spurs on their legs and sharpened beaks."

I stared at my torso. I looked like I had sprouted barbed wire with the black thread of stitches sticking out all over me.

He dabbed and wiped around the sutures with cotton balls. Some were crusted with gunk. "Yes, I know from the Philippines. Cockfighting is very popular there. Have you had a tetanus shot?"

I shrugged. "I don't know."

"You should get one. I put antibiotic ointment on the wounds. You must keep them clean with alcohol, mercurochrome, something like that. I think your tattoos will be ruined by scars, especially this dove you have. A shame, it's a nice one."

La paloma. "No sweat, that one was already ruined."

He moved up to work on my face. "No shower, just sponge bath. This lip is bad. You should see a doctor for that. The earlobe will be okay. It should heal over. I'll leave everything here so you can clean and change the dressings every day. The stitches stay in about a week. You need rest to let the body heal from the trauma. You lost a lot of blood. I will check back when I can."

He stood. I grabbed his wrist. "Fernando, I want to pay you."

He smiled. "Money is not necessary. You rest now."

After he left, I shuffled to the bathroom to check myself out in the mirror. Jesus. I looked like a mummy from one of those old cartoons. I was going to be real scarred up now, that was for damn sure. I wondered if I'd ever be able to kiss again with a chunk of lip missing. I took a piss and went out into the kitchen. Julio was busy at the stove. A mattress stood on its side against the kitchen wall. It hit me that I was taking up his bed. He musta slept on the floor.

"Julio, you can have your room, I can sleep on the floor."

He turned from the frying pan. "Don't worry about it. I've slept on worse. It's good to see you up."

"I'm a little lightheaded, but okay, feeling a little hungry." I sat at the table.

"That's a good sign. I got scrambled eggs and beans here. You want some?"

"Gracias."

He slid a plate in front of me, then served himself and sat down. I picked up my fork then put it down when I saw him clasp his hands on the table and close his eyes. He said a fast grace and we dug in. I ate a couple mouthfuls and rested my fork. I was full.

"Julio, I gotta ask you, why you doing all this for me? You don't even know me."

"I got help when I was down, so I gotta pay back God by helping others. We all need help sometimes."

"You got a lot of answers."

"Believe me, I been to hell and back and picked up a few tips both ways. You gonna eat that?" He pointed his fork at my plate. I pushed it toward him, and he switched it with his empty one. "I used to be hard like you, banging and shit, using anything I could plug into my arm, nose and mouth," he said as he chewed. "I didn't care nothing bout nobody, least of all myself. I never knew my father. My mother's boyfriend was always beating me down. I ran away when I was twelve and joined the clica. They became my family and the street my home." He pushed back his chair. "I'll have to save the rest of the story for later. I got an AA meeting at seven."

"You got a lot of meetings."

"Can't do without em. They keep me sober."

I was curious about how this AA shit got people to stop drinking. I wondered if Pops would ever go. I washed the dishes in the sink, then I cracked open the door to the front room and peeked in. Men stood in a circle holding hands, chanting something in Spanish. They all sat, and Julio started talking. A late arrival came in and slipped into the back row not far from me. Black ink tatts webbed his arms and his neck. A dark beanie covered his head. A homeboy, but not one of mine. I squinted to check out his tatts. I could make out an "S" in old English script on the inside of his forearm as he leaned forward with his arms on his knees and clasped his hands. Or was it a "5," as in 5150. My heart boomed. I closed the door and went to the bedroom.

I lay down and took a deep breath. It didn't mean anything if a 5150 was at an AA meeting. Julio helped anyone. Still, it got me thinking about my situation. I was feeling weak, but I was gonna have to bounce soon. The question was where to? I couldn't go back to my family, Gato's, the homies. It would put them in even more danger than before because I knew too much about Rico and Chivas. They could get to me by getting to the people I loved.

Rico had surely left me to bleed out in the park, although I couldn't figure why he'd bothered dumping me there instead leaving me near wherever I was, although maybe it was to protect his uncle's gallo business.

Whatever it was, he was gonna try to pin me as the shooter in the car with Blueboy. And if he knew I was alive, I'd end up the same as Blue, six feet under. The only answer was to get out of LA. I'd get my money at the yard and jet. Pain started throbbing through me so bad it blotted out my thoughts. I swallowed a handful of pills and sank my head into the pillow. I was hoping for oblivion.

My stitches were itching like a motherfucker. I ripped off the bandages and was sitting on the bed cleaning and soothing the wounds with alcohol when Julio called from the kitchen.

"You hungry? One of the señoras brought me rice and chicken."

"The chubby one? Sits in the front row, plays the guitar?"

"How do you know?"

"She never took her eyes off you the whole time you were saying misa that day." I shuffled into the kitchen.

Julio laughed as he tossed tortillas on the stove ring to warm them. "She's always the first to show up and the last to leave."

He set down two plates of arroz con pollo and the tortillas in a plastic basket on the table.

We ate without talking. I finished the whole meal and felt a rush of new life with the food.

"Know what I think?" I said.

"What?"

"You gotta go for this girl. She can cook."

"I don't know, man. I ain't had too much luck with women."

"Me neither."

I told him about Paloma without going into details.

"You got kids with her?"

I shook my head.

Julio took off his glasses and cleaned them with his shirt. "I gotta daughter. She'd be seventeen now. I ain't seen her since she was five. When I got out of el bote, her moms went back to her people in Zacatecas to get away from me. I was clean and I told her I was done with the street, but she didn't believe me. Can't blame her. I broke a lot of promises to her over the years. Still, it hurt. I was counting on having a family when I got out. Instead of using, I started drinking. It got pretty bad.

"One night I ended up passing out on the sidewalk. When I woke up, there was a flyer in my hand and a sandwich and a bottle of water next to me. The flyer was for the Church of the Redeemer. I went straight there. They got me into a rehab program, and I cleaned up for good. That was twelve years ago. And let me tell you, ain't a day goes by that I don't get that craving to use or drink, some days worse than others. Every single day I pray for strength to get through."

I didn't know what to say. I wondered if Pops felt that same craving.

He stood and took the plates to the sink. "I gotta get going. I hit the streets at night, handing out sandwiches, socks and blankets to the homeless, runaways, addicts, whoever needs it. When you're better, you can come with me."

"You're gonna be a saint."

"I gotta to buy my way through the pearly gates after all the shit I pulled."

I helped him carry a couple boxes of donated goods to a mini van parked in the alley. A lot of its forest green paint was peeled off and its front bumper was tied on with a rope. "This was a donation, too," he said, sliding behind the wheel. "But it runs. Hey, tomorrow's domingo. Your moms will be at church."

Sunday. I had lost all track of days and time. I suddenly yearned to see my family.

After Julio left, I figured this was my chance to get to my homeboys. They were probably at Gato's club, but I couldn't go there. Too many eyes.

My best bet was to make for Flaco's house and ask his moms or little brother to call him for me.

I threw a hoodie over my head and slipped out the back door. I walked as fast as I could, zig-zagging through the alleys.

I got to Flaco's in record time. I could see the TV on through the curtain and rapped on the door.

Andrés answered, as I hoped. His eyes saucered when he saw me. "Homie, you look real bad."

"I had a bad accident, lil homie. Can I come in?" He held the door open and I stepped inside. "Where's Flaco at?"

"He's out with Yajaira."

"Can you call him for me? It's real important."

I sank into a kitchen chair as he dialed his phone. I leaned my head against the wall and closed my eyes. I was exhausted.

"Mags is here. He looks real bad."

Andrés held out the phone to me.

Fifteen minutes later, I was getting in the Nissan outside Flaco's house. He stared at me. "Puta, the fuck happen to you, homes?"

I waved at him to drive. "I don't got much time, dog. We gotta go to the yard."

On the way, I told him what went down and where I been at.

"Motherfucker!" he said. "We got to the yard that night, found the dogs and shit. We got the fuck outta there and called Gato. I thought maybe it was some shit with the rides, Gato's wife's in-laws getting payback on getting cut out of the business, but he said it wasn't them. So that left Rico. We been keeping real lo pro, waiting to hear from you."

"You seen Rico?"

He shook his head. "I'm real glad to see you, dog. I was starting to think you were resting."

"I can't figure out how I ain't, why he didn't put a bullet in my head and leave me by the side of the road?"

"He prolly figured you were as good as dead and wanted to send a message to the barrio—if anybody spills about the driveby, that's what's gonna happen to them, or maybe he just wanted the cops to find you sooner so that would close the case faster."

We arrived at the yard. It had shiny new gates and razor wire on top of the fence. I hoped Gato hadn't got rid of the palm trees. I directed Flaco to turn into the back alley. "What's the play, Mags?"

"I gotta go in through the fence and get my shit. You wait here. Keep the ride running."

We stopped next to the oil drums covering the cut in the fence we made. Flaco helped me roll them out of the way.

I pushed open the flap in the fence and edged along the narrow space behind the shop til I got to the end of the building. I stuck my head around the corner. The yard was silent. The center area was bathed in white from the floodlight on the office roof, the rest in deep shadow.

Holding my breath, I checked the front of the shop. The palm trees were still there. I jogged over, dug out the bundles of cash and replaced the plants. I relaxed a little.

I went into the shop and got my duffel bag, stuffing the cash at the bottom and heaping clothes on top of it. I grabbed a couple candy bars from a drawer in the tool bench and a cellphone that I'd bought for Mouse but never had the chance to give him.

I closed the door to the shop and headed back to the fence. I paused. There was something else. I dropped the duffel and using the cell phone as a flashlight, squeezed along the narrow path along the fence behind all the parts. I wished I'd just bailed out through the hole into the alley. I prolly coulda outrun the twins since they weren't from around here.

I passed the pile where I thought I'd hid the piece and where they caught up to me. I walked further. It had to still be there unless Gato'd come across it. I didn't think so, though. He didn't mess around much with all this junk. It was his cover business.

About ten paces down, I spotted a lookalike heap of odd engine parts. I crouched and tossed them aside. The .22 was still in the envelope. I stuffed the packet in my waistband and sped back through the fence with my duffel. We rolled the drums into place and took off.

"Aight?" Flaco asked.

My mouth had gone dry. I nodded.

"Where we going now?"

"Back to the church. Now I got the feria, I can figure out the next step."

"You gonna book?"

"I got to, homes. You take over the business, aight? I seen you already got the Nissan."

I gave him a sideways look.

He looked worried. "No disrespect, Mags. Gato gave me the keys."

"Ain't no thing. I ain't gonna be around." I smiled, and his face eased. "Know what? I wanna make one stop before you ride me back."

When Paloma answered the door, my heart thumped just like when I saw her the first night I got out and came to visit Blueboy, the night that started everything.

Now she stood in front of me, her hair swept back in a messy knot on top of her head, loose strands falling around her face like a frame. She was wearing a cutoff sweatshirt that showed her belly button.

"I gotta ask you one thing real quick," I said.

She recovered from her shock fast, folding her arms. "Lemme guess—you're in some kinda trouble."

I pointed to my face. "You know how I got this? And this?" I raised my shirt. "I got more all over me, but you got the idea. Rico. I almost bled out in the fuckin park cuz you went and told him I was staying at the yard and he put his cousins, the bikers, on me. You know all about me and Rico, and what he did to Blueboy. Why'd you tell him where he could find me? You didn't think he was asking for a reason?"

Her eyes flickered with guilt, or so I wanted to think, then hardened again. "You mean you weren't with Yvette?" she said in a sarcastic tone. She knew about Yvette? Now it was my turn to be jolted. "Yeah, I know all about you and her. I went down to El Gato Rey to find you. I wanted to say I was sorry for how I acted and ran into Tweety. He told me to ask Yvette, she'd know where you were at. You were with her every night."

Fuckin Tweety! "Nena, Yvette means nothing to me, nada, zero.

You told me you didn't want to see me no more. It was just …"

"We have one fight and you gotta jump some puta's bones right away?" Her voice splintered. "My brother was murdered, Magdaleno, I was upset. You couldn't give me some time?"

"Nena, you blamed me for Blueboy, and you told me you didn't want a guy like me. Those were your exact words when you got outta the car that day. I wanted you, but you didn't want me." I could feel the hurt that I had papered over cracking inside me.

She said nothing, just stood there, wiping tears, shoulders hunched.

I lifted her chin gently so she could look at me. "Paloma, te amo con todo el corazón. Let's forget all this. I'm leaving town in the next day or so. Come with me, like we planned. I got money now."

Her face turned to flint, and she shook my hand off. "Yvette'll be happy to go with you. Or did she dump you? Is that why you're here?"

I gave it one last shot. "Nena, please. I'm begging you. I'm sorry for everything. We can't just throw everything away, everything we been through."

Tears trickled down her face. "It's too much, Magdaleno, everything is too much with you. I can't take it no more. I just can't." She turned and shut the door fast.

I banged on the door with the palms of both hands, threw my head back and screamed with all the strength I had in my lungs. "Palomaaaaaaa!" The dogs yowling next door were my only answer. It was done. It was over.

Flaco didn't say nothing when I slumped into the shotgun seat. He raised his eyebrows and turned the ignition key.

"I love her, homes, I always will."

He just nodded.

THIRTY-NINE

I woke up to the sound of singing from the front room. Church. Moms. I padded across the kitchen and cracked the door. It wasn't crowded.

Right away, I spotted her grey-streaked hair, wavy from her usual braid, falling to her hips. She was wearing a knee-length black skirt, flat black shoes with worn down heels and a purple patterned top. One of her church outfits.

I wanted to go to her so bad, lay my head on her shoulder and wrap her strawberry-scented hair around me, but I knew I couldn't. I had to forget about my family, let them forget about me. I stood rooted to the spot.

I didn't know when I'd see her again. She raised her arms to the sky and swayed as she sang and prayed. I watched her til the service ended. I felt a split inside me, and hurried to the bathroom to wash up before Julio came in.

I was taking a shit, thinking about Moms, when I noticed something about the bathtub in front of me. At the very corner, where the tub joined the wall and the floor, something was sticking out.

Paper. Dark green with a white edge.

After I flushed, I crouched down and took a closer look. It was what I thought it was.

Money.

I looked at the tub. It was one of them molded plastic kinds that come with the walls and all. You just put it right over the old tub and walls and you had a whole new setup without the hassle of taking out the old shit. The landlord did that one time when we had a cracked tub. Cash sticking out of the bathtub?

I tugged the corner of the bill. The strip of plastic sealant along the tub and wall peeled back a little. I pulled at it. It came off nice and easy in one big, long piece.

Then I pulled at the strip along the floor. Same thing. I yanked the corner of the tub siding a little and a grip of cash fell out. It was a stash.

I heard voices in the kitchen then somebody knocked at the door. I practically had a fuckin heart attack.

"Un momento," I called.

I replaced the sealant strips, pressing them back in neat and tidy, then grabbed the bills that had fallen out and stuffed them in my shoes and socks.

I flushed the toilet again, ran the faucets under my hands, dried them and opened the door.

Two women were in the kitchen. One of them was the lady crushing on Julio. I nodded at them and wheeled into the bedroom as fast as I could.

I unloaded the bills. They were all hundreds, a few fifties. A coupla Gs worth. I didn't think it would be missed. There was prolly a fortune lining the molded tub and walls.

I stuffed them in my duffle, inside a rip at the bottom, which wasn't a safe place but the best I could do right then, and lay back on the bed, thinking.

This wasn't no earnings from street slinging, small bills all crumpled and dirty from desperate junkie hands. This was bigtime, cartel plata for buys or whatever.

Julio was a bagman. Maybe he was in charge of the laundry, washing money to make it clean.

Whatever it was, he had the perfect front.

I had to hand it to them cartel vatos. They were real smart, smarter than Gato even.

They operated at a whole other level, staying in the shadows, revealing themselves to only those who needed to know. They were the real movers, dope, plata, weapons, women, whatever.

I figured that when Julio went out last night to give socks to homeless people, he was probably collecting or delivering. He prolly did hand out shit, too.

He came back late, I musta been asleep, and sealed up the cash in the bathtub, but maybe he was tired, got a lil careless and didn't notice he left a bill sticking out.

Whatever. It didn't mean shit to me, only that I had to book fast. It was only a matter of time til he noticed the sealant been peeled up. He'd know it was me. A rap on the door made me jump.

"Mags, Fernando's gonna come by before the AA meeting tonight and look at your stitches."

I opened the door. He was still in his pastor outfit, an open-necked white shirt and dark jacket and slacks. "Feel like taking a ride in a few?"

"Where at?"

"The cemetery over in East Los. I visit my moms on Sundays. It's kinda nice there, peaceful. Sounds weird, but it clears my mind."

At first, I was gonna say no, but then I thought less time I spent by myself, the less he'd suspect me of finding his shit.

"Matter of fact, I got someone I need to see there, too."

It was a sunny morning, sky a clear deep blue. On a day like today, I should be taking Paloma out, maybe to somewhere where we could see the ocean and eat fish tacos.

The back of my eyes stung.

I forced myself to concentrate on the murals of Aztec warriors and César Chávez on the walls of the housing project we were passing.

Julio glanced at me. "You aight?"

I turned to the window so he couldn't see my moist eyes. "Thinking about my girl."

"Yeah, I been there."

The cemetery was like a soft, green island in the middle of the asphalt jungle.

Julio left me at the entrance while he went off to see his moms, Bible in hand. "I got a lotta amends to make to her," he said.

I couldn't figure him out. Was he for real or was this all an act? If he was playing, he should win that big acting award. What was that shit called? Oh, yeah, the Oscar.

A lady was selling carnations from buckets outside the gate. At first, I bought just the blue ones, but since the flowers were the prettiest things I'd seen in a long time, I bought everything she had—

three buckets of white, red, pink, yellow. She stared at me like I was crazy, then seized the fistful of bills I was offering and stuck them in her apron pocket.

I found Blueboy's name on a list of graves near the gate and followed the path to it. Trees with leafy branches offered shade like umbrellas. The grass smelled hot and sweet. I guessed it was mowed recently.

It didn't take long to find his grave. It had a plain white cross with his name on it. I pictured Blueboy lying in a box under the ground, his single blue eye cold and still as a marble. His body lay there, but where did all the things that made him Blueboy go—the history of his life, the knowledge in his head, his donkey hee-haw, his one-shoulder shrug? They were just gone. Smoke in the air was all we were in the end. What was the point of life when it all disappeared like that?

I tossed the carnations one by one on the mound of dirt, so it turned into a blanket of flowers. Then I sat next to it, crossing my legs and hugging my knees.

"I didn't get to your funeral to say goodbye, Blue, so here I am. I know I fucked up everything. I don't blame you for nothing. It's all on me. Nothing turned out like I thought it would. I'm sorry, bro. I know that ain't shit, but it's all I got. I wish it all turned out different. All I wanted to do was get the fuck outta here with you and Paloma, open a business somewhere, something legit you and me could run like a family. But now you're resting, it's over with Paloma, Rico's got a green light on me, and I gotta fuckin jet solo."

I could feel him listening to me, like he always did, his breath warm on my arm.

"I'm sorry we didn't get to go find your viejo up in Salvador. I really wanted to do that."

I looked up and smiled at the sky, as if he was right above me. I closed my eyes against the raw white sun, but it dazzled them all the same. Then I knew. El Salvador was where I had to go. "You know what, Blue? I'm gonna go to Salvador. I'm gonna look for your viejo for you. I owe you that. And maybe I gotta go for me, too—go back to my beginning to find the way back to myself."

I sat there for a while, feeling my decision seep into my bones, then I stood. I didn't know how I'd took, and Julio might be waiting for me. As I walked back to the gate, I considered the plan. It was solid. Nobody would find me in El Salvador. I would leave that night, when Julio was at the AA meeting. I wouldn't tell him. I'd get on the bus to Tijuana and keep heading south.

FORTY

I got Julio to drop me off at home, though I didn't tell him that. I said it was my girl's place. I had a few things to pick up and I wanted to see my family one last time.

I smelled stale cooking oil as I climbed the stairs and entered the living room.

Pops was slouched in his chair, beer in his hand, watching an old Mexican western.

Vicente Fernández was dressed in a fancy charro suit riding a horse on a desert ranch. I got a pang, remembering how when we were little, Pops would sing along to Vicente's rancheras when he got drunk. We'd hide in the hall or the kitchen, peeking at him and snickering behind cupped hands. He never sang now.

"Hola papá." He stared at my cut-up face, turned his eyes back to the TV and grunted a greeting. "Mamá around, the girls?"

"At the hospital. Lissy went into labor." He took a swallow from his can.

Shit. The baby came early. "When?"

"This morning."

"She okay?"

He nodded. "Last I heard. First one takes a while."

"Frank?"

"Working."

I felt a lil worried about her, but there was nothing I could do. I knew Frank would be checking on her. I had to do what I came for. I went to the dresser and searched through the junk in the top drawer, but I couldn't find my passport and green card, which I thought were there. I did find Angel's card with his cell phone number on it. I tucked it in my pocket.

"Papá, you know where my passport is?"

He looked at me in surprise. "Shoebox in the closet." He raised his chin toward the bedroom.

I entered my parents' room and slid open the closet door, scanning the jumble of clothes, belts and shoes. A shoebox sat on the top shelf. I pulled it down and took off the rubber band holding the lid on.

The family's passports were in a bundle held with another rubber band. I took it off and shuffled through. I found mine, green card carefully placed inside the back cover. I slid it into my pocket.

Under the passports was a bunch of loose photos. I took them out. The colors were faded and the edges dogeared. Zully as a baby. Me and Frank, my grin showing no front teeth. Frank with Dumbo ears. Lissy, Frank and me, standing at attention in our Sunday best.

Young Moms and Pops, hair shiny, faces pancake smooth. Another of them: Moms cradled a baby—Frank, I guessed, and leaned into the umbrella of Pops' arm curled around her. His other hand rested on the baby. They both looked like they'd swallowed sunshine.

I couldn't ever remember seeing them so happy like that. I noticed a gold dot on the baby's earlobe, an earring. The baby must be Lissy. But they looked younger than the pictures of when they had Lissy. A niece or some other relative?

Would they be smiling like that for someone else's kid? It was taken in El Salvador. I knew that from the red-tiled roof house and the lush green trees in the background. I flipped over the photo. Nothing was written on the back.

"What do you need your passport for, vos?"

I jumped and almost dropped the box. Pops stood in the doorway.

"I'm going to El Salvador, papá."

"Two detectives were here the other day."

My throat tightened. "They say what they want?"

"They were from homicide. They wanted to know where you were on some night."

I met his eyes straight on. "I didn't kill nobody, papá. They're hassling me because of my record."

He gazed at me a moment longer and shuffled out. I shoved the photos and passports back in the box and put it back on the closet shelf.

He wasn't in the living room when I returned. I heard a noise in the kitchen. He was getting another beer.

"Papá," I called. "Tell mamá and the girls goodbye for me." No response. That old knife blade twisted inside me. I turned the doorknob.

"Wait," he called. I turned.

He entered the living room and handed me a slip of paper. "It's the address and phone of my brother, Salomón, in San Salvador. He'll take care of you. I told those detectives you were watching TV with me til late that night."

A late afternoon sunbeam streamed through the window behind him. He looked tired and withered as he stood in its shaft of light. I realized then that I'd prolly look like that too, if I'd gone through what he did. My breath caught and then rippled through my chest.

"Gracias, papá," I whispered, scared that if I spoke in a normal tone, my voice would collapse.

"Suerte, m'hijo."

It took me a moment to comprehend what he had said. Good luck, m'hijo. Mi hijo. *My* son. I gazed at him. We were different, but also the same.

We were both just trying to survive as a tide of events swept us along the river of life. I had to accept and respect him as a man, as he had to accept and respect me. We were both men making decisions in an unjust world. Some would be the right ones, others not.

"Papá," I blurted. "Perdóname por todo." Forgive me for everything.

"Perdóname a mi, m'hijo." Forgive me, my son.

A huge weight evaporated from me. He was my father. I could never change that. Then I did something I vowed never to do.

"Bendición, papá," I whispered.

"Dios te bendiga, m'hijo." God bless you, my son.

His eyes went velvet, and I felt myself imploding. I ran down the stairs and kept running, until I arrived, breathless and sore, at the church.

Through the front window, I saw Julio and Fernando setting up the chairs for the AA meeting.

I went round to the back alley and called Flaco, telling him to meet me in the alley in an hour. By then, the meeting would be under way and night would fallen.

I slipped in through the back door and passed through the kitchen into the bedroom. I was fishing out the duffel bag from under the bed when I heard voices in the kitchen.

I stuffed it back under and was standing up when Julio gave a brief knock and peeked in.

"Fernando's here. You want him to check your stitches?"

I sat on the side of the bed and removed my shirt as Fernando entered. He was wearing a pink shirt and a bag on his shoulder like a purse. I briefly wondered if Julio and him …

"How are you? You're looking much better," Fernando said.

"Real good, I think. These things are itching like crazy."

"That's good. That means they're healing. Go ahead and lie down."

Fernando took out gold wire-rimmed glasses from his purse and placed them on his squat nose. He peeled off the bandages and peered at the wounds.

"The ones on your face can come out, except your lip, but the ones on your body must stay longer. The superficial wounds look good."

He took out a small pair of scissors and started snipping the threads. I felt the creepy sensation of thread sliding through my skin. A little mound of black cotton bits formed on the nightstand.

"How many stitches you put in?" I asked.

"Sixty-eight."

"Damn."

"I've done more." He dressed the wounds again. "You'll be okay. In a few more days, the others will be ready to come out. Keep them clean, okay?"

I nodded. "I preciate everything you done for me, for real."

"Law of good karma. Do good, good will come to you."

He left to go to the meeting. I went into the bathroom to check myself out. I looked like a little kid took a crayon to my face. A line extended from my left eyelid up into my eyebrow. Another scar ran down the side of my nose. A couple of nicks on my cheeks. And I was going to have a forest of scars on my shoulders, chest and stomach. I was one ugly cabrón.

I didn't have time to mourn my looks. The sound of chanting came from the front room. The meeting had started. Flaco would arrive soon. I had one more errand to do. I returned to the bedroom and pulled out the duffel. I dug out the .22 package, stuck it in my waistband and rolled out the back door.

Nerves tingling, I threw up my hoodie and strode off. Two blocks out of the downtown area, I spotted a scraggly but thick bush growing along a wooden fence in an alley. I looked up and down. Nobody. I walked over and stood in the shrub like I was taking a piss. Then I pulled out the .22 from the envelope with the cuff of my sweatshirt, tossed it deep into the bush and kicked some leaves and dirt behind it. I walked fast back to the church, noting the name of the cross-street and chucking the envelope in a trash can on the way.

A voice droned from the front room as I entered the kitchen. Flaco should be here any minute. I went into the bedroom and closed the door.

My head was jerked back. A rope around my throat pulled tighter and tighter. I gasped, grabbing the cord to try to pull it off my windpipe. I rammed my left elbow back, hitting the guy in the stomach. The cord loosened slightly as the blow put him off balance, just enough for me to get my right hand under the rope and yank some slack into the noose.

He didn't let go but fell onto my shoulder blades. I wheeled out from under him, smashing him in the center of his back with a karate chop. He groaned as he buckled but didn't fall.

I grabbed the Bible on the nightstand and crashed a corner of it into his temple as he tackled me around the hips, shoving me back onto the bed. He was on top of me, his hands around my neck. I saw who it was—the 5150 from the AA meeting. His eyes glittered. "This is for Payaso, pinche huey."

With the heel of my right hand, I pushed up on his chin as hard as I could. We stayed locked like that, then I suddenly let go. His head dropped. I stuck a thumb in his eye, grinding into the squishiness.

The pressure on my throat lightened as he used one hand to seize my wrist and lever it down. I pushed him off me and jumped to my feet. I wrapped my right arm around his neck from behind, grabbing my left shoulder to lock it. With my left hand, I pushed the back of his head, forcing his throat into my arm. Then I slid my left arm behind his head to grab my right shoulder.

His neck was locked between my arms. It was a hold a cop used on me once and I never forgot it. I squeezed his neck between my arms as hard as I could. He gurgled. I kept squeezing, his limbs were doing a wild dance. The door burst open. Flaco, Tweety and Jackie.

"Drop him, Mags." Flaco said. "He's done." I let him go. He collapsed to the floor. I seized the duffel.

"¡Vamos!" I said.

We ran. Cojo was at the wheel of the Nissan, engine running. We piled in and took off down the alley with a screech of rubber, crashing a trash bin that flew into the air, spraying garbage everywhere.

"Where to, Mags?" Cojo said.

"Downtown, the bus terminals." I was panting, turning to check behind us. Nobody. "Damn, homies, you came right on the money."

"When we pulled into the alley, I saw that fuckin mini-van and tripped bigtime," Flaco said. "That was the same mini-van the 5150s were riding in that night going up to Elysian Park. I remember cuz the bumper was tied on. I called your phone. When you didn't answer, we went in."

"That fuckin pastor, Julio, ratted me out. That 5150 goes to the AA meeting at the church." Julio knew how the street worked. He knew I had to be in a real jam, showing up as I did, and that someone would be looking to finish the job. He asked around to see how he could trade me for money or favors.

"That's real cold," Tweety said.

"Was that homeboy breathing, Flaco?" Jackie said.

"Just barely, I think."

"Where you booking to, Mags?" Tweety brought me from the recent past into the imminent future.

"Right there." Their gazes followed my finger down the street to a bus with a sign saying "Tijuana" in the front window. The driver was loading bags in the compartments underneath.

Cojo pulled into the curb. "Looks like that one's the next to go."

"You really booking, homie," Tweety said as it sunk into him where I was going.

"If I stick around, I'll be resting in the boneyard."

We got out and stood on the sidewalk. Travelers hung around, burdened with backpacks and cheap plastic bags stuffed to bursting. Vendors peddled bottled water and snacks.

"I appreciate everything you done for me, homies."

One by one, we clasped fists and embraced, clapping each other on the back three times.

"You coming back?" Tweety said.

"Sure. One day."

"Ain't gonna be the same without you, homes," Cojo said.

"I ain't gonna be the same without my homies, neither. Who's gonna get me outta trouble?" Everyone smiled weakly.

"You stay in touch, if you can, aight?" Jackie said.

I nodded. "Down to you, now, dogs."

I entered the bus company office and bought my ticket and a bunch of candy bars. When I came out, they were still there, slouching with their hands pulling their pockets wide. I hugged Flaco, throwing an arm around his neck. I whispered in his ear what I'd found at Julio's. "Hit him when he's out giving socks and shit," I said. "It'll be like hitting el gordo with the lottery, plus a lil payback for ratting me out to the 51s."

He nodded.

Then I rolled fast to the bus. I could feel them watching me as I boarded. I walked down the aisle, ignoring passengers' stares at my raw face, and settled into a seat at the back. The homeboys and me stared at each other through the window til the bus pulled out and they faded into stick figures. I felt a ripping inside, like a sheet of paper torn into bits. Even if you taped the pieces back together, it would never be the same. Something had ended.

The bus lumbered through downtown and onto the San Diego Freeway. I tore open an Almond Joy and leaned my head back. Chewing slowly, a flashflood of thoughts rushed through my mind. Would I ever see my family again? I wished I'd had the chance to say goodbye to Zully and another chance to ask Lissy to forgive me for Benny's death. I wanted to thank Frank for all he done for the family. I was glad that I at least had a picture in my mind of Moms at church to take with me even if I couldn't hug her a last time.

The bus rumbled past Camp Pendleton, the Marine base, on one side, the vast blackness of the ocean on the other. We were getting close to the border. What lay ahead for me, I had no idea. All I knew was that I was truly on my own now, no backup, and I was going to stay that way.

I wasn't going to trust a damn fuckin soul from here on out. I had to operate for me and myself alone. I had to numb myself out. It was the only way to survive.

We reached the border and piled out to walk across the footbridge. I moved into a shadow and took out my cellphone. I was going to play my last card.

I dialed Angel's cell number, willing him to answer. He did.

"It's me, Magdaleno."

A pause. I could hear him wondering why I was calling. "What's up?"

"I got a tip for you bout that driveby, but it's gotta stay anonymous, and you gotta discharge me."

"You're discharged tomorrow anyway. That's your last appointment."

"I can't make it. So, we got a deal?"

He paused. "Okay."

"The five-o will find what they been looking for under a bush in an alley." I gave him the cross streets. "I don't know if it's got prints on it or not, but they might find it's got some 211s on it, too. They find the guy who pulled the robberies, they got the driveby shooter."

"Wait, how do you know this?"

"That's all I can say. The rest is up to the cops. So, am I discharged?"

"Yeah, you're discharged."

"Nice knowing you, Angel. You won't see me again."

I clicked off and dialed home. Zully picked up.

"Magdaleno, you're a tío. Lissy had a boy." She was real excited. "You should see him. He's so tiny. They got him in an incubator."

"Lissy okay?"

"Yeah, she's sleeping so we came home."

"I ain't got a lotta time, but you gotta tell Moms Julio is a fake, not to trust him. She gotta find a new church."

"Where you at? You sound funny."

"I gotta book for a while."

"I gotta tell you something."

"Rápido, girl."

"Lissy named the baby Benito Magdaleno."

She'd forgiven me. "Tell her I love her, too."

I hung up and dropped the phone onto the ground, stomping on it until it shattered. I threw the pieces in the trash and headed to the line shuffling through revolving gate.

I noticed a clock through an office window as I walked past the "Bienvenidos a México" sign with a hot wind breathing on my back, the staccato sound of Spanish everywhere. It was just after midnight. The sky was still black, but it was a whole new day.

Acknowledgments

I was inspired to write this novel after interviewing gang members deported from Los Angeles to El Salvador for a Colombian magazine. I was familiar with El Salvador as I'd travelled there several times when I lived in Guatemala during its own grinding civil war against Marxist guerrillas.

Years later, when I was working for the Associated Press in Los Angeles, I covered street gangs and the poverty and despair that leads to and empowers gangs. I went on to co-write a book on gang intervention, *Peace in the Hood: Working with Gang Members to End the Violence*, and finally the novel came together.

So my thanks goes to the young men and women who trusted me with their stories. They wished to remain anonymous back then and they still are. I'm also grateful to my creative writing students at California State Prison-Los Angeles County's A yard for reading the book and confirming its validity as a "firme job."

Besides my own reporting, I read many books that informed this work, including *G-Dog and the Homeboys* by Celeste Fremon, *Always Running* by Luis J. Rodriguez, *Tattoos on the Heart* by Gregory Boyle, *The Black Hand* by Chris Blatchford, *Inside the Crips* by Colton Simpson, *Monster* by Sanyika Shakur, *My Bloody Life* and *Once a King Always a King* by Reymundo Sanchez, *The Killing Season* by Miles Corwin, and *Ghettoside* by Jill Leovy.

About the Author

Christina Hoag is a former journalist who has had her laptop searched by Colombian guerrillas, phone tapped in Venezuela, was suspected of drug trafficking in Guyana, hid under a car to evade Guatemalan soldiers, and posed as a nun to get inside a Caracas jail. She has interviewed gang members, bank robbers, thieves and thugs in prisons, shantytowns and slums, not to forget billionaires and presidents, some of whom fall into the previous categories. Now she writes about such characters in her fiction. A former staff writer for the Miami Herald and Associated Press, Christina reported from fourteen countries around Latin America *for Time, Business Week, New York Times, Financial Times, Sunday Times of London, Houston Chronicle* and other media. Born in New Zealand, Christina lives in Southern California, where she has taught creative writing at a maximum-security prison and to at risk teen girls. For more about her, go to christinahoag.com.